Joe tried to reach that comfortable state of ennui

The one he liked to wallow in right before the start of a new school year. But everything felt as if it was slipping out of his grasp. As if Emily Sullivan had ripped all the self-indulgent pleasure out of his back-to-school misery and twisted it into something...something even more twisted than usual.

Ideas crackled through his brain like static. He couldn't stop considering all the possibilities, imagining all the delights of an ongoing ideological duel with a well-educated, intelligent adversary. The thrust and parry that could be played out before a captive but fascinated adolescent audience. It was tempting. It was intriguing. It was downright stimulating.

But Joe didn't want to be tempted or intrigued. He certainly didn't want to be stimulated. And definitely not by some chirpy student teacher with short skirts and big, wide eyes. Eyes with sparkly silver spikes that...

Stop right there. Get a grip, Wisniewski.

Joe took a deep breath, but regretted it instantly. There, just beneath the odors of musty texts and stale coffee, was a faint trace of something fresh and floral.

It was going to be a long, long year.

Dear Reader,

All of us have been touched, in some way, by special teachers who opened our lives to the possibilities beyond the classroom basics. In *Learning Curve,* Emily and Joe are given a chance to say thank-you for the lessons they've learned.

The teachers I tend to remember are those who shoved me out of my comfort zone and dared me to try something new. One of them told me I should try to write a book, and even though I laughed at the time and waited more than ten years to follow his advice, his praise meant enough to make me take that first uncomfortable step into a new world. This book is dedicated to him—my own small way of saying thank-you.

I'd love to hear from my readers! Please come for a visit to my Web site at www.terrymclaughlin.com, or find me at www.wetnoodleposse.com or www.superauthors.com, or write to me at P.O. Box 5838, Eureka, CA 95002.

Wishing you plenty of happily-ever-after reading,

Terry McLaughlin

LEARNING CURVE
Terry McLaughlin

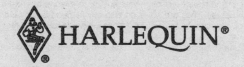

TORONTO • NEW YORK • LONDON
AMSTERDAM • PARIS • SYDNEY • HAMBURG
STOCKHOLM • ATHENS • TOKYO • MILAN • MADRID
PRAGUE • WARSAW • BUDAPEST • AUCKLAND

ISBN 0-373-78093-1

LEARNING CURVE

Copyright © 2006 by Teresa A. McLaughlin

For Professor Tom Gage, who told me I could write—
and then made me believe it, too.

CHAPTER ONE

JOSEPH P. WISNIEWSKI listened to the slap and shuffle of his Birkenstocks echo along the empty corridor of Caldwell High School. He knew where his steps were taking him, but he wasn't sure why anymore. That echo seemed to ping around the empty spaces inside him, searching for the answer.

He'd give himself until the end of the term to figure things out or hand in his resignation. To quit teaching.

He navigated a crooked course along the wide vinyl hall dulled by Mr. Stenquist's ineffective floor wax, avoiding the sunlight flooding through the open classroom doors to nurse his hangover in the shadows. It wouldn't be so easy to detour around the back-to-school business with his fellow faculty that was sure to nudge his early-morning headache into a midafternoon migraine.

"Suck it up, Wisniewski," he muttered, rubbing a hand over the last batch of four-day stubble he'd feel until deep into Thanksgiving vacation. "This is why you get paid the big bucks." Steeling himself to confront another school year, he shouldered his way through the office door.

Linda Miller glanced up from her command post behind the reception counter. "Well, look what the cat dragged in."

Joe's grimace eased into a smile. The middle-aged secretary's crusty personality masked a gooey cream center. Linda might be mouthier than the average clerk, but she anted up pay phone coins for teen crises and found more niches for hopeless grads than the local armed forces recruiting office. "Hey, Linda."

"What? No tan from the tropics? No handwoven shirt from Nepal? No bruises from a dustup with a jealous husband? Exactly what kind of summer vacation did you take?"

"The restful kind." He turned to pull two months' junk mail and memos out of his office box. "And I told you that black eye was a misunderstanding. Pamela was legally separated. The divorce decree was in the mail."

"Hmmph." She came around the counter with her nose in the air, sniffing with a smirk. "Aramis. A seductive scent. With undertones of Excedrin and Scope that almost disguise the subtle hint of too much Scotch."

"Come on, Linda. Even you can't smell Excedrin."

"No, but I can see that whatever you took isn't living up to its advertising." She pinned him to the wall with a look that made him feel like he was ten years old and smeared with enough incriminating evidence to get grounded for life. "Just look at yourself. What a waste of tall, dark and handsome, not to mention all that education. Have you ever once used those over-the-top looks or that under-the-radar charm to pursue anyone suitable to be the mother of your children?" She shook her head. "You know, your brains are interesting enough when they aren't pickled, and your conversation's kind of pleasant when you bother to move beyond the grunting stage."

Because he was just about to grunt a response before moving out of firing range, Joe stood his ground, resigned to taking a few more lumps. Knowing Linda, they were coming.

"Shame on you. Forty years old and nothing much to show for it."

"Thirty-nine."

"The way you look today, fifty would have been a generous guess." She wagged a scolding finger under his nose. "Well, it looks like you're finally going to pay the piper."

The waving finger made his stomach pitch and roll. "I'm really not in the mood for a lecture on over-indulgence at the moment."

"That's right—when it comes to lecturing, you're the pro. But I'm not talking about talk."

Something about the gleam in her eyes set off alarm bells that intensified the throbbing in his head. "What is it? What's going on?"

The phone interrupted. Linda's lips spread in a smile that hinted of hell on earth. "Duty calls," she said, patting his arm before she retreated to her post. "Duty calls us all, sooner or later."

He followed her into the cramped area behind the counter, dumping his unread mail into the wastebasket. Carefully nudging the clutter on her desk aside with one hip, he settled in to wait while she recited the late registration litany for a new parent.

"...Yes, I'm sure that would be all right, Joyce." She tried to wave him away, but he dodged and stuck. "Donny can take the forms home Monday after classes."

"Tell me," he said with a growl when she dropped the receiver back in its cradle.

She folded her hands over a stack of fall sports schedules. "Maybe if you kept in touch, you wouldn't come back to nasty little surprises."

Behind him, another door clicked open. "Joe?"

"Speaking of nasty little surprises," Linda muttered under her breath.

He turned to see Kyle Walford, Caldwell's principal, step out of his office. Joe's headache shifted into migraine mode ahead of schedule.

"Joe, buddy. Looking good." Kyle swept a hand through his hair and smoothed down his tie as he moved toward the reception area. Joe wondered, not for the first time, how Kyle's wife got the greasy stuff out of his ties. Then he wondered if there was any way to get out of grasping that same hand when Kyle offered it in greeting.

"Where have you been?" said Kyle. "I tried calling you all day yesterday."

"That's odd. There was no message on my machine."

Kyle threw a companionable arm around Joe's shoulders, an awkward position for them both since Joe was several inches taller. "Well, you're here now, and there's someone I'd like you to meet."

"I was going to check on a few things before the faculty meeting." Joe dug his heels deep into his Birkenstocks, resisting Kyle's attempt to maneuver him into the principal's office. "I don't want to be late."

"You can't be late if I'm not there," Kyle pointed out, flashing even, white caps.

Joe remembered that Kyle's smile had been bartered for a local dentist's outfield billboard. He didn't smile back. "Who is it that's important enough to keep everyone waiting?"

"Well, Joe…it's your student teacher."

It wasn't often that Joe got angry enough to worry about high blood pressure. But he could feel the adrenaline pumping through his system now. There it was, coiling in his gut and rippling along his jaw. He didn't want his classroom turned into some sort of petri dish, didn't want a stranger probing into the hows and whys of what he did—especially when he didn't know how and why himself anymore. He just wanted to get his job done and make his escape every afternoon shortly after three o'clock. "I don't have student teachers, Kyle."

"Plenty of teachers do, sooner or later." Kyle playfully punched Joe's arm. "And now it's your turn."

"I don't have student teachers, Kyle."

"You've got one now." Kyle's fingers twitched a bit as he smoothed his already smooth tie. "Come on into my office and I'll introduce you."

EMILY SULLIVAN RECROSSED her legs, right over left this time, and reminded herself not to swing the suspended foot. Bruising the principal's shins wasn't the way to make a professional impression.

She reached down to tug at the hem of her skirt and watched it snap back into place a couple of inches above her knees, just like it had snapped back the other six times she'd tugged at it. Maybe she should have gone with the ankle-length skirt. Oh, well. No use second-guessing her morning fashion decision—and she did tend to step on that longer skirt and trip when getting out of chairs. Tripping and falling flat on her face probably created a less professional appearance than swinging a shin-bruising foot.

How could anyone relax in the principal's office? Okay, the principal probably managed just fine. And at least she wasn't staring at the fake walnut paneling from a juvenile delinquent's point of view.

A delinquent adult's, maybe. Her family certainly seemed to think so. That was why she had to clinch this student teaching assignment. It was her last, best chance to launch her grown-up life—even if, at twenty-nine, she was rusting on the launch pad. She'd studied subjects from anthropology to zoology, she'd waited tables in Dublin and sold perfume in Marseilles. She'd done just about everything but decide what to do with her life, blithely hopping from one campus, one major, one country, one job, to another. Now it was time to choose a career and stick with it. She'd run out of hopping room.

Kyle walked in, wearing his alligator-on-campaign grin. A dark, rangy man trailed him into the room, closed the door, and slouched against it, his hands in his pockets. Emily got a brief impression of worn jeans, wrinkled white shirt, black hair in need of a trim and waves of hostility.

"Emily Sullivan," said Kyle, "meet Joe Wisniewski."

She rose, hand extended, lifting her chin to look her new master teacher straight in his bloodshot eyes. So this was The Wiz, the infamous seducer of impressionable young minds and restless older women. He was exactly what she'd imagined, right down to the scruffy sandals.

What she hadn't imagined was the potent appeal tucked inside the Heathcliff packaging. The sexual left hook knocked the wind out of her before she saw it coming.

"How do you do?" she managed to ask when she got her breath back.

Silence. Emily fought the urge to tug at her skirt until it morphed into a shroud. She wanted to wear it as she slipped into the hole in the ground she felt opening beneath her. And just when the absence of sound or movement had stretched her nerves to the snapping point, The Wiz shrugged away from the door and took her hand in his.

"Fine," he said. His dark laser beam stare locked in on Kyle. "Just fine. Thanks."

Emily slipped her hand out of his oversize grip and sank back into her chair. She would have preferred to dive under it instead, to tuck her head in the emergency position and pray that the impending nuclear blast didn't spew too much radiation in her direction. Something was wrong—understatement alert. The tension in this office was a palpable, living thing. A thing with pastrami breath and a sinus condition, camped at an open fire. Which would explain why it was getting so warm in here. And hard to breathe. She tried to swallow without gulping out loud.

"So..." Kyle's smile wavered a bit at the edges. "You might remember Emily's brother, Joe. Jack Sullivan?"

Another marathon silence followed the question. Then, with a flick of a glance in Emily's direction, Joe grunted. "I might."

"He was a senior the first year you taught here at Caldwell, wasn't he?" Kyle didn't wait for Joe's answer. "You made a big impression on young Jack, I hear. A big impression."

The Wiz might have been carved in stone, except for the tiny muscle rippling along his jaw.

Kyle vaulted over another conversation chasm. "Jack Sullivan, Senior, was mighty impressed, too, I understand."

"Is that so?"

Emily winced. She supposed that "impressed" was one way to describe sputtering, splotchy-faced outrage.

Actually, the member of the Sullivan clan who was the most enthralled, the most entranced, the most *impressed* by The Great and Powerful Wiz was impressionable thirteen-year-old Emily. She would sit in her spot at the Sullivan dining room table, swinging both feet, quietly devouring Jack's civics class quote of the day and the delicious debates that followed like servings of dessert.

She'd never taken her turn in the classroom of the man behind the uproar. Shortly after Jack's graduation, her parents had moved from the tiny mill town of Issimish to shorten Dad's hour-long commute to his job in Seattle. And her fascination with the infamous Mr. Wisniewski had tangled with her fantasies into a knotty teenage crush.

Joe shifted his attention in her direction. "Is that so?" he asked again in that soft, dangerous voice.

"Yes, it is." Time to focus on her goal, stiffen her backbone, and turn on the charm. She smiled her best Innocent-Your-Honor smile. "Quite an impression. In fact, that's what brings me here."

JOE CLIMBED THE STAIRS to the second floor of Caldwell's main building that afternoon and headed toward his room. He shoved his hands into his pockets, silently cursing the unnatural alignment of crater-plowing asteroids, planet-destroying supernovas, galaxy-sucking black holes and all other cosmic disasters that had sent Ms. Emily Sullivan into his path, not to mention his classroom.

God. If there was one thing he couldn't stand, it was chirpiness. Emily Sullivan could give chirping lessons to a million yellow puffballs carpeting a commercial chicken incubator. And, as if her own big-blue-eyed version wasn't bad enough, she'd gone and spread it like a virus, infecting the male portion of the Caldwell High faculty within minutes of bouncing into the conference room. She'd had them eating out of her fluttery little hands—right after they'd finished tripping over their tongues at her long-legged, short-skirted entrance.

Ed Brock, senior class adviser, had never been so animated about homecoming plans before Emily piped up with a few suggestions. Russell Strand, head math geek, almost choked in his own bow tie when she giggled a wrinkle-nosed giggle over one of his DOA puns. And the football coach couldn't speak at all for a few moments after Emily's blond curls brushed over his cheek as she reached to collect her complimentary season pass.

Even the female faculty members weren't immune

to Emily's enthusiasm, applauding her proposal for a benefit debut performance of the annual spring play. Joe hated contagious enthusiasm almost as much as chirpiness, especially when it was the fund-raising kind. Most fund-raisers were a big waste of time, as far as he was concerned. They played havoc with scheduling, burned holes in the ozone layer and brought in approximately seventeen cents per hour of mental and manual labor. And now he was stuck with trying to round up student volunteers for the theatrical benefit.

Stuck. Stuck with a student teacher he hadn't expected and didn't want. Stuck with the administrative duties for a social studies department chair sidelined with complications from a difficult pregnancy. He was tempted to dump his student teacher on his chair's long-term sub. It would be his personal social chemistry experiment: mix one part ignorance and two parts incompetence. No danger of an explosion—the school board had sputtered along for years on a similar formula.

He popped another couple of pain relievers and slipped through his classroom door, hoping to turn the lock for a few moments of peace and privacy. But Ms. Sullivan had already invaded this space, too. There she was: probing.

He watched her bend over to read the caption of a faded political cartoon pinned to the bottom edge of one of his bulletin boards. And he tried, he really did try not to notice the way that short skirt slid up the backs of those long, shapely thighs, or the way one of those blond party streamers slipped across her forehead to tease the tip of her turned-up nose.

God. Even her hair was chirpy.

Because he resented having to roll his own tongue off the floor and back into his mouth, he growled a bit more than usual. "There must have been an incredible flood of last-minute student teachers this year. I thought the university avoided placing them in out-of-the-way districts like Issimish, especially when there are so many more options closer to Seattle."

"That's right." She straightened and turned to face him. "I was the one who suggested Caldwell. I asked my university adviser to pull some strings to get me assigned here. Specifically, to work with you."

"Why?"

She twisted her hands together. "Because of what you did to my brother."

"Jack?"

"Yes."

Joe pulled his hands out of his pockets. "What did I do to Jack?"

"You inspired him."

"No." Joe felt something like panic welling up inside. "I didn't."

"Yes, you did." She took a step forward. "You changed his life. For a little while, anyway. But you did."

He frowned and moved away from her. Around behind his desk, where it was safe.

She followed, facing him across its scarred oak surface. "You encouraged him to think, for the first time, his own thoughts, to question all the ideas that had been handed to him." She ran a finger along a crooked gouge. "It may have been a brief deflection, but it was an important one. I think it was very important—downright momentous, in fact—that Jack took those first wobbly steps off the family's well-beaten path."

Joe didn't want to be held responsible for anyone's first wobbly steps, or for anything momentous. And he really didn't want to be a human detour sign. Not unless it meant he could make Emily Sullivan disappear.

She turned back to the bulletin board and pointed at the curling slips of yellowed paper. "I'll bet some of these headlines are the same ones you pinned up on your bulletin board the first year you taught here. The same ones that were here when Jack was sitting in this room."

"I'm not big on redecorating. If you want the bulletin update job, it's yours."

Joe regretted the offer the moment he heard himself make it. It sounded like he was knuckling under and accepting the situation. But what else could he do? There she stood with those big blue eyes and those tousled curls and those odd little curves at the corners of her mouth that made her look like she was smiling even when she wasn't.

She couldn't be smiling all the time. Could she?

And what had he been regretting and resenting before he got sidetracked? Oh, yeah—there she stood, in her newly assigned spot, expecting some newly assigned duties. "There." He waved in the direction of a particularly ragged display. "If you decide to stay, and if I decide you can—and that's a couple of big ifs—there's your first assignment."

Emily laughed. Joe watched her nose scrunch up and felt a throat-constricting kinship with Russell and his bow tie.

"I wouldn't dream of touching these bulletin boards," she said. "They're absolutely you. Look at this." She walked over to one and then turned, crooking a finger in invitation.

Joe didn't want to deal with overt invitations. Or covert invitations, or invert invitations, or any other kind of invitation that would lure him too close. "I know what's on my walls."

"Come on and take a look." The finger kept curling, tugging at him with hypnotic pale pink nail polish. "Please."

He scuffed across the room and leaned down to squint at a faded editorial on Ford's pardon of Nixon. It was hard not to notice her fresh, floral scent competing with eau de chalk dust and essence of floor wax, but he thought he was doing an admirable job of blocking it out. "Yeah. Ford. Nixon. So?"

"There's nothing here about Nixon going to China. I checked."

"Try a little word association with just about anyone you meet. Nixon, Watergate. Nixon, crook. Not Nixon, China."

Emily straightened, smiling her tilt-edged smile. "That's my point, exactly."

"Glad you made it. I'd be even gladder to get it."

She leaned in a bit and lowered her voice. "You are, and I quote, 'a corrupter of innocent young minds.'"

"Jack Senior, right?"

He thought he saw her wince before she nodded. "Yes."

"You asked for this teaching assignment to upset your father?"

"Actually, my father finds my choice of a student teaching assignment…fascinating." She linked her fingers under her chin and gazed up at him with something that looked suspiciously like admiration. "I want to inspire students, the way you inspired my brother. I want to watch you in action, to try to figure out how you do it."

"No." He rubbed a hand across his mouth. The look on her face was drying up all his spit. "I mean, I don't know for sure that I do it. If I do do it, I'm not sure how. And even if I thought I could do it, and knew how to do it, I know for sure I don't know how to show anyone else how to do it."

Time out. Time to stop right there, before he started making even less sense. But he should definitely stop before her naive enthusiasm—and that soft, dreamy look on her face—made him feel any more stiff and empty, old and dried up.

He shuffled back to his desk and dropped into his chair. "I don't want to do this, Ms. Sullivan. I'm sorry if you've been led to believe differently, but the truth is, I didn't agree to have a student teacher this year. I don't work with student teachers anymore. I haven't for a long, long time. I didn't even know about your assignment here until a few moments before I met you this morning. And I don't think this is a good idea, in spite of all your expectations and your obvious enthusiasm." He slumped lower in his seat and stretched a hand across his forehead. "Or maybe because of them."

Emily flipped one hand in the air, brushing aside his touching little speech. "Okay," she said. "I knew coming into this it was going to be a tough sell." She cleared her throat. "What I'd like you to do is to view my student teaching assignment as an opportunity for a kind of personal and educational renewal."

"Renewal?"

"A chance to revisit your philosophical underpinnings. To sharpen and highlight the contrast between your views and those of another educational professional—just for the sake of argument."

"And I suppose the person I'd be contrasted with would be you." Joe straightened in his chair. An old, familiar feeling was spreading like heartburn through his gut. The kind of feeling he got whenever he pictured William F. Buckley squinting at him from the cover of the *National Review.* "And just what are these 'ideological underpinnings?'"

"Let's see if I remember the legend according to Jack Junior." Emily raised her hands to tick off the items. "Joseph P. Wisniewski—the *P* an ongoing and entertaining mystery to your students. Raised at an Oregon commune and Rainbow Family gatherings. Homeschooled, for the most part, with extracurricular activities at antinuke demonstrations. High school years spent in San Francisco, where an early growth spurt grabbed the attention of the basketball coach and landed you a college sports scholarship."

Emily ran out of fingers and crossed her arms beneath attractively perky breasts. "You joined the Peace Corps after graduation and took up teaching when you got back to the States."

Dozens of years summarized in less than a dozen sentences. It didn't matter—he'd lost track when she mentioned the Peace Corps.

Guatemala. *Rosaria.*

He shut his eyes against the old wounds, and then opened them to confront the new irritant: Emily Sullivan, a living, breathing reminder of what he'd been like when he started teaching at Caldwell. That first year, before the crushing news from Guatemala, before Rosaria's death. The year he'd been fired up with purpose and filled with enthusiasm.

It was hard to look at her. Hard to look back. But he forced himself to meet her eyes, to smile, to nod. "An impressive performance. I think you managed to hit most of the highlights."

"Thank you."

Joe leaned back in his chair, which creaked a warning to keep his voice low and his wits sharp. "So you want me to agree to share my liberal, left-wing soapbox with a…" He gestured for her to fill in the blanks.

"A woman who was raised on Air Force bases and Reaganomics." Emily leaned down and settled her hands on the edge of his desk. "A conservative Republican."

"That's redundant," he said.

"That's predictable," she answered.

He shifted forward and noted the tiny flinch before her smile widened. He waited and watched as her knuckles turned white from her grip on his desk. But she didn't back off, and she kept her eyes steady on his. He had to give her points for sheer spunk. "Oh, I don't think you've got me completely figured out yet," he said.

"Good. That'll just liven things up." She took a deep breath. "Come on, Wiz. Take me on for a couple of rounds. You've got nothing to lose but the right edge of that soapbox."

He could see the freckles scattered across her nose, and the shards of silver ringing her pupils. One curl slipped forward over one of her eyebrows, and he caught his breath. Such an appealing package wrapped around such repulsive politics. He could reach out and strangle her. Or tip forward just a couple of inches and nibble on those smug, curvy lips. The first would earn him a prison sentence. The second would probably get him fired.

He was sure about one thing. Sexual harassment of a student teacher wasn't part of his personal politics or his philosophical underpinnings. He leaned back and rubbed a finger across his mouth. "You know, a soapbox can have a pretty slippery surface. And I may have a few surprises left up my sleeve."

"Sounds like a challenge—or a bargain. Either way, I'm taking it." Emily slapped her palms against the top of his desk. "That's the spirit. That's The Wiz I've heard about. This is going to be great, just great," she said, backing toward the door. "And don't worry, we can work out the details later."

She sidestepped into the hall. "I have a few surprises up my sleeve, too. See you on Monday—bright and early!" And then she was gone, taking most of the classroom's oxygen with her.

Joe sighed and slouched deeper into his complaining chair. He closed his eyes and tried to reach that comfortable state of ennui he liked to wallow in right before the start of a new school year. But everything felt like it was trickling out of his grasp. As if Emily Sullivan had ripped all the self-indulgent pleasure out of his back-to-school misery and twisted it into something...something even more twisted than usual.

Ideas crackled through his brain like static. He couldn't stop considering all the possibilities, imagining all the delights of an ongoing ideological duel with a well-educated, intelligent adversary. The subtle—no, the visceral thrust and parry that could be played out before a captive but fascinated adolescent audience. Hmm. It was tempting. It was intriguing. It was downright stimulating.

But Joe didn't want to be tempted or intrigued. He certainly didn't want to be stimulated. And definitely not by some chirpy student teacher in short skirts and big, wide eyes. Eyes with sparkly silver spikes that rayed out into sky-colored irises rimmed by beautiful navy rings....

Stop right there. Get a grip, Wisniewski.

Joe took a deep breath, but regretted it instantly. There, just beneath the odors of musty texts and stale coffee, was a faint trace of something fresh and floral.

Damn. It was going to be a long, long school year.

CHAPTER TWO

BRIGHT AND EARLY. Those two words certainly seemed made for each other, Joe thought as he shuffled through the main hall of Caldwell High at 7:45 a.m. on the first day of school. Sort of like black and blue. Or battery and assault.

He tucked a stack of folders under one arm and rammed his hands into his pockets, focusing on the floor to avoid eye contact. Eye contact could lead to conversation, which often led to dodging requests and other forms of aerobic exercise. And he wasn't looking for a workout.

Two sleek, high-heeled shoes bounced into his path. By the time Joe's gaze roamed over sexy ankles, shapely calves and knees that hinted at more interesting items above a no-nonsense hemline, he knew what he'd find at eyeball level: Emily Sullivan, his own personal triathlon.

She beamed up at him, her smile nearly blinding him with white-toothed enthusiasm. He hoped she came with a dimmer switch. "Good morning, Mr. Wisniewski."

"Is it, Ms. Sullivan?"

"Well, of course! Don't you just love the first day of school? All the energy, all the possibilities."

She sighed a happy little sigh and scrunched up her nose, oblivious to the staggering and chest clutching going on behind her back. Her prim sweater set and that twist thing she'd done with her hair wasn't going to fool the local male population. Might as well go for truth in advertising and hang a flashing neon *Hot Babe* sign around her neck.

"I was wondering," she said, "if I could sit in on all your classes today, since it's a noon dismissal schedule."

"If you want to. It's going to be pretty routine, just handing stuff out. Texts, course schedules. Threats."

"Anything I can do to help?"

There it was, punching him right between the eyes in the first five minutes of the first morning of the school year: one of the many reasons he didn't want a student teacher, even one who didn't look like Emily Sullivan. It was going to be a lot of work for him to find work for his student teacher to do. "I could probably come up with something," he muttered.

"Great!"

Great. It was going to be like training a puppy. An eager, squirming puppy that followed him everywhere, licking his shoes, looking up at him with big, wide puppy eyes no matter how many times he scolded or stepped on it. He hated stepping on puppies, but it usually happened sooner or later, because the damn things always managed to get right under his feet. Crowding him.

Might as well kill two puppies with one stone, so to speak. Give her something to do, far away from him. He pulled the folders from under his arm and chose some prep work. Emily could do it. She could feel useful and needed, a valuable partner on the educational team. She could establish a meaningful relationship with the copier. "Do you know where the copier is?"

"Linda showed me."

Probably during some female bonding ritual involving office equipment. "Class rosters are inside. Copy the assignment sheets and reading lists, with a couple extra for each class, okay?"

"Okay. I can handle that." She hesitated, her smile dimming just a bit around the edges. "But do you think I'll be finished by the time the first bell rings?"

Squish. "If not, we'll finish up at the break—my prep period is right after that. Don't worry about it."

Emily's beam bounced back. "I'll see you in class."

Joe stood rooted to his spot, watching her blond twist bob through the hall, wondering how he was going to get through five class periods of puppy eyes following his every move.

"Hey, Wiz."

He turned as Matt Zerlinger, a senior in his Government and Current Events classes, motioned with his chin toward Emily. "Heard you got a student teacher this year. That her?"

"Yeah."

"Whoa."

"Yeah."

Matt grinned. "Shit happens."

"Yeah." Joe sighed. "And because I have a student teacher, and I need to set a better example, I have to warn you to watch the language in the halls, Matt."

Matt's smile widened. "This is going to be fun."

"Shit," said Joe.

"Oh, that reminds me." Matt cast a glance down the hall. "Dornley was looking for you."

The athletic director. Probably looking for another sucker to coach another orphan team. "Damn."

"Yeah. Just thought I'd warn you."

Joe clamped a hand over Matt's shoulder as they headed toward the stairway. "In addition to running interference for Dornley, I see you've registered for two periods with me. What's the angle?"

"An awesome recommendation for Berkeley."

"So, you're going for it." Joe squeezed Matt's shoulder before dropping his hand back into his pocket. "Is Walt going to come through with the funding?"

Walter Mullins was Matt's latest stepfather. Matt's mom went through husbands like she went through bottles of cheap vodka, but Walt seemed to have some staying power.

"I've been working on him," said Matt, "but it's

too soon to tell. Gonna have to hit the scholarship scene pretty hard."

"Let me know what I can do to help."

"Count on it." Matt shrugged his backpack higher on his shoulder. "Walt says since this is all your idea in the first place, the least you can do is find a way to help pay for it."

Joe knew it wasn't wise to get too attached to a student, but Matt had snuck under his emotional radar as a scrawny freshman using his wits to keep pace with the upperclassmen on a backpacking trip. Matt was still a little on the scrawny side, but once he filled out the gangly frame and ditched the lab tech look, the womenfolk would start paying more attention. "Hey, two smart guys like us should be able to come up with some college funds."

"Yeah." Matt scrubbed the toe of a stiff new Birkenstock against the floor. "Wonder if that hot new student teacher would be of any assistance."

"The student teacher's name is Ms. Sullivan. And she's not going to seem so hot after she starts handing out detention slips and essay tests."

"I don't know." Matt shook his head. "Hot is hot."

"She's too old for you, Matt."

"I don't want to date her. I'm just going to enjoy the scenery. Besides," he added, "the student betting pool is placing the best odds on Walford to make the first move."

Real pros, those student bookies. "He's married."

"Yeah, but it's kinda shaky right now. His wife went to Boise to visit her mother right after the Fourth of July picnic, and she hasn't come back yet." Matt shook his head. "And he's enough of a loser to hit on the hired help."

Hitting on the hot new student teacher—the worst kind of power play. And where power was involved in a relationship, it opened the door to some pretty ugly things, with exploitation heading the list. Good thing Joe kept reminding himself of the potential for disaster. Good thing bright and bouncy Emily Sullivan wasn't his type.

The first bell sent Matt jogging back to his locker and Joe trudging toward the stairs. He tried to focus on his first period class, but all he could come up with was visions of wide blue puppy eyes and the student bookies branding his forehead with an *L* for Loser.

EMILY WAS SURE that most people never realized how much energy it took to be energetic.

She turned down Main Street shortly after a late lunch at Al's Pizzeria, so tired she was afraid she'd lose the steering wheel tug-of-war with her battered, bullying '92 Chevy pickup. It was a good kind of tired, though. The kind that carried a kick, with sparks of self-satisfaction snapping beneath the layers of exhaustion.

She had moved a mountain of texts up a mountain of stairs, had overseen a pile of photocopying and a fist-bruising stack of stapling. There had been enough paperwork to tie up the State Department in a red-tape bow, enough crises to keep a soap opera afloat for a season and no chance for a coffee break. Her back hurt almost as much as her feet, and she suspected her bladder had stretch marks.

But there had also been dozens of shy smiles and friendly greetings. Her welcome to campus had been so warm, so *energizing,* that if someone asked her, at this very moment, to shift her growling truck to light speed, she was pretty sure she could pull it off.

Cast in the afterglow of all this goodwill, the heart of Issimish sparkled. Main Street's shop windows reflected the polish and flair filtering down the interstate from Seattle's suburbs. Even the town's rough and rowdy origins were getting a stylish makeover, something a little more quaint and a little less quirky.

She thumped over the railroad crossing at the edge of the new industrial park and sped out through orchards lining the old county road, rolling down the window to inhale the ripe tang of a football season afternoon. Houses thinned, separated by acres of bramble-edged fields instead of neatly fenced yards. The pickup's treads whined over the ragged pavement, their vibrations humming through her in an edgy accompaniment.

Emily planned on keeping the buzz buzzing with a liquid caffeine recharge and the semisweet chocolate bar she had hidden in the back of her kitchen junk drawer. Her schedule until the end of her college term, at Christmas, was a tight one: high school observations in the mornings followed by the lengthy commute to her university classes in the afternoons and evenings. She only had a few hours left to pound out a paper on Piaget due in tonight's Ed Psych class. And she should record her impressions of day one in her Social Studies Methodology journal before day two hit.

Impressions. Joe Wisniewski, still and self-contained, striking a deceptively lazy pose. Hitching one hip over the edge of his desk, those dark eyes scanning the room for student outlaws. Gary Cooper, calmly lecturing 'til high noon.

Okay, so she was still a bit impressed by The Great and Powerful Wiz, thrilling to his slow grin, or the quirk of an eyebrow, or the rumble of that deep voice. Her adolescent tingles and twinges had matured into, well, more mature tingles and twinges.

There she sat, tucked into the corner of a classroom she'd dreamed of joining at thirteen and clawed her way into at twenty-nine, echoes of her adolescent longings tumbling through her insides while her outsides calmly took notes. Studying his every move, pondering his every word—and wondering what was wrong.

Maybe it was the contrast of her own excitement with Joe's apparent lack of enthusiasm, maybe it was his laid-back ease and deadpan delivery, but nothing had been quite what she'd expected. He'd been a bit too laid-back, a bit too deadpan, not exactly the inspiring educational model she'd hoped for.

Still, he seemed to have a quiet rapport with his students. And he definitely had a subtle magnetism that tugged at her on every level. Her instincts told her there was something there, beneath the surface, something he was holding back.

But what if those instincts were nothing more than the kind of fantasizing she'd engaged in as a teen? What if this attraction turned into a major distraction? She needed to analyze his effect on her and his other students, not simply sit there and enjoy it. She needed to focus on her job, to evaluate his classroom management style, not get sidetracked by wide shoulders and lean hips.

She tightened her grip on the steering wheel. She wouldn't let it happen. Couldn't let it happen. There was too much riding on this assignment: her career, her family's approval, her own self-esteem. Her future.

She was in charge of her educational experience, not The Wiz. If he didn't offer the inspiration she'd hoped for, she'd work harder to find it elsewhere. Maybe, with time, she'd find what she needed within herself, wrapped in her own dreams and abilities.

In the meantime, if she had to spend several months observing a subject, it might as well be a good-looking one. "Can I pick 'em, or can I pick 'em?" she asked no one in particular as the truck rattled over a series of potholes.

Daydreaming of dark eyes and a deep voice, Emily pulled into her gravel drive and swerved to avoid clipping the fender of a silver Volvo sedan.

Uh-oh. Mom alert.

Emily frowned. What was on Kay Sullivan's agenda today? More questions about her daughter's career choice? Doubts about her living arrangement? A reconnaissance mission to check on the refrigerator's contents or the dryer's lint trap?

At the moment, Kay was plucking weeds from the box of overgrown petunias on Emily's front porch. She straightened and waved. "Yoo-hoo, Emily!"

Emily sighed. As if anyone could miss the tall, slim blonde in a bright red double-breasted dress with coordinating red lipstick and shoes. Kay's was the only coordinated ensemble in the ragtag front yard—although the brownish patches of rust on the gutters did match the brownish patches of gopher mounds in the grass.

"Hi, Mom." Emily hopped down from the truck, plotting a way to fast-forward through the visit so she could attack the Piaget project before it reached critical mass. Kay had a languid Louisiana way of drawing out an afternoon chat until it felt like a two-week delta cruise into the Twilight Zone.

Emily pointed to a wire-handled shopping bag near the doorstep. "What's in there?"

"Cookies and milk, just like old times." Kay's cheek brushed Emily's with the scent of gardenia. "To celebrate your first day of school."

"Oatmeal and butterscotch?"

"With extra chips."

Kay did have her good points—a couple dozen of them, judging from the size of the bag. Butterscotch could fill in for chocolate, in a pinch. And oatmeal counted as nutrition. She could chew fast, shorten the visit and skip dinner. "Sounds perfect. Except for the milk. I don't drink it anymore."

"I remember. But it goes with the cookies."

Of course. Just because neither of them would actually drink the milk didn't mean that the afternoon snack of cookies would be offered without the appropriate beverage. It simply wasn't done. After all, Kay Sullivan was the high priestess of family food rituals. She packed a picnic luncheon every Fourth of July, even when it rained. Spread coconut frosting on the Easter cake, which everyone scraped off. And labored over a jellied tomato aspic every Thanksgiving, though no one had yet worked up enough courage for even one taste. That, too, was tradition: the untouched aspic, trembling on the table in virginal apprehension.

"You know," said Emily, "they drink tea with cookies in England."

"I suppose they do." Kay picked up her package. "It would be rather continental, wouldn't it?"

"Come on, Mom," Emily said as she unlocked her door. "Let's live dangerously. I'll put the kettle on to boil."

She caught her mother's quick, discreet appraisal of the empty walls and curtainless windows as they stepped over the threshold. "My goodness," Kay drawled. "It's so refreshing, the way you're using all this natural light and the open floor plan."

Emily bit back an excuse and led the way to the kitchen.

"It's probably best not to invest in things that may be discarded. This is simply a temporary situation, after all." Kay's smile was a hopeful one. "Who could possibly know how long you'll be here?"

Emily dodged the question and arranged the cookies on a paper plate in the center of the tiny kitchen table. She knew her parents didn't understand her decision to dip into her savings to make the move out of their Seattle condominium.

A change of subject was called for, and Emily knew just the tack to take—her sister-in-law's pregnancy. "How's Susan doing? Getting rounder?"

Kay's eyes went soft and dreamy at the mention of her first grandbaby. "Just imagine, my little Jack, a father."

"Someone new for you to spoil."

"I never spoiled you and Jack."

"I was talking about Dad."

Kay laughed. "Oh, yes. I'll admit to plenty of

spoiling there. Although it always seems to work in both directions."

Emily turned to snatch the screeching kettle off the burner. Oh, how she wanted that for herself, that deep affection glowing beneath the patina of years spent rubbing along together. A husband might be a low-priority item on her list of short-term goals, but she intended to have her own glow one of these years.

She poured boiling water over tea bags in her two least chipped mugs, set them on a tray with some folded paper towels and paper plates and snuck a peek at the pig-shaped garage-sale clock before carrying everything to the table. Three o'clock—time to get this visit moving toward the finale. "So, let me give you the completely condensed version of my first day at school. It was great."

Kay cautiously lowered herself into a plastic lawn chair. "That's wonderful, Em. But then, you've always been able to find some degree of success in whatever you choose to do. All those different jobs—every last one of them."

Emily sighed over the references to her short attention span and lack of commitment and then piled her plate with cookies and spooned three helpings of sugar into her mug. "Well, today, my successes included photocopying, collating and stapling."

"My goodness." Kay sipped her tea and managed to look impressed. "That sounds ever so productive."

"It *sounds* as awful as it was. But it had its moments." Emily wrapped her hands around her mug and leaned forward. "I wish you could have seen the students' faces—all those expectations. I'm going to love it, I just know it. If I survive the planning, the teaching, the paperwork, the assignments for my university classes and all the extracurricular activities I plan to squeeze in."

"Oh, you'll survive. You thrive on hard work. You always have." Kay smoothed a hand over the paper in her lap as if it were fine linen. "Now, when are you going to let me take you shopping and buy you something special to brighten up this place a bit?"

Emily blew on her tea to cool it. She wasn't surprised by the shift in topic. Her mother was far more comfortable discussing homemaking than career planning. "Somehow I knew that's where this conversation was heading all along."

"Conversations are like the wind. They go where they will." Kay rose from her seat. "Sometimes they're wild and stormy, and sometimes they're just as fickle as a little breeze, blowing every which way and never keeping to any one direction."

"And sometimes they're as steady and predictable as a trade wind." Emily knew better than to assume that Kay's meandering didn't have an eventual destination. "Is that why you drove all this way out from the city this afternoon? Because you were looking for a fresh excuse to drag me out on a shopping trip?"

"Not entirely. I wanted to see for myself if my

youngest chick was healthy and happy." Kay leaned down and placed a kiss on her daughter's head with a loud smack.

Emily smiled. "Definitely both."

"It's working out then?" Kay carried her mug to the sink. "This teaching assignment?"

"After just one day filling in at that naval base classroom in Naples, I knew I was meant to be a teacher." Emily twisted her mug in a circle. "This is the one career that will make the best use of all my studies. And all my travels and experiences."

She sipped her tea. "I wanted this assignment at Caldwell with Joe Wisniewski, and I did everything but hold my breath until I turned blue to get it."

Kay found a dish towel to scrub over the counter. "How is The Wiz? Do they still call him that?"

"Yes, he's still The Wiz."

She watched her mother fussily fold the dish towel and then shake it out to start the process again. Emily was surprised to see a blush creep into her cheeks. "Mom?"

"Is he still a hunk?" Kay dropped the towel over the edge of the sink and faced her daughter. "He used to be. Is he still? A hunk?"

CHAPTER THREE

HUMILIATION ALERT. Did Kay know about Emily's adolescent fantasies? Did she suspect they were the real reason for this student teaching assignment? Not that a tiny crush had anything to do with anything, Emily was quick to reassure herself.

"Well, is he?" asked Kay. "A hunk?"

"Oh, yes." Emily sighed. "He's definitely still a hunk."

Kay slipped back into her seat and leaned forward in conspiracy mode. "Rumor had it he was carrying on with Ginny Krubek, all those years ago."

"Ginny Krubek?" Emily frowned. "Wasn't she the stylist at The Cow Lick?"

Kay nodded, and then broke a cookie in two and put half on her plate. "The Wiz came roaring into town on his motorcycle late that summer, looking like sin on wheels."

"I saw him walk out of the post office one morning." Tall and tanned, so dangerously different than everyone else on the street. "I remember he had a ponytail."

"He had Ginny cut it off the second week of school."

Kay lowered her voice to a whisper. "That was the same week Patsy Velasco started telling anyone who'd take the time to listen that Wiz had a tattoo. Of course, plenty of people around this town had plenty of time to gossip over information of that nature."

Gossip temporarily knocked Piaget off the list of priorities. "I never heard anything about tattoos," said Emily.

"That's what made Patsy's news so interesting. She said it wasn't exactly available for public viewing."

Imagining middle-aged Patsy Velasco viewing any of Joe's less public places was doing something nasty to the butterscotch in Emily's stomach. "Go back to the part about Ginny Krubek."

"Oh, yes. Well," Kay said, crossing her arms on the table, "like I said, rumors were flying fast and thick that there was something going on between Wiz and Ginny, too. Ginny was sure talking it up around town, at any rate."

"Wasn't there a Krubek in Jack's class?"

"Yes, Steve Krubek. And the principal back then, Mr. Rockman, was fit to be tied. He threatened to withdraw Wiz's contract. After all, Ginny's husband was a school board member back then. I'm sure the poor man was putting a lot of pressure on Mr. Rockman, behind the scenes."

"I knew there was something weird going on." Emily drummed her fingers on the table. "I figured there had to be more than one reason Dad was always getting so upset about that new teacher."

"Your father liked Wiz just fine, in spite of all their political disagreements. I think those two rather enjoyed arguing with each other. Dad used to say Wiz was one of the few intelligent life forms this side of Seattle. He did think Wiz could have been a little more discreet, though. Or at least discouraged Ginny's attentions. I always thought she was inventing most of what she was spreading around. Maybe even all of it. Who knows for sure?"

Emily finished off the broken cookie. "Why would Wiz put up with Ginny's big mouth? Or Patsy's, for that matter?"

"I got the impression that Joseph P. Wisniewski wasn't the kind of man who would give a hoot what other people said about him. Or thought about him, at any rate. That's one of the things the women found so exciting." Kay shook her head and laughed. "Lord, we were all so jealous of Ginny and Patsy back in those days."

"Even you, Mom?"

Kay straightened in her chair and brushed at the front of her dress. "You forget I'm married to a hunk of my own. I have neither the time nor the inclination to notice anything about another man. Even if he does look like a gypsy with the very devil in his eyes."

Emily grinned. "That's still a pretty good description."

"Oh, I imagine he's even more attractive now. Men get that chiseled look to their faces when they get a little older. Unless they go doughy. I can't imagine Wiz ever getting doughy, though. He was already a little chiseled to begin with, and besides, he had plenty of room for some more meat on those bones." Kay twitched a wrinkle out of the tablecloth. "Is he going gray? Losing his hair?"

"I don't think gray hair or male pattern baldness are in the picture yet."

"Oh, that's right." Kay shook her head and settled back. "He's only about ten years older than you, if that. He always did seem so much older, even back then. Some people do, you know."

Emily thought for a moment about all she'd heard of Joe's unconventional lifestyle and his reckless choices in women. Living like that would probably age anyone—and not the way a fine wine aged. "Well, he's had an interesting life."

"Yes, he certainly has, hasn't he? Up to and including the moment he decided to settle down to teach at that tiny school in this speck of a town. Why a man like that would ever choose to live in a place like this has always been a mystery to me."

Kay nibbled a bit more on her cookie and stared out the window. Emily studied her mother, certain now that Kay had just pulled off another fast one. This afternoon's meandering conversation had ended up precisely where she'd meant it to end. With a subtle warning to steer clear of any involvement with a man who was completely wrong for her daughter under any circumstances.

Emily had already figured things out for herself: Joseph P. Wisniewski was bad news. As a master teacher... well, she was prepared to give him another chance. Or two. After all, he hadn't wanted her in his classroom. But as a prospect for a romantic relationship outside the classroom? There was no evidence he was capable of anything resembling romance or a relationship.

Not that she should be entertaining thoughts about a romance or a relationship in the first place. Either one would jeopardize this assignment. And she couldn't disappoint her family again, not with another failed attempt at a professional career, and not with a questionable choice for her personal life.

She flicked a glance at the pig and tried not to wince. Half past time to drag her mind away from tattoos and tackle tonight's university assignment.

If there was one thing Kay could field like a major league champ, it was a social cue. She peeked at her watch and gasped. "Look at the time! I've truly overstayed my welcome. And I'll be lucky to make it back to the city before that awful rush hour traffic starts up." She stood to smack a little air kiss near Emily's left ear. "You're such a gracious hostess, dear, putting up with this interminable visit from your mother."

"I enjoyed every minute."

"Yes, the gossip was delicious."

"So were the cookies. Thanks."

Kay turned at the door. "Don't be a stranger, Em. Let's get together again, soon."

"Okay." Emily gave her mother a quick squeeze. She was pumped up on butterscotch and gossip now, ready to take on Piaget. She could even face the prospect of a discussion on decorating. "How about a shopping trip the weekend after next?"

"Call me."

"I will."

Emily stepped out on the crooked little porch and waved as the silver sedan backed into the county road. "I will," she promised them both.

JOE HEADED THROUGH the main doors of Caldwell High the following week and made an immediate about-face, hoping to escape Volunteer Friday before anyone noticed. No such luck.

"Hey, Wiz!" Sophomore Lindsay Wellek waved him toward a card table wrapped in gaily painted butcher paper and stacked with pamphlets in more somber, politically correct recyclable shades. "A lot of people have been checking us out. I think the Garden Project is really going to take off this year."

The Garden Project—the sole survivor of his misbegotten attempts at service learning, and the one extracurricular commitment he'd kept to ward off the possibility of a more strenuous assignment. "That's good to hear," he said.

He recognized the light in Lindsay's eyes, that heady mix of altruism and activism that fired the soul with strength and confidence in cause and self. He'd seen it in the mirror, not that many years ago. But now, surrounded by all this energy, with the scent of pledges and possibilities wafting through the corridor and the bustle at the tables humming like the soundtrack for *Norma Rae,* he felt as if the last embers of his fire had gone cold a lifetime ago.

When had he become more concerned with logistics and permission slips than with the basic joy of being a part of something good? When had he lost the ability to bask in the contentment of counting for something, of mattering to someone?

At what precise moment had he turned into one more member of the establishment?

Hell, he wasn't even a good bureaucrat. He'd forgotten about this morning's activities.

"This looks great," he said. "Did you paint this sign yourself?"

Lindsay's blush clashed with her red hair. "Yeah."

"Hey, Wiz." Matt stopped at the table, shrugged his backpack higher on his shoulder and reached for one of the pamphlets. He studied the information with great care, ignoring Lindsay's wistful glances.

Joe rolled his eyes at the teen angst tableau. He wanted to say something, to shove Matt off the curb and into the rush of oncoming female traffic, but he reminded himself that matchmaking was against one of his religions.

Besides, he'd nearly been sideswiped himself recently.

He settled a hand on Lindsay's shoulder. "You need to get yourself into Mrs. Mazza's art class next semester. I'm sure she'd appreciate having a student with some natural talent for a change."

Lindsay's blush deepened, and he gave her shoulder a tiny squeeze before straightening to level a long stare at Matt.

"What?" Matt asked.

"Get your nose out of that pamphlet and enjoy the scenery."

He turned and started a zigzag path through the crowd, checking in with the club officers stationed at other tables. And noting Emily's bold, spiky signature on far too many of the sign-up sheets. She was probably deep in chirp heaven this morning, spreading enthusiasm like pepper spray at an Earth First protest. Spreading way too much of her energy far too thin.

She'd learn her lesson soon enough. Extracurricular activities were education's answer to Chinese water torture. They wore teachers down, drip by time-consuming drip.

He hoped she wouldn't cry on his shoulder when the going got tough, or expect him to bail her out when she started to sink. One more reason he didn't want a student teacher.

There she was now, pausing at the table advertising winter term cheerleading tryouts, scribbling in the bulging organizer that seemed to be a detachable part of her anatomy. There was no way in hell he'd help her with a cheerleading commitment.

"How's it going, Wiz?"

He turned in time to catch Mitch Dornley's admiring glance at Emily's legs, and he shifted position to block the athletic director's view. "Fine. It's going just fine."

"Wish I could say the same."

Mitch hesitated, waiting for a response, but Joe let him sweat. He knew what was coming. It was the same routine every year.

"We've got another vacancy on the coaching staff, Wiz."

"That's tough."

Mitch hesitated. "It's a tough one to fill, all right."

Foreign languages like Innuendo lost a lot in the translation for Mitch. He scratched his bald spot and stuck to his game plan. "It's the JV girls' basketball team. They're a little low on talent this year, since we had to promote a few to fill in the gaps on Varsity. And those girls' JV teams are always kind of touchy. All those hormones and stuff."

"Nasty things, hormones."

Mitch nodded, obviously relieved to have escaped the ravages of estrogen. "I was just thinking…well, you did play hoops in college."

"I played, Mitch. I didn't coach."

"You coached track. The first year you were here."

"The post-traumatic stress episodes are finally tapering off," said Joe. "I'd like to keep it that way."

"Good morning, Wiz." Emily breezed into the conversation. "Hi, Mitch."

"Hey there, Emily." Mitch arched back and sucked in his gut. "I was just trying to talk The Wiz here into coaching JV girls' hoops."

"Really?" Emily seemed surprised. "Why?"

"He played hoops in college."

"Playing isn't the same thing as coaching, Mitch," Emily pointed out. "Coaching takes special skills. Not everyone has them."

Mitch puffed up again. "That's right."

"I coached track once." Joe couldn't explain why that had popped out. Maybe the puffing was contagious.

"You did?" She stared up at him. "Imagine that."

"Can't you?"

She smiled politely. "Not really, no."

Sheesh, where was a little chirpiness when a fellow needed it? "Well, I did. My first year here."

"Oh." Emily brightened. "That explains it."

"Explains what?"

The day's first bell set off slamming locker doors and last-minute pamphlet grabbing.

"Sorry," Emily said as she turned to go. "Can't be late taking first period attendance."

"Catch you later, Wiz." Mitch jogged up behind

Emily, catching her by one arm. He leaned down close to her ear and whatever he said had her laughing and shaking her curls against his shoulder.

Joe stood in the hall, students and staff churning around him like salmon headed upstream to spawn, and watched Emily disappear up the stairs. What in the hell was all that about? What did she mean, she couldn't imagine him coaching? Didn't she think he was patient enough? Sensitive enough? Inspirational enough? Did she think he was too lazy? Too irresponsible? Too out of shape?

Okay, so he probably was—or wasn't—a lot of those things. But just because he thought so didn't give her the right to entertain the same opinions. She certainly didn't know him well enough yet to catalog or appreciate the impressive list of his negative qualities. The fascinating backstories, the intriguing layers, the varied nuances—the mud-splattered tapestry of his soul.

He stalked into the office, snatched his mail out of his box and dumped it all into the nearest trash container. He stood there for a moment, visualizing himself kicking the can, imagining the whump of the metal, feeling the thwack against his sandal. Ahh, that was better. Slightly less violent, definitely more mature, and the next best thing to actually putting a dent in the can. Or picking it up and heaving it at the nearest window—or Dornley's head. Whichever got in the way first.

"Well, if it isn't another wonderful, wonderful day," Linda practically purred from behind her counter. "Good morning, Wiz. And how are you doing?"

"Can it, Linda."

"You've already handled that little chore." She held up a note. "I managed to rescue this before you went through your daily filing routine. You might want to answer it before Blob Dixon threatens to cut off the funding for whatever he's promising to fund this week."

He grinned at Linda's pet name for Bob, part owner of Dixon's Hardware and full-blown parental plague on Caldwell High. Bob also happened to be Joe's landlord, a fact he repeated every couple of weeks or so, just in case the concept hadn't yet lodged in the one short-term memory cell of Joe's brain. "What does he want this time?"

"A parent-teacher conference."

"It's only the second week of school."

"He has some concerns about your student teacher."

There was another reason he didn't want a student teacher. Now he was going to have to deal with all the parental concern issues Emily dragged to his classroom door. "He just wants to check her out," he said. "Up close and personal."

"Blob and every other red-blooded single male in the school community. Some of the married ones, too." Linda shot a slitted glance at Kyle's door, and then rested an elbow on the counter, waving the message.

"Tell me, what's it like mentoring the Student Teacher Most Likely to Cause a Traffic Pileup?"

Joe took the memo and crammed it into his pocket. "You're really enjoying this, aren't you?"

She laced her fingers beneath her chin. "Oh, yeah."

"Well, for your information—and for Blob Hardware's, and for anyone else who asks—she's doing fine. Just fine." The second bell rang. "She's up there right now, taking roll. She'll probably march the troops through maneuvers and drill them on essay responses before I arrive."

"I've heard she's a take-charge gal. I also hear she's got a date for every dance-chaperoning duty this fall."

"Yeah, well, things'll quiet down once everyone gets used to everyone else."

"Hmm."

He narrowed his eyes. "What was that supposed to mean?"

"What?"

"That 'hmm.' I know that 'hmm.'"

"Oh, nothing." Linda rubbed at a speck on the counter. "Better get up there, Wiz. High school students have been known to eat student teachers and subs for breakfast, especially since most of them don't eat anything before they get here."

"I thought that's what the candy in the snack machines was for."

"Hyped up on a sugar fix and ready to rumble," said Linda. "Either way, things could get ugly."

He shook his head. "I don't think anyone'll try anything. They've been pretty easy on her so far. If I didn't know better, I might start believing some of these crazy rumors going around."

"I heard her dad is a three-star general who used to send her to basic instead of summer camp."

He grinned. "You wouldn't happen to know where that rumor got started, would you?"

She inspected her nails. "Not a clue."

"Speaking of military types, how's Alice?"

"Your department chair? Still AWOL. Having a real tough time with this pregnancy, from what I hear." She paused. "I don't think she's going to make it back at all this year."

"Damn." Joe took a deep, resentful breath and let it rush out in despair. "I'm sorry to hear that."

"I'm sure you are."

"I guess I'd better get up there." He glanced at the ceiling. "Things may be nice and quiet right now, but what really worries me are the crazy ideas Ms. Sullivan might be pouring into those empty heads."

EMILY STARED at all the hands in the air, exhilaration and terror churning in her stomach along with her leftover pizza breakfast. She wished her university adviser was here to observe how well she was directing this American History discussion. And she hoped Joe wouldn't tell her adviser he wanted her out of his classroom because she directed discussions just like this.

"Does anyone disagree with what Matt just said?" she asked, looking for someone who hadn't yet had a chance to speak. "Angie?"

"No way!" Angie twisted in her seat to face Matt across the room. "I mean, it's so obvious that the Boston Tea Party was totally an anarchy thing. You know, like those people who smashed the windows in Seattle."

"Yeah, but at least those Seattle dudes didn't wear disguises," added someone from the back row.

"Starbucks coffee and English tea," rumbled Joe's soft voice from the classroom doorway. "Hmm."

Emily winced at the ominous sound of that *hmm*. She turned to see him lounging against the wide wood trim. One corner of his mouth slid into a wry grin. The kind of grin that could mask any number of things: irritation, amusement, her imminent dismissal. The kind of grin that scrambled her pulse and scattered her thoughts.

"Guess some people can get a little violent about their caffeine addiction," he said. "But anarchists? That's an interesting take on the Sons of Liberty."

She cleared her throat and pasted on a bright, confident smile to mask her panic. "We were discussing how some British taxpayers might have been angry about the actions and beliefs of some of the American colonists. Considering a different point of view."

"Is that so?"

"Just for the sake of argument," she added.

"Well, now. That sounds…fascinating. Sorry I missed it," he said. "How about a little review of the highlights?"

He slipped his hands into his pockets and settled into one of those deceptively negligent poses. "Just for the sake of argument."

CHAPTER FOUR

AN HOUR LATER Emily faced Arnold, the copier, her fingers hovering just above the green start button. "Okay, Arnold. Time to boldly go where no copier has gone before."

"Arnold?" Linda leaned against the doorjamb, a cup of coffee in one hand. "As in Schwarzenegger?"

Emily shook her head. "As in Kitchener. Not the Terminator—the Tormentor, in third grade. He used to trip me and steal my snack at morning recess. Then he got a crush on Alexa Poukopolis, and I got to keep my Twinkies."

"Men." Linda sipped her coffee. "Food and sex."

Emily nodded. "Hit and run."

The copier clunked once, twice and then flashed a jammed code. Emily sighed. "Is it just me, Arnold? Or do you treat all the girls this way?"

"It's the colored paper. Can't do anything creative on this machine." Linda opened the front compartment and ripped a shredded piece of paper out of the gears. "Did Wiz ask you to do this?"

"No, this is for the hospitality committee. Double-sided." Emily refilled the feed bin with a thick stack of plain white paper. "Wiz wouldn't use green paper for a handout."

"Guess not." Linda reached past her to punch Reset. "But it might be fun to see what would happen if you brought him a stack in hot pink. I have a secret stash of neon stuff. You could tell him we ran out of white."

"Are you trying to cause problems for me?"

"Just looking for a little more entertainment. I enjoyed hearing about the show you two put on yesterday. Maybe I'll get lucky and see your next spat live."

"What spat was—oh," Emily said. Her cheeks were getting warm. "That was just—well, I was—"

"Marcy told me there was a fight in the faculty room." Linda set her coffee on the counter and hoisted herself up next to it. "But I didn't believe it until Russell came in, shaking his head and saying he'd never seen Wiz get red in the face before. I'm just sorry I missed the opening round."

"There wasn't any opening round." Emily keyed in the copy commands and punched Start. "We were having a simple, civilized, philosophical discussion."

"I heard you two were going at it in the hall during break."

Emily's face grew uncomfortably hot. "We weren't 'going at it.' Not exactly."

Not unless you counted intense hissing from nose-to-nose range.

Linda looked unconvinced. "Maybe not in the

halls. But in the faculty room, definitely. I heard it from a couple of sources who had ringside seats. What was that about him being a jerk?"

"The word was knee-jerk. As in response."

Linda's smile was beatific. "Hmm."

Emily sighed. "Here I am giving my master teacher a bad time when he's been nothing but generous and patient with me."

"Pull-eez. Joe's patience is laziness in disguise. And generous?" Linda snorted.

"I'm trying to be grateful here," said Emily.

"How about honest? What's he been generous with besides copying duties?"

"That is part of the job."

"A very small part."

Emily pushed aside another batch of misgivings about this internship assignment and pulled the feed bin open to slip the printed papers in, sunny side up. "Maybe he just needs time to get to know me better."

"And maybe he's keeping you at arm's length precisely because he doesn't want to."

"He made it pretty clear he didn't want me here." She muttered a quick prayer to the copier gods and hit Start again. "I figure he needs another couple of weeks to come around. Eventually, he'll have to get used to the idea of sharing his classroom."

"Don't count on it."

Emily leaned against the counter and crossed her arms. Beside her, papers slapped and settled into the side tray without a hitch. "I can be very persuasive when I set my mind to it."

"That's what's going to make this so much fun to watch." Linda sipped her coffee. "And I'm not the only one looking forward to the fireworks. Most of the faculty think you're the best thing to happen to Joe Wisniewski in years. More than one witness to yesterday's 'philosophical discussion' mentioned how good it was to have the old Joe back, even if it was only for a few minutes. We all thought he'd dried up and fossilized way ahead of schedule."

"The old Joe?"

"Lord, yes." Linda flapped her hand. "He was hell on wheels his first year here."

"I've heard some stories."

"He used to drive us nuts with his causes and his arguments. I think he won most of the debates just by wearing down the opposition. He had more energy than any three of us put together. He was like a walking vibrator. You could get a buzz just from being in the same room with him."

Emily pulled the papers out of the tray, trying to imagine Joe's laid-back charm hyped up into killer charisma—The Wiz she'd known through her brother's tales and her parents' reactions, The Wiz she'd daydreamed over. "So, what happened?"

Linda frowned down into her mug. "I don't know. He never talked about it. He took off work for a while that spring—which was a shock, because he'd never taken so much as a sick day. And when he came back, he was sort of…I don't know. Defeated. Dull. It was like all the life had drained out of him. He never told any of us what was wrong. What had happened."

"That's so sad."

"Yeah." Linda took another sip of coffee. "The old Joe—the Joe that I remember—that Joe never came all the way back. But a couple of teachers saw a bit of that old fire in his eyes when he was arguing with you."

Emily started in on a second batch of copies. "I wonder what happened?"

Linda shrugged. "Like I said, it's a mystery."

Joe was turning out to be a mysterious man. And Emily never left a mystery unsolved—it was so careless, so untidy. Besides, whatever had happened to Joe all those years ago had affected his teaching, which was affecting her internship.

She hesitated to dig too deeply into his private life, particularly when the public parts were so… well, scandalous. Maybe she wouldn't need to unlock the secrets of his past to get him fired up again. There were other ways she could help him rediscover the joys of teaching or the excitement of a worthy cause, to help him find happiness.

"A mystery, hmm?" she asked Linda. "Sort of like the *P* in Joseph P. Wisniewski."

Linda smiled along the rim of her mug. "I happen to know the solution to that little mystery. But before you start in on me," she said, holding up her hand, "I have to tell you I'm sworn to secrecy."

"Come on. Not even a hint?"

"You'll never guess. Not in a million years. And that's the only hint you're going to pry out of me."

"Ms. Sullivan?"

Emily glanced behind her to see Kyle standing in the workroom doorway.

"Yes?"

"May I see you in my office?" He frowned at Linda, lounging on the counter. "When you're finished with your work here."

A summons to the principal's office. Disaster alert. Plague, pestilence and another dose of fake walnut paneling. "I'll be right there."

"Thank you." The door clicked shut behind him.

"Oh-oh," said Linda. "Watch out."

"Why?" Emily's pulse rate spiked. "What's going on?"

"Nothing." Linda narrowed her eyes at the spot where Kyle had been standing. "And that's what has me worried."

"Did someone call with a complaint?"

"No. You're doing fine. He's probably just fishing, that's all."

"Fishing?"

"His wife never came home from her little summer trip, you know. And he's been sighted at the local watering hole on more than one weekend evening."

"His wife left him?"

"That's the rumor." Linda slid down from the counter. "So, watch out."

"For what?"

"For a move."

Emily shuddered. "Yeeuchh."

"It shouldn't be too tough to spot," Linda said. "Kyle may think he's smooth, but he never made it past the slippery stage."

EMILY WALKED down the short hall as if it were the plank. She knocked on Kyle's office door and waited for his "Come in" before entering.

"Emily!" He smoothed his tie as he rose from his chair and walked out from behind his desk. He waved at one of the padded chairs in front of it. "Have a seat. Make yourself comfortable."

She tried to do just that, settling back and tucking her feet beneath her. The blinds behind his desk carved daylight into slits, and the dust motes blinked SOS as they floated on their oxygen ocean. The stuffy space smelled of floor wax and freshly applied cologne.

Kyle leaned back against his desk, crossed his arms and smiled down at her.

She smiled back and waited for him to speak.

And waited some more. And smiled a bit harder. And hoped her cheek muscles wouldn't start to spasm.

"How's it going so far?" he asked.

"Fine," she said. "I really like it here at Caldwell."

"That's good to hear." His smile didn't change as he nodded or spoke. It seemed to be molded out of some substance that looked like flesh and bone but couldn't quite capture that genuine, lifelike quality. "I want you to be happy here," he said.

"I am so far." Up until about five minutes ago, anyway.

"Any problems with any of the students?"

What was he fishing for? What had he heard? Calm down, she ordered herself. If Linda didn't know why she was in here, no one knew. And as for Linda's theory about what Kyle was after... Emily shuffled that thought out of the way.

"Problems with the students?" Emily asked. "None. No problems at all." She pulled one foot out from under her chair and crossed one knee over the other to get more comfortable.

"So, no problems," said Kyle. "Glad to hear it. We're proud of our students here at Caldwell."

"They're terrific."

"And the staff? I hope they've been helpful."

"Oh, yes. Extremely."

"Good, good." He smoothed his tie again. "We want you to feel like part of the team here."

"Thank you."

He cocked one hip against the edge of his desk, shifting his weight to one foot and letting the other dangle near her knee. When Joe made that same move, it was fluid and casual. Kyle's version was posed and calculated. She tried to ignore his loafer's subtle invasion of her space and her urge to shift out of reach.

"You're probably aware, Emily, that there are several staff members who are single, like you."

She nodded, hoping Linda's theory wasn't about to become fact.

"And many single people these days meet and get to know each other at the workplace," he continued.

She nodded again, feeling like a bobble-head doll.

"I was wondering if there might be any circumstances in which you would consider a friendly, social interaction with a member of this staff. A social relationship, outside of school."

"Well." She cleared her throat. "I'd certainly be willing to attend any parties for the faculty members."

Kyle tilted his head back and laughed a forced little laugh. "I'll make sure you get an invitation."

Emily laughed, too. Hers sounded a bit strangled.

"Actually, Emily…" Kyle hesitated, and the smile disappeared. His hand passed once more over the silk of his tie, a long, teasing stroke. "I was wondering how you might feel about the possibility of developing a…a personal relationship with someone on staff."

Think diplomacy, she told herself. Think tact and subtlety. And if that doesn't work, think Sherman tank blasting a hole in the walnut and leaving caterpillar treads on the splintered furniture and the splattered principal on the way out.

She smiled a neutral smile. "I hope to develop

personal relationships with several of the members of this staff before I leave. I think I've already begun to form some friendships. And I'd like to develop some mentoring relationships, too." She settled back a bit and spread her hands. "There's a lot I can learn from many of the people here."

"Yes, of course. That's something we can discuss at some other time."

He rubbed at his chin. "The reason I asked to see you today is to find out whether or not you might consider dating one of the staff members."

"Dating? No." She shook her head. "That wouldn't be appropriate."

Kyle's plastic smile was back. And something else, too. Something in the way he leaned forward and glanced down at her neatly crossed kneecaps.

Something fishy.

The vision of her suspended foot swinging up into Kyle's carefully positioned crotch was strong and clear and too tempting by half. She uncrossed her legs and tucked her feet beneath her chair. "I have a personal rule against dating coworkers," she said. "It seems the best policy."

"Yes. Simple and tidy." Kyle nodded. "I can certainly see how it might seem that way."

Emily had no intention of hanging around so Kyle could ask her to indulge in some friendly social interaction just to test the limits of her simple, tidy rule. "Well," she said, setting her hands on the arms of her chair and edging toward escape. "Is there anything else you wanted to discuss?"

"No. I just wanted to touch base," he said, and paused to let the words hang between them. "To see if you're happy here."

"Thank you for taking the time to check with me," she said, ignoring the remark about touching base as she stood to go. He didn't move, and she was forced to dance a quick sidestep to avoid brushing against him.

"If there's anything I can do for you, Emily," he said, following her to the door, "anything at all, you let me know, okay?"

"I will. Thanks again." She felt his eyes on her back as she fled toward sunlight and fresh air.

JOE MUTTERED A CURSE as he stepped into Caldwell's quad at lunch break. Drifts of smoke carried the stench of burning byproducts, piles of refuse dotted the lawn and something that was supposed to be music throbbed from the speakers behind an oversize grill. Another football season hot dog barbecue in all its glory.

He carried his curried-chicken-and-brown-rice salad across the quad to a twisted fir tree, found his favorite napping space between two root bumps and stretched out on his back on the grass, his head cushioned on his hands. He gazed up through the tree limbs and contemplated saying something to someone about the song lyrics, but decided it was such a petty thing compared to the unrecycled waste and charcoaled carcinogens surrounding him. He simply closed his eyes to shut it all out.

"Pardon me."

Emily. He turned his head toward the sound of her voice and opened his eyes. She was standing above him, sunlight rimming her curls in a blinding corona. He squeezed his eyes shut, but her afterimage danced in a negative exposure. "Yes?"

"Is this exposed root taken?"

"No."

He cracked one eye open to watch her sink to the ground, cross-legged and skirt-draped.

She held out a can of soda. "You looked thirsty."

He crossed his ankles and shifted his hands more comfortably under his head. "I was hoping I looked asleep."

"Nope." She set the can down near his elbow. "I could see your eyes twitching."

He watched her sip her soda, her mouth puckering around the rim of the can and her long neck arching back in a grateful curve. She swallowed, lowered the can and ran her tongue along her moist upper lip.

Joe looked away. He wasn't feeling drowsy anymore. He was feeling far too awake. And far too aware of Emily's throat and tongue and lips. "What do you want, Ms. Sullivan?"

"To buy you a soda. To say thank you for agreeing to this internship."

She lifted the can of cola and offered it again. It wouldn't have been polite to refuse.

"To have a simple, friendly conversation," she added.

He wondered if this was a student teaching assignment. Have a friendly chat with your master teacher sometime during the first month of classes. Report due on Monday.

Then he glanced up at her and saw the nerves behind her smile.

God, he was getting cynical in his pre-middle age. He really ought to apologize for any number of things: for not initiating a friendly chat himself, or for his bad habit of suspecting ulterior motives. For not seeming more grateful for the offer of free carbonated chemicals. For spending half his time plotting to get rid of her and the other half visualizing her naked in his bed.

This was why etiquette had been invented—to safely channel all manner of primal urges and sociopathic aberrations into G-rated clichés the whole family could enjoy. "Thank you," he said as he took the can.

"You're welcome."

"So." Joe set his soda on the grass beside him, shifted to his side, braced his head in his hand and prepared to engage in something simple and friendly. "What are your plans for this weekend?"

"Short-term or long-term?"

A two-tiered plan for a two-day weekend? Why did

he think any conversation with Emily could be simple? "Forget I asked."

"Okay." She shoved a hand into her skirt pocket, withdrew a folded wad of paper and waved it under her chin. "New topic. I have here a list of names beginning with *P*," she said.

He groaned. "Believe me, I've heard them all."

"Not, apparently, *all* of them." She shifted and wriggled her curvy rear end over the root to torture him. "I figured I could arrange the search in either alphabetical order or categories."

"Categories?"

"Categories makes the most sense to me, too." She smoothed her paper over her lap. "I thought I'd start with Polish names. Just in case someone overlooked something that goes with Wisniewski. Names like Pawel? Piotr? Prosimir?"

He shook his head. "No, no and nope."

"Prokop. Parys. Pankracy. Pius. Pielgrzym. And this one," she said, handing him the paper. "I don't know how to pronounce it."

Przybywoj. "Neither do I."

"Oh, well." She took her list back with a sigh. "I didn't expect to get it on the first try."

He watched her refold the paper and carefully shove it back into her skirt pocket. They sat for a moment in silence, watching students materialize and vanish through the grill smoke.

Emily picked up her soda and sipped, and then

gestured with the can to encompass the scene on the quad. "So, is this where you picture yourself in ten years?"

Joe narrowed his eyes. "Why should I?"

"Because this is where you want to be, what you want to be doing." She cocked her head to one side with a bright smile. "Because you find teaching challenging and satisfying. Because it makes you happy."

He stared at her seemingly innocent expression, searching for a trick. Strange that she'd ask him the one question he'd been ducking lately. "Happy?"

"Happiness is a worthwhile goal." She set down her can. "I'm hoping teaching will bring me happiness. For any number of reasons."

Her idealism itched along his conscience like a rash. He frowned at her and grabbed his soda. "Do you have another list in your pocket?"

"No," she said with a laugh. "And we don't have to talk shop if you don't want to."

Thank God. "What will we talk about?"

"Oh, I don't know. Life, for instance. Specific or generic. Past, present or future. For a start."

"For a start," he said. "Would that fall under the short-term or long-term goals for this conversation?"

She smiled one of her widest smiles, the one that twisted and tickled something deep inside him. "Any topic, Joe. Any or all of the above. You could start with the easiest one first."

"Don't you have something else to do right now?"

He rolled onto his back and set the can of soda on his chest before closing his eyes. "Someone else to interview about the meaning of life?"

"No. I don't have university classes on Fridays, so I thought I'd hang out here for the rest of the day. Maybe find another opportunity for a friendly chat."

Joe groaned. "Lucky me."

He listened to her laugh and couldn't suppress a miserly smile. He enjoyed hearing her laugh, and he liked knowing that something he'd said was the reason. He enjoyed her company, and her chatter, and her scrunching nose and pinwheeling hands. And he liked this simple, friendly feeling. It was…nice.

He really hated that particular four-letter word, but there it was: nice. He couldn't come up with a better term for this warm and fuzzy friendship he felt settling over them just the way he imagined grandma's favorite afghan might feel—soft and familiar and scented with something other than barbecued pork extract. Warm, and fuzzy, and safe. *Nice*.

He hadn't planned on it, hadn't been looking for it, hadn't been working at it, but there it was. And what was extra nice was that he was fairly sure Emily felt the same, too. The sound of her laughter was a good sign. That and the fact that she hadn't given up on him and moved away.

So he made the effort to straighten up, chance a sip of the soda she'd given him and take the simple, friendly conversation to another level. "You know,

Ms. Sullivan, not everyone chooses happiness as a life goal. Some people put other people's happiness ahead of their own."

She tilted her head. He knew that tilt. It meant his philosophical underpinnings were about to be run through the wringer.

"And doesn't the creation of that happiness give a deep sense of accomplishment and satisfaction to the happiness causer?" she asked.

He shifted forward. "What about pure altruism? Doing good for others at the risk of complete self-sacrifice?"

"Does it have to make you unhappy to be pure? Can't an act still be altruistic even if there's a little niggling shred of satisfaction mixed in with the sacrifice?"

"So, in your world, self-satisfied self-sacrifice is, in essence, a selfish act?"

Emily leaned closer. "What is self-sacrifice without some degree of self-satisfaction?"

"Altruism."

"Or martyrdom." She tilted her head again. "So, Joe, which kind of teacher are you? A slightly impure altruist? Or a chest-thumping martyr?"

"Neither. And I have the paychecks to prove it."

Damn. She'd snuck in under his guard and landed another sucker punch. She'd gotten his brain in gear, his juices flowing and forced him to examine his motivations for teaching. He was feeling bruised, and confused, and annoyed, and something else he didn't care to label at the moment, because it felt like one of those feelings that would get him fired if he followed through on it.

He settled back against the ground and closed his eyes to shut her out and end the conversation. "It's just a job, Emily."

When she didn't respond, he cracked one eye open to see her smiling down at him. One of her admiring smiles. The kind that made him squirm.

CHAPTER FIVE

EMILY PERCHED on her bar stool a week later and surveyed the Friday-night scene at a university area pub: a room packed with hopefuls looking for hookups. The stale beer, the stale peanuts and the stale lines were standard issue atmosphere.

Next to her, Social Studies Methodology classmate Marilee Ostrom ran a red-lacquered nail along the edge of her margarita glass and licked the salt from her finger. Then she leaned forward and set her elbows on the glossy pub bar, crossing her arms to neatly frame her ample breasts for the male art critics on the other side of the counter.

"Okay, you're right. Nice moves," said Emily. "But it's the cleavage that makes it work."

"You've got cleavage."

"Barely."

"There's nothing bare about it tonight," said Marilee, glancing at Emily's gray turtleneck sweater. "You won't land a live one if you don't get your hook in the water."

Marilee tossed her lush auburn hair over her

shoulder with a sensual shrug. Everything about Marilee was lush and sensual and made for red. Not a sophisticated burgundy or a down-to-earth rust, but a sex-served-straight-up, sirens-screaming, fire-engine red. "Besides," she said, "your reel will get rusty if you don't play out a little line every now and then."

All this fishing talk was reminding Emily of Linda's theory about Kyle. "Can we drop the fishing analogies? And besides, I'm not interested."

"I've always believed that the best way to top off a girl's night out is with a man in the morning." Marilee tipped her glass in a discreet gesture. "That one, over there, the one with the dark green sweater- -he looks like your type."

Emily glanced at a lanky all-American candidate with squared-off shoulders and a squared-off jaw. "Yep, he sure does."

"So, give him some encouragement," said Marilee.

"I don't want to encourage him."

Marilee rolled her eyes.

Emily stared down at her drink. "It's complicated."

"Is there someone else?"

"Why does there have to be someone else?"

"Because Chad, or Blake, or Whoever over there is seriously cute."

Marilee smiled at the dark and brooding guy in black leather at the other end of the bar, and he smiled back through a ribbon of cigarette smoke. Dark and brooding would suit Marilee, Emily thought.

They watched him send up another smoke signal. "Go ahead," Emily said. "Go fish."

"And leave you crying over your mysterious someone else?"

"I'm not. I won't."

Marilee rolled her eyes again. "You've got all the symptoms. Sighing, dressing like a nun. Ignoring Troy in the green sweater."

"Maybe I'm just picky." Because she could feel a blush coming on, Emily turned to stare out at the crowd.

Marilee shook her head. "I've got you pegged. And your cheeks are turning bright pink. You're like a human traffic signal. Stop. Go. Go away."

Emily reached back to pick up her wine and took a big sip of avoidance.

Marilee gasped. "I know who it is. It's your master teacher. The tall, dark and cranky one with the troubled past. You like him."

"Of course I like him."

"No. I mean, you *like* him. As in 'I like what I see and I want to see more.'"

"I couldn't do that," Emily said. Marilee lifted one auburn eyebrow, and Emily's cheeks got warmer. "It's complicated."

"We've already established that." Marilee toyed with her straw. "So he's your master teacher. So you've got an itch for him that can't be scratched till the end of the term. Doesn't mean you can't brush up against him every now and then in an innocent social setting. Find out if he's a little itchy, too."

Emily spun the stem of her glass. "No way. He's my teacher *and* my job supervisor. That's two big check marks in the hands-off column."

And she'd better remind herself about those check marks whenever she started feeling a little warm and rashy. Joe would be evaluating her performance during the next few weeks. Things could get sticky if either of them acknowledged a sexual attraction or, worse, followed up on it.

The smart thing to do would be to get herself re-assigned to another school—it might not be too late in the term. But there were mysteries to solve, and things she wanted to help Joe rediscover. And there were other things she still believed, deep down in her heart, only Joe could teach her.

"So there are some complications." Marilee shrugged. "I don't see anything here a little time won't cure."

The smoker slid off his stool and sauntered to an empty booth, casting lures in his wake. Marilee's lips bowed in a smug curve. "Unless the complica-tions on the personal level are complicating things on the job level," she said.

"What do you mean?"

"All that photocopying and note-taking you're stuck doing while the rest of us are enjoying some one-on-one time with students." She set her drink on the bar. "Are you letting the personal complications get in the way of the job?"

Maybe she was. Maybe she'd been distracted by Joe's good looks and his mysterious past. Maybe she'd been a little too admiring, a little too curious—and a little too passive.

Maybe it was time to be more assertive, time to stop settling for copier crumbs and grab a bigger share of the classroom pie. Maybe the only way she'd ever find out if she could handle the challenges of a teaching career was to challenge Joe on his own turf.

While she was considering all the maybes, Marilee slid off her bar stool and slipped her purse strap over the shoulder of her bright red dress.

"You can't just open up a can of worms like that and then leave me here," Emily said.

Marilee waggled red-tipped fingers in farewell. "Fish or cut bait, Em."

JOE CONFRONTED another restless Friday night. The end of another week of teaching, another week of trying to figure out if making an effort was worth the effort. One week closer to the end of the school year and the decision whether or not to sign another contract.

He stood at the living area window in his cramped apartment tucked above Dixon's Hardware, staring down into the glowing puddles ringing the street-lights along Main Street, and poured the last half inch of a bottle of Merlot into a large goblet. He swirled it, watching the wine glide down the curved sides. Good legs.

Legs. Female legs. Long, satiny and tangled with his. The perfect distraction from thoughts of the job.

He could phone Dolores over in Orchard View. He'd buy her a few drinks, and she'd offer her warm bed and willing body in exchange. She always did. Dependable, divorced Dolores. Maybe tonight he'd take her up on it.

He frowned down into his glass, knowing the company of a forty-five-year-old shopping network addict wasn't the cure for this particular case of restlessness.

Maybe he'd make a plan. Short-term, just for the next few hours; long-term, to get him through Saturday night, too. Maybe he'd open another bottle of wine and settle in at the piano, spin out whatever blowzy, bluesy tune the vintage suggested. Ambivalence in the key of Burgundy.

He turned from the window, set the goblet on a side table and stretched out along the oversize sofa squeezed into the undersize space. The secondhand-shop leather cushioned him like an old ball glove, and he focused on the comfort as he willed himself to relax.

The clock struck nine, and the room dimmed as the shop lights beading the street below winked out. Rain splashed over the gutter, and the furnace whumped and hissed. He tapped one foot against the other, adding to the sullen syncopation.

So, is this where you picture yourself in ten years?

He swung his feet to the floor with an oath and flicked the switch on the side table lamp. Light spilled over his empty goblet and beside it, his cell phone.

Conversation could be a cure for restlessness. He'd had a taste of conversation, of connection, in the quad with Emily, and the sample had left him hungry for more.

He lifted the phone, hit the first number on his automatic dial and waited through the electronic clicks and trills to hear the voice of his aunt in San Francisco. Anna Green, his one and only family member. An activist with a heart as deep as San Pablo Bay and enough political savvy to fill it ten times over.

"Anna," he said when she picked up. "It's me."

"So it is." His aunt's gravelly voice sounded like his childhood—earthy, basic, and a little rough around the edges. "Where are you, kid? Anywhere close?"

"Here at home," he said.

"Friday night, single fella, stuck at home. What's wrong with this picture?"

"It was a rough week."

"Aren't they all?" she asked. Joe could hear papers rustling in the background and pictured her fidgeting with her work. Anna never did one thing at a time when she could do two.

"The first couple of weeks of school don't usually

hit this hard." He didn't usually have to deal with a fresh and lovely young woman probing into his intellectual and emotional nooks and crannies.

Joe slouched down and rubbed his free hand over his face. "What's on the political agenda these days?"

"SUVs. Elitist weapons of death." He listened for a few minutes while she read him an abbreviated version of her current riot act. The follow-up literature would probably hit his mailbox within a week. Anna didn't write, she pamphleted.

But he'd always been able to derail her from her one-track speeches for the critical moments of his life. And she'd managed to keep him fed and clothed, disciplined and educated after his mother had abandoned him on her doorstep. He was grateful for the care she spared for her nephew in the midst of her greater quest to care for humanity.

He waited for her to wind down, waited for an opening. "Is it all worth it? What you do, I mean."

"That's one of the most ridiculous questions you've ever asked." Her exasperation sputtered through the wires. "What's wrong with you?"

"I don't mean the causes. Or the effort," he said.

"What do you mean, then?"

"I mean…" What did he mean? "Does it—does your work make you happy? Are you happy, Anna?"

"Why the hell wouldn't I be?" No more sputtering now. "It's what I choose to do, every day. It's my life—it gives my life meaning and direction. There aren't many people who can say that about what they've chosen to do."

Anna's words rippled through his dark and empty spaces. Something coherent struggled to take shape, but he was too weary to concentrate. Too much wine, too much rain.

"This is an interesting series of questions," she said. "I'm wondering what inspired it."

"A conversation I had this week. About altruism."

"Hmm." The paper rustling slowed. "I think that, to some degree, I need to feel good about myself. About what I do. What about the job you do? Some folks might call teaching an altruistic profession."

"But I get paid to do it."

"So do I. All my causes put food on my table. Just because they're bigger than a classroom doesn't mean they're any more important."

Joe rubbed tiredly at his face and silently cursed Emily Sullivan for making him feel like a project with a due date. Short-term, long-term, end-of-term—any way he looked at it, he was going to have to define himself as a teacher and a human being before he could help guide her through the process. And he had a feeling he wasn't going to like the answer to the big essay question waiting at the bottom of the page.

"So, what's the real reason for the call?" Anna asked.

"Nothing special. I just wanted to talk."

"About the justification for our existence? Most

folks start out with something simple, like, 'How's the weather down there?'"

He thought of Emily's simple, friendly chat. "Maybe I'm a little rattled. New school year, remember?"

"Yeah. Any changes? How about a new principal?"

"No, still stuck with Kyle."

Joe smiled at Anna's inventive curse. She'd met his boss once; survivors of the disaster scene still cringed at the memory. "Word is his wife left him."

"Smart move."

"There's more." He stalled for a moment, and then dived into the news he realized he'd wanted to share with her all along. "I've got a student teacher."

"It's about time, kid." The paper rustling stopped. He had her complete attention now. "Here's your chance to make a bigger impact. Mold another teacher to fight the good fight."

Joe quickly blocked the image of his hands molding Emily's curves. "I don't think that's going to happen. She comes from a military family. You know the type—solid, upstanding, old-fashioned. Big-time conservatives."

There was another pause. A long one. And then Anna did something she didn't do very often. She laughed. A rolling, raucous, riot of a laugh. The kind of laugh he hadn't heard from her since that *Love Boat* actor decided to run for Congress on the GOP ticket. He could hear Anna's partner, Carol, in the background, ask what was going on.

Anna finally managed to ask, "Is she pretty?"

"What does that have to do with anything?"

"Is she?"

"What if she is?" said Joe. "She's not my type."

"What do you mean, she's not your type? Is she mine?"

"No!" Joe stalked to the window and lowered the blinds. "I mean, I don't think so. *No*." God, no.

"So, what's she like?"

"Think Shirley Temple on speed."

There was that laugh again. And when Anna repeated his description for Carol, he got to hear it in stereo. "So glad I could provide this evening's entertainment," he said.

Anna sighed a settling-down sigh. "God, I'd love to meet her."

"Yeah, I'll bet you would." He grinned at the thought of Emily deconstructing Anna's underpinnings. "She'll be at Caldwell until the end of the semester."

"That's only, what, months away?"

Joe shut his eyes. "God."

"You know how time flies when you're having fun," said Anna.

"This isn't fun."

"Yin and yang, kid," said Anna. "Find the right balance, achieve harmony."

Joe grunted. When it came to Emily Sullivan, his take on yin and yang was probably something a lot more physical than what Anna had in mind.

"It's getting late," he said. "Thanks, Anna."

He said goodbye and disconnected. The sudden silence magnified the emptiness of his dark apartment.

He snatched his empty goblet from the side table and carried it into the kitchen. No more wine tonight. And less wine in the nights to come. He needed to keep a clearer head.

Damn it, he hadn't asked for a session of self-analysis. He'd been reasonably content with his life before Ms. Emily Sullivan barged into it and started asking all her questions about goals and happiness. Okay, maybe not content, exactly, but resigned. Resignation was a good thing, especially for his mental health. It meant he'd faced his mistakes and learned from them. That he was doing everything in his power to keep from making them again.

Which meant he never should have allowed Ms. Fresh and Lovely Sullivan to step one foot in his classroom door. But there she was. Probing.

Tempting.

He cursed and swung back into the living area, scrambling for control. He was the authority figure here, damn it. What he needed to do was to start acting like it. He'd probably be sore. He hadn't used those particular muscles for a long, long time.

Better sore than sorry.

From here on out, the honeymoon period was over. Fini. Kaput. He wasn't going to let her get to him again, to get the upper hand again. He'd take the lead in their conversations.

These first few weeks of her part-time internship were supposed to be an observation phase in her student teaching year—well, she could damn well observe. Nothing more. Let her sit out there with the other students, far away from his desk. Far away from him.

When it was time for the next phase, he'd set up separate discussion groups, separate projects. No need for teamwork. Keep her moving in baby steps, carefully placed. That was the plan. The end of the term would be here before she knew it.

Better still, there might be some way to get rid of her. He'd make a few phone calls, talk to a few people. He'd ease her out, before she realized what was happening. Before she could shake him up like this again.

Before she wormed all the way under his skin and drove him completely over the edge.

There you go, Emily, he thought with a smile. Plans. Short-term and long-term goals, neatly outlined and ready to be implemented.

He walked over to his piano and stared down at the keys. There it was again—the tune that had been teasing through the back of his mind all week. All it needed was a different tempo: lazy, with a touch of the blues.

He stretched one hand over the keys and began to pick out the first few notes of "Animal Crackers in My Soup."

CHAPTER SIX

ON MONDAY MORNING, Joe watched Emily hunch over her observation post in the back corner of his second-period Current Events class. She was doing an admirable job of ignoring the bright blue Skittle wobbling on top of the radiator a few inches from her elbow.

Her neighbors were having a more difficult time ignoring the results of an incident involving a dangling backpack, an open box of candy and Emily's swinging foot. Every once in a while someone shifted, and another Skittle scuttled across the room. A discussion on the European economic union couldn't compete with the subtle soccer matches going on in the aisles.

When the bell rang, she stood with the other students and began her end-of-observation routine: double-checking her schedule in her organizer before closing it, arranging her pens in a predetermined order in the pen compartment of her briefcase, marking her place in her journal before slipping it into its special slot.

She adjusted the strap over her shoulder and turned

to leave, but Matt stepped into the aisle, blocking the path from her desk to Joe's. "Hey, Ms. Sullivan."

Emily gave him one of her more businesslike smiles. "Hi, Matt."

Joe turned to wipe his lecture notes off the board and give them both a little privacy. He suspected Matt had a bit of a crush on her. There was a lot of that going around. She'd have to learn to deal with it on her own.

"I heard you're going to coach the JV girls' basketball team," Matt said.

The eraser scudded across the board and flopped on the floor in a little puff of chalk dust. Joe swiveled to scoop it up and caught Emily's quick, guilty glance.

She cleared her throat. "Uh, yes, Coach Dornley and I have been talking. But that's all—just talking." She flicked another glance at Joe. "Nothing's been decided yet."

"Okay." Matt shrugged his backpack higher on his shoulder. "Just curious."

She followed Matt down the aisle, toward the front of the room where Joe waited, one hip cocked against the edge of his desk.

"If you do decide to coach basketball," Matt said, "I'd be happy to help. Team manager, stats, that kind of stuff."

Emily's smile was overly bright. "Thanks. I'll let you know."

Matt nodded and strolled out the door.

Emily took a deep breath. "Wiz?"

"Hmm?"

"Do you have a minute?"

"Actually, there's something I'd like to discuss with you." He swiped his chalky hands on his jeans. "What's this about you talking to Dornley about the JV girls' basketball team?"

"They really need a coach," she said. "Practices are scheduled to start in a few weeks."

"Dornley'll handle it."

"He's going to coach?"

"No. But he'll find someone. He always does."

Emily wrapped her fingers around her briefcase strap. "He doesn't seem too sure about that."

"Dornley never seems too sure about anything." He shrugged. "But that's his problem. Not yours."

"Don't you think I could do it?"

He suspected she could do just about anything she set her mind to, and the concept terrified him.

He moved around his desk and sank into his chair. "It doesn't matter whether or not you can do it. It matters whether or not you have the time to coach."

"If I didn't think I could make the time, I wouldn't be considering taking it on."

Emily slipped her briefcase off her shoulder, settled into the nearest student desk and folded her hands neatly on the top. She looked very serious. Too serious. The little hairs on the back of Joe's neck prickled.

"When I took this student teaching assignment,"

she began, "I planned on getting involved in the school. That includes extracurricular activities."

"Coaching isn't an extracurricular activity. It's a prison sentence. And a cell mate with a multiple personalities disorder."

"I think it could be rewarding and educational," she said in a prim and proper voice. "A way to interact with the students on a different level than in the classroom."

"Trust me," he said, leaning back in his chair. "You don't want that kind of interaction. With them or with their parents."

She nodded, obviously considering his arguments. There was something different in her expression, something that had him worried. Something that looked suspiciously like calculation.

"I want that kind of interaction, Wiz. That's why I'm here. To learn about *all* the aspects of a teaching career, including the extracurricular ones."

She had no idea what she was letting herself in for—which meant he'd probably get stuck mopping up after her. But that's not what had him worried him at the moment. It was the prim and proper bit. Emily's enthusiasm was never this cool and restrained.

He picked up a piece of chalk and drew it through his fingers. "Why don't you just stick with the classroom basics until you're ready to move up to the big time?"

"The basics?" She smiled and widened her eyes in her best I'm-not-as-naive-as-I-look look.

He hated that look. It usually meant he was about to get backed into a corner.

"Do you mean, the real teaching basics," she said, "like making copies, and collating, and stapling?"

His fingers stilled. "Is that why you're thinking about coaching? Because you're bored?"

"Were you thinking of giving me more responsibilities in the classroom?" Emily asked. "Is that why you're so concerned about me taking on extras?"

The walls were already closing in on him. "Maybe."

"Maybe?"

"Probably." The hinges squawked as he tipped back, and he flinched.

She stood and stalked to his desk, and then placed her hands on the edge and leaned over it. He hated when she did that, too. He had trouble deciding how to focus at that angle. Her breasts were most directly in his line of sight, so he had to shift his concentration to her face. More distractions: the silvery blue eyes beneath her lowered lashes, the tiny freckles dashed across her nose, the even white teeth biting into her pouty lower lip.

"You know," she said, "if you're really worried about me being able to handle all of it, you could help. You could help coach, for instance."

The casters on his chair slammed down on the floor as he fell forward. Was she insane? Did she really think he wanted to extend his school day into the evening and squander his weekends in the gym?

Spend hundreds of hours of "quality" locker-room time with sweaty teens and hundreds more socializing and arguing with their pushy parents?

Did she actually think he'd agree to spend countless hours more consulting with her, huddling close to map out plays? Taking off with her on road trips, or working up some sweat of their own tossing a ball around on the court?

Was he insane to be imagining, for one satisfyingly detailed moment, doing all of that sweaty, huddling stuff with her, and more?

He shifted his feet and a Skittle rolled out from beneath his desk. Emily discreetly nudged it back, and then straightened away from his desk. "Or I could help you coach. You're far more qualified and experienced than I am."

"Emily, I never—"

"I know what's bothering you," she said with one of her dismissive waves. "That day in the hall, when you were talking to Dornley—"

"Wait a minute—"

"—and I said I couldn't imagine you coaching the JV girls' basketball team—"

"—I never said I—"

"—Oh, Joe," she continued. "I'm so sorry I said what I said. Do you want me to try harder?"

"Harder?"

"To picture you coaching the JV girls' team. Because if you're thinking about coaching—"

"No!"

"You're not?"

"No." He raked a hand through his hair. "God, no."

"Well." She smiled and slid back into her front row desk. "Then I guess I should do it."

"No!"

"Well, someone has to do it."

"Someone," he said, rubbing his face. "Just not you."

Now he'd done it. He'd hurt her feelings. He could see it in the way she folded her hands again, just so, on her desk. Now he'd have to do something, promise her something, give her something to make it up to her. Just not basketball. Anything but that. And not the upcoming activity on the United Nations. Or global warming. Those were his babies.

"I guess you don't think I can handle that kind of responsibility." Her whispery voice filleted him like a flounder.

Okay, she could have the United Nations. "I don't think that at all."

"Thank you, Joe." She sighed. "That means a great deal to me."

She peered up at him through her lashes. Okay, she could have global warming, too. But not basketball. No way in hell was he going to coach.

There. A stand on an issue. Maintaining control over the situation and keeping his student teacher in her place.

God, what a wimp.

He stared at her innocent smile and wondered what kind of scheming sorceress lurked behind it. How many other victims had Emily Sullivan lured to their dooms with her wide-eyed glances, or that little sighing shrug thing she did just before she flounced into a chair? She was dangerous; she was lethal. She was Attila the Honey.

Here he was, scrambling to regroup, and she was getting ready to cut him a deal. He could see it in the way she settled back in her seat, in the way her lips pressed down to keep her next smile under control.

"I guess I could tell Coach Dornley you've got some special projects for me in your classroom," she said. "I wouldn't have time to coach if I had other things to handle."

"Something tells me you could get around that problem, too." He slumped deeper into his chair and waited to hear her first offer.

She stood and reached for her briefcase. "I could probably handle a class or two. Or a unit, if you'd like." She slipped the strap over her shoulder. "I think it's time for me to take on a few more teaching responsibilities. I'm sure my adviser would like to see that, anyway."

"I'm sure he would." He should have known she wouldn't leave a loophole unplugged. "So, we might as well get this over with. How are things so far? Got the copier situation under control?"

She nodded. "Nailed that on day one."

"Atta girl."

"What was that I just heard?" She leaned forward, cupping a hand behind one ear. "A little positive reinforcement? Why, you almost sounded like—no. It couldn't be."

"What?"

"You almost sounded like a…well, like a coach."

She may have been a witch, but she was a sexy witch. A challenging witch who made the job fun, which it hadn't been in a long, long while. And her teasing made something swell inside him. Something young and energetic and nearly carefree. Something that made him snatch a piece of paper from the recycle tray, wad it and toss it at her head.

She dodged, laughing. "Imagine that."

"Imagine this, Sullivan." He leaned to one side and grabbed the lesson plan book next to his coffee mug. "You can start with a current events discussion on Monday. Foreign or domestic. Pick one. It's yours."

She froze. "Oh, Wiz, really?"

"Why so surprised?"

"I was just thinking…well, after…"

He liked knocking her off balance, even if she tended to bob right back up. "The coaching thing? The Skittle thing?"

"No. The Boston Tea Party thing."

"Ahh." He'd almost forgotten about the tiny,

panicked flicker in Emily's eyes when she'd seen him at the classroom door a couple of weeks ago. But he hadn't forgotten that he'd walked in on a group of students engaged in a lively, wide-ranging discussion. Hell, he'd enjoyed going along for the ride. As an opening act, he'd have to give her an A. "The great taxation vs. representation debate, revisited," he said. "Not bad."

She fisted her hands on her hips. "Not bad?"

"Okay, it was good. Damn good. Now, wipe that smug smile off your face and let's see what else you've got up your sleeve." He offered her the lesson book. "Here's the time frame. What looks good for you?"

She unloaded the briefcase. "I need to check my calendar, too."

Of course. Wouldn't want to make a move without checking the planner.

He leaned back and watched her go through her organizer routine. It never ceased to amaze him how someone so organized and methodical could seem so impulsive at times. He might tolerate a bit more disarray in his life, but at least he had firmer control over his impulses. To prove it, he dragged his eyes away from the spot where her sweater outlined the curve of her breast.

He looked down at his plans for a review of recent American interventionist activities and wondered what Emily would choose to highlight when it was her turn to discuss the news. He hoped she'd call on him if he raised his hand to participate.

Just for the sake of argument, of course.

EMILY STARED OUT her kitchen window a few weeks later, watching fickle red leaves ditch their maple tree partners to swirl away in the arms of a late-October wind. She wished she could be outside stomping through heaped-up piles of leaves, reveling in the riotous hues and crackling textures. Instead, she was stuck inside with a university assignment.

Beside her, Marilee paced from the flecked Formica counter to the stubby refrigerator. They were supposed to be preparing a presentation for their methodology class. Instead, Marilee was planning a party. She spent a great deal of time planning activities involving food, fun and the opposite sex—though not necessarily in that order.

Right now food was the top priority as Marilee opened the refrigerator door and examined its contents. "You're not planning on doing anything to this place over the next couple of weeks, are you?"

"Not if I can help it." Emily sighed. She knew it was true that nature abhorred a vacuum, because everyone who stepped through her front door seemed determined to fill the empty spaces on her walls and floors. Even the spiders worked overtime trying to soften the corners. "I'm leaning toward a minimalist look, but only if I can keep the pink pig clock."

"Minimalism denotes some conscious choice about a style." Marilee rummaged through the fruit juice bottles to score the last soft drink. "This place is not minimalist."

"How about existentialist? This place exists."

"Yes, it does." Marilee twisted off the cap and took a healthy swig. "It's a blank canvas. It's perfect."

"I want you to tell my mother what you just said." Emily ripped a piece of paper from her notebook and started her grocery list with the first item: soda.

"Please." Marilee rolled her eyes. "I don't deal with other people's mothers. Dealing with my own is enough torture."

She dropped into the chair facing Emily. "Back to business. You know, this place would be perfect for a party."

"We're having a party? Here?" Emily thought of the shopping, the cleaning, the yard work. "It's too far out of the city."

"Throw a party, provide free food, and grad students will beat a path to any door." Marilee tipped the can back for another long sip. "Look, there's hardly any stuff to move out of the way. We can easily add to your collection of plastic lawn furniture. And I know some theater arts people who could turn this place into just about anything we come up with."

"Just as long as they turn it back into my place when the party's over," said Emily.

"Don't worry, they know how to strike a set. We'll change it from something back into nothing."

Emily put her laptop to sleep and closed the cover. "What did you have in mind?"

"I don't know, yet. But something different than the usual skeletons and jack-o-lanterns."

"Wait a minute. You're talking Halloween? That's next week. One week from today."

"What's wrong? Short-term notice? Short-term strategy? I know it pains you to have two shorts in one plan, Em, but look at it this way—at least they coordinate. Which is more than I can say for your kitchen furniture."

Emily shrugged. "It's temporary."

"Thank God."

"You sound like my mother."

"Shoot me now," said Marilee.

"Maybe I should, before the invitations go out."

"Too late. I told Sarah in Ed Psych."

Emily frowned. "The one with the big mouth?"

"Cheaper than postage, and more effective."

"So, it's on for sure."

"All but the details," said Marilee. "I thought I'd leave those to you, since you live to obsess."

Emily sighed. "You make me sound like such a bore."

"If the penny loafer fits…" Marilee twirled the can between her hands. "Okay, how about this—beads and incense and tarot cards. Alternative carnival chic."

"And this is something that can be organized in one week. A week that includes calculating first quarter scores, writing the methodology presentation and staging a student council Halloween rally."

"Am I detecting a note of skepticism here?"

"This isn't skepticism," said Emily. "This is the obsessing over details part."

She took a sip of her cider. Fruit and spice and childhood memories of Halloween distilled in the taste. The cold kiss of October's last evening on her cheek, the pleasing weight of her pillowcase stuffed with treats. Her father's large, warm hand wrapped around hers. Things had been so much simpler then.

Everything had been simpler then. Her mother had planned the parties. "We'll need a gypsy to do the readings."

"I'll do it." Marilee tapped a bright red nail against her chin. "We could drape some fabric from the front room light fixture, make it look like a fortune-teller's tent."

"Do you know how to read palms?"

"I could fake it. It'd be a fun way to meet everyone." Marilee waggled her eyebrows. "I'm definitely looking forward to meeting your master teacher."

"The Wiz?"

"Sounds like he'll fit right in with the party theme."

"But not the party itself." Emily pushed her cider aside. "I don't think he'll come, even if I ask him."

"You've got to ask him. I'm asking my master teacher. And her boyfriend."

"How many people are invited to this party?" asked Emily.

"We can probably keep it under fifty."

Emily's stomach rebounded from the floor. "Fifty?"

"Okay, forty." Marilee finished her soda and thunked the can down on the table. "Now, are you going to ask The Wiz to this party or not?"

Emily carried her mug and Marilee's can to the counter. "I don't know. It's complicated."

Marilee groaned. "Not this again."

"Things are better now. Going pretty well, actually. I don't want to do anything to compromise the working relationship."

"This is a party, not an assignment. This has nothing to do with the work. Or with the working relationship."

"I know. But it might…I don't know. Blur the edges."

"What's been going on?" Marilee leaned forward. "Have you been picking up signals?"

"Signals?"

"You know what I mean. Signals. Man-woman signals."

"No. I—" Emily hesitated. Had she caught a few glimpses of heat in those dark eyes? A minute shift in attitude? Or was her vivid imagination making too much out of a glance or a grin? *"No."*

"You know, this party could be the perfect chance to figure that out, once and for all."

"I'm not taking any chances. Not with this assignment."

But when the assignment was over, did she want to take a chance on Joe?

CHAPTER SEVEN

A LATE OCTOBER THUNDERSTORM was working up to the pyrotechnic stage, but Matt's eyes didn't stray to the rattling windows of Wiz's classroom. There was more interesting stuff to watch when Ms. Sullivan was teaching. Not the show in front of the class, although watching her long legs pace and her pretty hands wave around was definitely entertaining. No, the real fun was watching The Wiz watch his student teacher.

First he'd shift around in his student-size desk, trying to tuck those long legs of his out of the aisle. Next he'd play the avoidance routine, tricks like staring at her when she turned to write on the board and then glancing down real fast at the papers on his desk when she faced the class. You could tell he had a case for her.

It was no big surprise, the way she looked and all. She was smart, and funny, too—and no boyfriend hanging around, as far as anyone could tell. But it was still kind of ironic, considering how different she and Wiz were.

And that was the best part of the sideshow in

Current Events—all that squirming Wiz'd do whenever Ms. Sullivan came up with one of her right-wing zingers. Sometimes, if the light through the window was just right, Matt could see those little muscles along Wiz's jaw that rippled when he got real upset about something.

The way they were rippling right now.

Matt had never seen Wiz lose his temper, but Ms. Sullivan could sure push him right up to the edge. Matt enjoyed the suspense, wondering if today was going to be the day Wiz jumped off the cliff.

In the next seat, Lindsay Wellek was scribbling notes. Lindsay scribbled a lot of notes. That was one of the things about her that intrigued him—how much she cared about things. She had this way of chomping down on something and not letting go until it got finished, or resolved, or settled, or made better in some Lindsay-designated way. He admired that about her.

He also admired the way she looked. Funny, how he'd never really looked that close before. At first glance, Lindsay was just your basic girl, just a basic size and shape dressed in basic baggy clothes, with long reddish hair and a blush that could turn neon-pink. But lately he'd been noticing the details. Like how her eyelashes were tipped with blond, and how amazingly sculptured the tip of her nose was. How she sort of leaned forward and tipped her head to one side when she was talking to her girlfriends, but pulled back like a turtle when one of the guys was around. He admired that about her, too, the way she wasn't always on the prowl like so many of the females in the building. She was kind of cool, once he thought about it.

A guy could get to feel comfortable around someone like Lindsay, if he could ever get her to stop the turtle act around him. He wouldn't mind discovering how it would feel to have her lean in a bit and tip her head toward him. He wouldn't even mind a bit of Lindsay-chomping, if it meant she cared.

The new kid in front of Lindsay had his hand up in the air again. Lindsay frowned and settled a little lower in her seat, shifting into turtle mode.

She wasn't the only one who could sense trouble. Matt had picked up on it right away, the way the guy sauntered in late and smirked at Ms. Sullivan when he'd handed her his admit slip. And the way he'd said "Thank you, ma'am" when she'd pointed to his assigned seat. He probably thought she was an easy target, someone to score points off and prove what a tough guy he was.

Todd Sommers, new kid. And from what Matt could tell so far, a king-size jerk.

Right now, Ms. Sullivan had no choice but to call on him. "Yes, Todd?"

"I didn't quite hear that." Todd was speaking a little too loud, a little too politely and wearing that kiss-ass smirk. "Could you repeat it again, ma'am, so I can copy it down in my notes?"

A couple of losers in the back corner snickered.

"What do you want me to repeat?"

"Well, all of it. It's all so very interesting." Todd glanced at the jocks over by the window and smiled. "Ma'am," he added.

The jocks smiled back. Ms. Sullivan took a deep breath and twisted a ring on her hand.

Matt looked back at Wiz. Muscles were rippling like ocean swells along his jaw now. He shifted forward in his seat, an elbow on the front of the desk, one hand rubbing over his mouth. Then his legs bunched beneath him, and Matt held his breath, waiting for Wiz to launch himself out into the aisle and prowl along the rows with that silent intimidation.

But Wiz's hand stilled. He shifted back, crossed his arms over his chest and stared down at his papers while Ms. Sullivan summarized the structure of the UN Security Council.

Todd's hand went up again. Ms. Sullivan tried to ignore it, but that was only asking for a different kind of trouble. He started clearing his throat, real loud, and a few seconds later, she had to call on him again.

"Yes, Todd?"

"Well...*ma'am*," he drawled, waiting for more reaction from the crowd in the corner.

Ms. Sullivan didn't give him a chance to finish his question. She tilted her head and batted her eyelashes. "Yes, honey chil'?" she drawled back in a thick Southern accent.

There was a moment of stunned silence before the class erupted. Everyone laughed and turned to stare at Sommers, who flushed a dark red and sank deep into his seat.

All right, Matt thought. Sommers had dug himself a good-size hole, and Ms. Sullivan had shoved him in, face-first. He'd probably be "Honey Chil'" for weeks—even months—before he earned a different nickname on his own.

Matt turned to catch The Wiz's reaction. He was frowning down at his papers, but it wasn't an unhappy frown, or a mad frown. Just a thoughtful kind of frown. Matt hoped Ms. Sullivan could tell the difference.

She didn't look like it, though. She looked a little shaky. She divided the class into small groups to discuss the questions on a worksheet and then retreated to the rusty old chair behind Wiz's desk.

When the bell rang ten minutes later, she was one of the first people out the classroom door. Another bad sign. Usually she hung around, taking an amazingly long time to pack all her things in that big bag of hers while she snuck glances at The Wiz. Today she crammed her stuff into her case and fled.

Matt tossed his things into his own pack and dashed out into the hall to follow her. "Damn," he muttered when he fell behind a straggly group of too-cool-to-move freshmen and lost sight of her in the crowd. He stopped near the top of the stairs, leaning over the railing, searching for blond curls.

Lindsay edged in next to him, up tight against his side to avoid the flood of students headed toward the cafeteria for break. "Looking for Ms. Sullivan?"

"Yeah."

"I saw her go downstairs and head toward the parking lot exit."

Lindsay smelled good, in a distracting kind of way. Better than plain shampoo and soap could make a person smell. He knew he should go after Ms. Sullivan, but he lingered for another moment, just to breathe in deep. "Thanks."

She looked right at him, a little pink-cheeked, but not turtling up, either.

She cared. Not just about Ms. Sullivan, but about him, too. The reality of it moved through him like a bunch of butterflies, all darting wings and tickling antennae. "I've got to go," he said.

"I know."

He didn't want to leave, but he knew he'd disappoint them both if he stayed. "Wait here, okay?"

She smiled and nodded.

Matt jogged down the steps, darting through openings and dodging backpacks, feeling like he could fly if he wanted to. Right now, because he knew Lindsay was waiting for him, he felt like he could handle just about anything. He reached the door in time to see Ms. Sullivan run through the rain and climb into her old beater of a truck.

He waited, peering through the drizzle, but the

truck's taillights stayed dim. He could see the outline of her head in the rear window, and the rain sliding down the glass like tears.

Somebody should do something to help her. Matt didn't have a fix yet on what that something would be, but it had to happen.

Matt could tell Wiz where she was. Not that Wiz had acted like he cared or anything, leaving her to fend for herself against that Sommers creep.

He ran back up the stairs, looking for Lindsay at her spot by the railing as he got near the top. She wasn't there.

JOE RUBBED Emily's American History homework assignment off the board. Now that she had survived her first big test, he should probably find her and reassure her that she'd handled the situation fairly well. As well as these things could ever be handled. Some days you didn't manage the classroom, you survived it.

He turned to see Matt storm back into the room. He tossed his backpack toward an empty desk, but it skidded across the seat and fell to the floor. "Ms. Sullivan went out to her truck," he said. "Just in case you wanted to know." The look on Matt's face said he thought otherwise.

"Did she leave?"

"Not yet. She's just sitting there. At least, she was when I saw her."

Joe hitched his hip over the edge of his desk. "Thanks."

Matt stalked over to his backpack and bent to shove scattered papers back inside. "Yeah, well, gotta go."

"Matt." The papers were getting mangled. *"Matt."*

"Yeah?"

Joe crossed his arms. "What do you want me to do?"

Matt shot to his feet, his hands fisted at his sides. "Give that Sommers kid detention or something. Go tell her she did okay." He tossed his hands out to his sides. "Hell, I don't know."

"You want me to fight her battles for her, Matt? Just like you asked me to fight yours for you three years ago?"

Matt stabbed a finger toward Joe's chest. "This has nothing to do with you and me."

Joe stared at his student's face and knew this had everything to do with the two of them, and with the young student teacher they were both attracted to. And with something else, too. Something that had hit Matt hard enough to hurt.

"I didn't think that stepping in and helping her was the best thing to do," Joe said.

"I thought you cared about her."

"I care about her plans for a teaching career. And I respect her."

"That's official bullshit," said Matt. "You like her."

"No, I don't. I can't. I can't let myself have those kinds of feelings for her." It should be easy enough—

all he had to do was remind himself of that fact a couple of dozen times a day.

Joe shoved off the desk and took a step closer. "I thought you knew me better than that."

"I do." Matt's struggle flickered across his face. He took a deep breath, and his shoulders sagged with a shrug. "Sorry, Wiz."

"Hey. It's okay. A woman who looks like that, well, she can drive a guy a little crazy."

"Yeah. I guess so."

"And I do like her. As a student teacher." Joe blew some of his tension out on a deep breath of his own. "She's okay."

"Then how could you just sit there and let her take it like that?"

He'd asked himself the same question, over and over while it was happening, and a dozen times since. The answer didn't go down any easier now that things had turned out for the best. Righteousness and helplessness were a noxious mix. "She took care of it, didn't she?"

"Yeah."

Joe slipped his hands into his pockets. "Don't you think the students should see her get herself out of situations like that?"

"Yeah. But you just sat there, watching." Matt stuffed his hands into his own pockets. "It hurt to watch."

"Yes, it did." Joe walked over to the window and stared out at the rain. "Just like it hurt to stand by and watch Ryan Simms shove you around on that back-packing trip. It just about did me in, waiting for you to work up the nerve to shove him back."

Matt was silent for a moment. "I'm glad you waited."

Joe sighed. He felt tired and much, much older than he had when he got out of bed that morning. "And I'm glad you came in here to tell me where to find Ms. Sullivan. So," he said, turning to face his student. "What do you think I should do? Do you think I should go out there and talk to her? Or do you think she needs some more time to calm down?"

Matt opened his mouth to reply, but then shut it on a frown. "I don't know."

"Hard to know what to do sometimes, isn't it?"

"Yeah." Matt stared down at his feet and kicked at a scar in a vinyl tile. "So, how do you figure it out?"

"One moment, one day at a time."

Joe grabbed his keys off his desk. "Better get your things."

Matt swept his backpack off the floor and headed for the door.

"And Matt?"

"Yeah?"

"It might look like I've got things figured out. But I don't," said Joe. "Half the time, I don't have a clue. I wait so long trying to make a decision that things get themselves sorted out before I have a chance to muck them up. The rest of the time, I just get lucky."

Matt stared at him, and then nodded and walked out.

Joe locked up behind him and headed out through halls littered with the break crowd, hoping to find Emily before she left for the day. Reason number three hundred and fifty-four why he didn't want a student teacher: too much emotional commotion, too much disruption. Mess and muck on top of the extra work.

On the other hand, maybe she was so torn up she'd quit or look for another assignment. This could be his best chance yet to get rid of her. Maybe all she needed was a little nudge in the right direction: gone.

Matt was right. It hurt watching that scene. He wasn't looking forward to more of the same, and it was bound to happen. He didn't want to see those high-wattage smiles get dimmer, or all that enthusiasm disappear until she ended up just like...

Just like him.

He didn't want a bright-eyed mirror held up to his darkened soul. Better for them both to send her packing.

EMILY GLANCED at her watch. Ten more minutes until the end of break. Ten more minutes to struggle against the threatening tears and pull herself together. Then she had to go in there again, just to prove she could.

Whatever had made her think she could do this job? Or skate through an entire term without a single flub? Or, when the inevitable mistakes occurred, that they could remain quiet and private and be handled with discretion? Was there any other job that offered so many opportunities to go down in flames before an audience? Okay, outside the entertainment business. And politics. Although entertainers and politicians seemed to thrive on disaster.

So, public self-immolation must be an exclusive teaching perk.

She reached for the door handle, and then collapsed back against the seat to stare down at her hands. They still trembled with the aftershocks of the scene with Todd.

She took a deep breath and shifted her focus, staring at the fat rain splatters that blurred the view through the windshield. It smelled safe inside her truck, a musty blend of wet wool and the pine forest deodorizer dangling from a knob on the dash. She could hear the muffled whump-whumps from a nearby car where a student with a deaf wish was probably sneaking a smoke between classes. Another outlaw sharing the hideout.

Someone approached the truck, materializing through the rain. Emily slid lower, striving for invisibility, but the figure stopped just outside her passenger door. She glanced up to see Joe, rain dripping from the ends of his hair. Something painfully sweet welled up inside her, pressing at her chest and stinging the backs of her eyes.

He rapped on the window. She could just make out his voice through the wet staccato on the glass. "Can I come in?"

She leaned over and popped the lock. He opened

the door and slid inside, stretching his long legs under the dash and rubbing his hands over his pants legs to dry them. She couldn't help noticing the lean muscles of his thighs outlined by the damp jeans and the dusting of dark hair on the backs of his long-fingered hands.

She waited for him to say something, anything, but it appeared he was going to wait her out. Typical. It was such a nasty, unfair tactic. Joe could probably outwait a priest in a confessional. She, on the other hand, had never won a round of the Quiet Game in her life. "Look at me," she said with a wobbly little laugh. "My hands are still shaking."

"Upset?"

"I'm mad, that's what I am. Mad at myself." She punched at the steering wheel. "And, okay, I'm mad at that Todd Sommers, too. Why did he have to pull a stunt like that?"

"Oh, any number of reasons." He shoved dripping hair out of his eyes. "Maybe because he got transferred to a new school at the start of his senior year. Or maybe he's worried he might not get to keep his usual spot on the football team."

Emily swallowed. She'd been thinking only of herself and her problems, while Todd wandered new school halls filled with strange faces. A good teacher would have sought him out and tried to talk things through, to try to understand.

And she hadn't been that teacher.

A fresh wave of guilt rushed through her and made it impossible to respond with anything other than a jerky nod.

Joe lifted a finger and traced the path of a raindrop down the passenger side window. "Or maybe Todd thinks the quickest way to align himself with the student 'us' is to take a quick, dirty shot at the teaching 'them,' and you just happened to be the most convenient victim." He frowned and shifted against the seat back. "Or maybe he's just a troublemaker."

She cleared her throat. "Yeah. Maybe."

He nodded. "Maybe."

A sudden gust of wind drove rain against the windshield like a spray of machine-gun fire. She shivered, though it was so warm in the truck the windows were starting to fog up.

Joe slouched down until his knees knocked against the dash and his head rested against the top edge of the seat. "When was the last time you woke up in your parents' house, begged for money and checked for zits before going off to face the possibility of total social annihilation before the lunch break?"

"A lifetime ago." She smiled and shook her head. "Poor monsters."

"Most of the time, the kids who lash out are just using a teacher for a target because they can't get at the real ones. Maybe they've had a fight with the old man, or they've just broken up with the love of the moment, or they're afraid they're going to get benched at the next game. It's not about us. We're just in the way."

Emily's hands had stopped shaking. It was nice in here, a little too close and a little too stuffy, but comfortable. Joe made it that way, with his soft, soothing rumble of a voice and his easy words. Insightful, compassionate, educational words.

It was incredibly kind of him to come out here, looking for her. Knowing him, as she did now, she knew he hadn't wanted to open up like that. All his advice meant so much more, because she understood what he was sacrificing to give it. "You know what, Joseph P. Wisniewski? Under that cranky exterior, you're really a very nice man."

"Hey." Joe plucked his wet shirt away from his chest and frowned. "Don't mess with the image."

Emily twisted, as far as the steering wheel would let her, to face him. "I'll bet this is the best talk about discipline issues that any student teacher has had with a master teacher so far this year. Can I do a report on you?"

"What?" He shifted in her direction and let his arm fall across the back of the seat. "Do I look like a punching bag?"

They smiled at each other. Outside, the wind moaned and plastered a few soggy leaves against the glass before they started the slide down to the hood. Lightning streaked somewhere behind them, flashing the parking lot like a strobe. It was getting too warm in the cab, and Joe was probably uncomfortable in his wet things, but she wasn't ready to go back into the building. She didn't want to lose this sense of connection.

She twisted the ring on her left hand. "You know, what Todd was saying, and the way I handled it—that wasn't the worst of it. And it wasn't my doubts, or the second-guessing. Or looking at all those kids out there, the ones who were horrified for me, and the ones who were enjoying the jabs."

She peeked to check Joe's reaction to her confession, but he was staring out the windshield. "The worst part was knowing you were out there, taking notes for my evaluation. It was like a bad dream, a dream in slow motion."

She tipped her head back and closed her eyes. "I could feel my heartbeats. I could count them, and it seemed there were way too many of them ticking by before I could think of something to do."

"It didn't last as long as you thought. You did fine."

She heard the rumble of thunder and the rustle of his shirt sleeve moving along the back of the seat. The cool draft of the storm pressed through the crack in her door, and then the soothing weight of Joe's fingertips brushed over her shoulder.

She'd seen him touch his students like this dozens of times. She'd never seen them react as if they'd been touched by fire. But that's what Joe's touch was like. In one instant, it flared and blazed through all the layers of teenage crush and womanly yearning. It torched a path right through to the emotional core of her attraction to him—to his challenging intelligence, and his rusty charm, and his gentle generosity.

And in the next instant, when everything else had burned away, she was left with a staggering awareness of him as a man.

CHAPTER EIGHT

JOE FELT HER TINY FLINCH beneath his fingers, and it whipsawed right through him. When her eyes flew open, what he saw in them told him that touching her had been a big mistake. Because right there, right then, in the way her lips fell open on a little gasp of sensual surprise, and a faint blush spread from her throat to her cheeks, he knew she was feeling the electrical storm inside this truck every bit as much as he was.

It scared him spitless, and he pulled back. Not far enough or fast enough to frighten her, but enough to scare himself. He didn't want to put this much space between them, he needed to. Needed to—that was what terrified him.

She smoothed her hands over her skirt, and he could see they were trembling again. The reassuring little smile she gave him was strained around the edges. She might be fooling herself with those casual, normal motions, but nothing was going to be casual or normal between them, not anymore.

Things were shifting around inside him now, opening fissures and tilting his foundation. There was the shift in his attitude toward the whole student teaching situation. Where just a few minutes ago he'd been hoping she'd leave, now he wanted her to stay and fight. More than that, he wanted to fight right beside her. He wanted to protect her, and guide her, and watch her become the teacher he knew she could be.

And then there was the shift in his attitude toward a personal relationship. He wanted one now, bad. Nothing like a little encouragement to get a man's interest up and locked on target, and he'd felt enough encouragement in that little flinch, that quiet gasp, that faint blush to keep him primed for a while.

Forget it. Bad idea, bad situation. He knew it, he knew all the reasons. Too bad his body wasn't buying any of the propaganda his brain was putting out.

He sucked in a breath of supercharged, super-heated air and struggled to get back on track. "Emily," he said, and then he cleared his throat so his next words wouldn't sound quite so strangled. "If you're anything else but human, how can the kids relate? Perfection can be rough on everyone."

She reached out to grab the steering wheel in a white-knuckled squeeze. "But I want to set a good example. That's what makes me the angriest with myself. I poked fun at Todd, right back at him. I humiliated him in front of the class." She shook her head. "Guess this is my day for making one faux poo after another."

"That's *faux pas*," he said with a smile.

"Not when it involves stepping in deep shit." She flipped one of those exasperated little waves in his direction. "Go ahead. Laugh. You're not the one suffering here."

"Sorry. I forgot I was trying to be sympathetic and supportive." He settled more snugly into the lumpy springs of the truck bench and crossed his arms over his chest, grateful for the shift in mood. "Give me a moment. I can do this."

She twisted to face him. "Seriously. How do you deal with it all? Why do you do it, year after year?"

He stifled a groan. Not another self-examination session with the student therapist. Not when he'd been thinking, just moments ago, of what they could be doing in this roomy old truck to steam up the windows so thick they wouldn't be found for days.

He scrubbed a hand over his face and tried to think of an answer. She needed him to be a good example, *her* good example, and he wanted to do it, for her. He could curse her later for making him care that much, and for forcing him to drag his good intentions out of their deep freeze. "Remember all those faces that were horrified for you?"

She grimaced. "Yeah."

"Want to get up in front of those faces again tomorrow? Share some really deep, important ideas with them?" He could see some of the light coming back into her beautiful eyes, and he smiled. "Find out what's going on in some terrific young minds?"

"Yeah."

Yeah. It didn't sound like such a bad idea, now that he thought about it. Not such a bad idea at all—and wasn't that a surprise?

"Good," he said. "Now, blow your nose and let's get back in there. Don't let the monsters think they've won."

She pulled her jacket hood up around her face and grabbed the door handle, and then she turned back toward him. "Thank you, Joe. You're a good friend."

He stared at her wide, happy smile, a smile that warmed all his empty spaces, and he knew he was quickly sinking into something a whole lot stickier than friendship. But somehow the sinking feeling didn't seem to matter. Nothing seemed to matter, as long as she'd keep smiling at him just the way she was smiling right now. As long as he could be the one to put that look on her face, and she could be the one to keep him warm. "Ready?" he asked.

"As ready as I'll ever be."

They jumped down from the truck and ran, heads down. Emily laughed when he splashed through a puddle. He wanted to splash through another one just to hear the sound again, but soon they were dashing through the wide doors and into an empty school hall.

He raked his fingers through his hair, sending water drops flying. "By the way, I liked the Southern accent. Nice touch."

"Really?"

She beamed up at him, and he stood there, basking in it. Then he reached out and tugged her jacket hood from her head.

For one agonizing, intoxicating moment, he thought he might not let go. He thought he might step toward her, and pull her forward, closer, against him, and lower his mouth to hers. God, he wanted to do it, wanted to taste that mouth, wanted to wrap his fingers in those curls, wanted to soak up her heat, wanted...her.

"Yeah," he said as he straightened one last fold and withdrew his hand. "I think I might write about the effective use of humor as part of your discipline method in my next evaluation."

God. He was supposed to evaluate her. If he ever made a move on her, she would always wonder if his evaluation was based on merit or on whatever had happened between them.

"Really?" she asked.

"Yeah," he said, after he'd swallowed the ugly aftertaste of his thoughts. "Really. You're doing okay. Most of the time, anyway, and that's all any of us can hope for."

"'Okay' sounds good," she said. "I'll take it."

"A woman with low standards. How lucky can a guy get?"

"Joe, I—"

She hesitated, and he made a mental note to cut any teasing that might be construed as flirting.

"I'm having a Halloween party for a bunch of the student teachers at my place," she said. "Saturday. Some of them are inviting their master teachers. Will you come?"

No. No way. Bad idea. "Maybe," he heard himself say, as he looked down into her expectant face. "I'll think about it."

"Oh. Okay, then." She smiled uncertainly. "I'll, uh, I'll just go check the office mailbox before I leave. See you tomorrow." She started down the hall.

Damn. Could he have been any clumsier? "Emily."

"Yes?"

"About the party." He shifted from one foot to the other. "I don't—"

The bell rang, signaling the end of break. Students poured into the hall. He stepped closer to her and leaned in so he could lower his voice. "I want to go. I'm just…sorry. Hope I didn't make too big a faux poo."

"Don't worry about it. The shit wasn't deep enough." She tossed him a tiny, reassuring grin and walked away.

Joe stood in the hall, watching her make her way toward the office. "I'm not so sure about that," he muttered. "I think I'm standing knee-deep in it."

"Joe?"

He glanced over his shoulder to see Kyle standing behind him.

"Got a minute?" The principal looked past him, toward the spot where Emily had just disappeared.

The thing about shit was it could get deeper when you least expected it.

Joe turned, wondering how much of that touching little scene Kyle had witnessed, and what he might read into it. When he gestured down the hall, toward his office, Joe could almost smell the manure.

He followed Kyle into the stuffy space and closed the door behind him, and then angled his arms across his chest and slouched against the jamb, ignoring Kyle's wave toward the visitors' chairs. He knew his subtle defiance was petty, just as he knew it made Kyle nervous to have Joe tower over him, even after he took his power seat behind the command center.

"Everything going okay, Joe?"

"Yeah."

Kyle leaned back and laced his fingers behind his head. "And why wouldn't things be going okay, with such an able-bodied assistant?"

Something about the way Kyle said the words *able-bodied* had the hairs on the back of Joe's neck gathering spears and clubs. *Down, boys,* he ordered. "She's very helpful."

"She looks helpful." Kyle swiveled slowly, back and forth. "She looks like she could handle just about anything you gave her."

Joe told himself Kyle didn't have the brains or the sophistication to engage in double entendres. Too bad he wasn't buying it. "What did you need to see me about?"

Kyle tapped a pencil against the desk top. "Your department chair just called."

"Alice? When is she coming back?"

"She's not." The tapping increased in tempo. "Her doctor ordered her to stay in bed for the duration of the pregnancy. She's out for the rest of the year."

"Are you going to switch Hanley's sub position to long-term?"

"That's what I need to talk to you about, since you're now the department chair."

"No," said Joe. "I'm not. Alice is the chair."

"Alice is out for the duration. And after that?" Kyle shrugged. They both knew she'd considered making her maternity leave permanent even before the start of the problems with the pregnancy. "The department needs a chair. You're the logical choice."

Kyle must really be desperate to be making this offer. Beyond all the bad history between them, beyond the battles over curriculum and the dustups over Joe's extracurricular projects, beyond the political maneuvers and the rumor-mongering, there was a deep and mutual animosity.

"What about Coop?" asked Joe. The P.E. teacher filled in with two periods of World Geography.

"I want a chair who's full-time in the department, not a part-timer whose head's in the locker room." Kyle set the pencil down. "I know you've been avoiding this, buddy, but it's time. You always had more seniority than Alice, anyway."

"She wanted it. She was good at it." Joe pulled his hands out of his pockets and crossed his arms. "I didn't want it. I don't want it now."

"Joe." Kyle spread his hands. "You've got it. I wish there were another option, but there's not, and you know it."

"There's Coop."

Kyle leaned back in his chair. "Do you want me to ask him?"

Joe felt the responsibility pressing in, the noose looping around his neck. Alice wasn't coming back, Hanley was settling in for the long haul and Emily had her fluttery hands on the lever of the gallows drop hatch. "No."

"I knew you'd understand." Kyle stood and reached across his desk. "Thanks, Joe. And congratulations."

Joe shook the outstretched hand. "You're welcome."

"There's the stipend, of course. I'll see that Linda puts through the paperwork. We'll make it retroactive." Kyle settled back into his chair. "Looks like this is your year for unexpected bonuses, eh?"

Joe nodded, slowly. "Guess so."

"I'm sure Ms. Sullivan will be very helpful with the additional paperwork, if you ask her."

Joe didn't respond. He needed to get out of this office as quickly as possible. "Hanley?"

"Talk to him. Do a casual evaluation, then offer him the spot if he wants it. Long-term sub, not probation. He'll have to apply for a position, just like everyone else."

Joe nodded and turned to go.

"Oh, and Joe? About Ms. Sullivan. Emily." Kyle's voice oozed around her first name as he swiveled in his chair. "Things seem to be going well between you two. It certainly looked that way in the hall earlier."

Joe's fingers curled into fists. "Things are fine."

"Glad to hear it. I'd like to keep them that way." Kyle fingered the pencil. "Her placement here establishes some good contacts with one of the local universities. I'd like to see those contacts expand, maybe pull in some more student teachers next year. Put Caldwell on the map, so to speak."

The noose tightened.

"Anyway, I thought I'd come in, do a couple of observations, write a letter of recommendation myself."

Joe ground his teeth at the thought of Kyle dropping by his classroom to ogle Emily. "That's good of you, Kyle."

"No trouble." He flashed his expensive dental work. "I'd enjoy observing Ms. Sullivan. I'm sure the experience would be very…educational."

"I DON'T CARE IF your mom dragged you through all the secondhand shops in the greater Seattle area," said Marilee as she emptied another bottle of rum into the punch. Marilee's idea of last-minute party prep was adding more of everything, but Emily was grateful for the help. "It was worth every torturous minute. That dress is stunning."

"You don't think it just hangs on me like a sack, do you?" Emily reached up to adjust the tissue-thin neckline of her black beaded flapper gown. "I've thinned out some since high school."

"The way that thing sort of slips around and floats and shimmers when you move?" She circled a finger in the air, and Emily spun around, beads clacking. "And the way it dips in the back? Pure, unadulterated come-on. I can't believe your mom let you wear that to your senior prom."

"Well, it was either this or something pink and puffy. Or blue and clingy. Or arguing with me about puffy and clingy for the rest of her life." Emily plucked an olive from a tray—to even out the pile—and popped it in her mouth. "The moment I saw this, I knew it was my prom dress. And that was the end of that."

"You were into vintage before vintage was cool. I'm impressed," said Marilee.

"What's really cool is that I still find chances to wear it. I wasn't lying when I told her it wouldn't hang in my closet forever, collecting dust."

Marilee reached up to tighten her bright red scarf. She was a fiery gypsy, with big gold hoops in her ears and oversize spangles stitched to her peasant blouse and striped skirt. "Wonder what Joe will think of that dress?" she asked.

Emily shrugged. "Nothing, since he probably isn't coming. And not much, even if he does show up."

She opened a package of paper napkins and started slapping them down in a fan-shaped arrangement at one end of the buffet table. "'I'll think about it,'" she muttered, narrowing her eyes at the memory of his response. "'I'll think about it…' one of these years."

"Don't abuse the party goods." Marilee snatched the napkins away and handed Emily an empty bottle. "You probably just caught him by surprise. Got him all flustered. It's kind of cute, when you think about it."

"You think anything I tell you about Joe is 'kind of cute.' You haven't even met him yet. How do you know he's 'cute'?"

"He sounds cute."

"He doesn't sound like anything. Except grumpy," said Emily.

"Grumpy is cute. Especially the way you tell it."

"I don't tell it cute. I tell it like it is—grumpy."

"I always thought Grumpy was the sexy dwarf," said Marilee. "All that repression, all that pent-up passion. Imagine what he would have been like in bed when he finally lost control." Marilee waved one of the napkins at her face. "Hot stuff."

Someone knocked at the door. Emily shoved the empty bottle back at Marilee. "Hi-ho, hi-ho," she said, and went off to greet the first guest.

Soon the house was filling with people, and the drinks were pouring, and the food was disappearing, and the fizzy blend of costumes, laughter and vintage jazz was taking the edge off Emily's annoyance with Joe. That, and the three glasses of wine she'd somehow managed to consume. No annoyances, no worries, no nothing but the low-key hum of social interaction.

Nothing the least bit edgy, until a pair of dark eyes locked on hers.

CHAPTER NINE

AT FIRST, she didn't recognize him: slicked back conservative haircut, slicked-up conservative suit, striped tie and smoke curling about his face—smoke from the conservative cigar stuck in one side of his mouth. But his height gave him away. That, and the jolt of awareness that sliced through her when he looked at her. Just looked at her, with the peculiar intensity that Joseph P. Wisniewski could put into a simple stare.

Hot stuff.

She could feel that stare licking along her skin like a flame. She could douse it; she could match it. What she couldn't do any longer was ignore it.

She wove through the crowd to where he stood, framed in the kitchen doorway. "Hello, Wiz."

"Hello, yourself." His eyes traveled the length of her filmy black shift. "Aren't you cold?"

"Nope. Aren't you strangling in that tie?"

He shook his head and blew a stream of smoke toward the ceiling. "The cigar is handling the asphyxiation tonight."

"I didn't know you smoked."

"I don't. But it's Halloween."

"Mmm-hmm."

They stood for a moment, an island of two in a crowded sea. The teasing alto of a classic big band number washed up against them like waves. Someone brushed by her to get into the kitchen, and she stepped closer to Joe to let him pass. Faint scents of party punch and Joe's soap were layered beneath the pungent smoke.

He waved the cigar toward the crowd cramming the makeshift bar in the kitchen behind him. "This is a costume party, right?"

She smiled. "I get it. The cigar is part of your disguise. I did have a bit of trouble recognizing you, at first."

He grinned. "Then it works."

"So, who are you?"

"The scariest, most loathsome creature imaginable."

"And that would be…"

"Rush Limbaugh."

She laughed and made an appropriate shudder. "I hope you don't start a stampede for the nearest exit. Nobody would be left here but us Republicans."

"And you'd bore yourselves to death in about five minutes."

She didn't know whether it was the teasing in his voice or the temptation in his eyes—or the aftereffects of the wine—but suddenly she wanted him all to herself. She held out her hand and waited for him to juggle his cigar and plastic punch cup to take it. "Let me whisk you out of sight," she said. "And get that cigar some fresh air while we're at it."

He glanced down at his hand clasped in hers, and then back at her face as she tugged him through the crush to the sliding glass doors that opened to the narrow back porch. The smile that crept across his features spread a giddy warmth across her midsection. She told herself it was just her metabolism plowing into her alcohol limit ahead of schedule.

She slipped her hand out of his and set her cup of Chardonnay on the railing. "Has anyone guessed your identity yet?"

"No, but the redhead at the front door thought I came here straight from my job at a stock brokerage. That was almost as much fun."

"You're a real party animal, Wiz."

"That's me." He placed his cup next to hers and reached for her hand. "Want to dance?"

"Are people dancing?" She shifted to peek through the glass doors.

He pulled her close and slipped an arm around her waist. "We could start a trend." He curled her hand against his chest and began to sway to Sinatra. "You know, I've got this thing for women in beads."

One of his cuff links brushed against the slope of her breast. Just a piece of metal making accidental contact, but it set off sparks.

She cleared her throat. "Beads, huh? I'll alert the local Camp Fire Girls."

"That's the community spirit."

She couldn't think of a snappy comeback. It was hard to think of anything other than the sensations of his fingers fanning across her bare back and his legs moving against hers. Hard to think of anything other than the solid, substantial feel of him—the heat he radiated, the scents of cigar and rum, the width of his shoulders shifting beneath the pinstripes, the sound of his feet shuffling with hers on the decking. He was Joe, but not Joe. Not only her master teacher, but an attractive man at a holiday party. A very attractive man who fit against her in a way that made her want to try him on for size.

The noise of the crowd faded, and the world shrank to the shape of his face. That wonderful long, rugged face. She thought she had known every inch of it, every expression, but there was something disturbing in the landscape tonight, something dangerous glinting in those impossibly dark eyes. She watched the crinkles in their corners smooth out as his smile disappeared.

"Song's winding down." He dropped his arms and snatched up his drink, emptying it in one swallow. "Drink's empty. Time to hit the buffet."

Cold air rushed over the spaces he'd warmed, leaving her chilled and off balance. "You sound like a man on a mission. Eat, drink, be merry and take no prisoners."

"Got to watch out for us party animals." He nodded toward the guests hovering over the buffet table inside. "Don't want to miss out on all the goodies. Looks like you've got a hit on your hands, Em."

"Go ahead then. Mingle a bit, Rush."

He raked his fingers through his hair, mussing the carefully combed effect. "Okay. Just for a bit. Can't stay too long."

She reached up to smooth a strand back in place, and then snatched her hand back, embarrassed by the intimacy of the gesture. "You cut your hair."

He grabbed for her hand before she could pull it completely out of range. "Had to eventually. Thought it would add to the disguise."

He toyed with her fingers a bit. His were warm and rough. She imagined them streaking up her arms, cupping her shoulders, pulling her close again. Drawing her into his heat.

"Don't you like it?" he asked.

Yes. No. "What?"

He smiled. "The haircut."

The haircut. Not the way his touch made her pulse pound. "It's a bit of a shock." She cocked her head to one side and considered. "But it's a good look for you."

"Now you're scaring me."

She knew she was playing with fire. She could feel it, singeing her fingertips where they laced with his. But it was Halloween, and they were both in disguise.

She laughed and tipped up on her toes, leaning forward. "Boo."

He tugged, the merest fraction of an inch, on the hand he still held, trapping her in place for a long moment before she could tip back down to earth. His eyes dropped to her mouth, a few electrified inches from his. She felt his warm, punch-scented breath rush over her face, felt his fingers tighten on hers as he held her still, motionless, fixed in a stationary orbit at some breath-robbing, head-lightening altitude, for the space of three thundering heartbeats.

Behind them, Tony Bennett began to sing about the way his woman looked tonight, and a burst of laughter competed with the yap of a dog in the distance. The evening breeze carried an autumn musk of smoke and loam, and swirled crisp leaves against the glass doors. Her dress fluttered against her legs, and another strand of his hair lifted out of place.

She should have been cold, but she wasn't. She should have been thinking of the party, and her responsibilities to her guests, but she wasn't. For a moment, she thought she might just lean in a bit more, and he might just dip his head a bit lower. And the world might just spin off its axis.

Then Marilee stepped out on the porch, and Tony's crooning rose above a crescendo of brass, and her heels touched down and the universe slipped back into familiar patterns. Joe brushed his fingers down her arm, a gentle, hesitant parting. He plucked his empty punch cup off the deck railing and stepped away. A world away.

"We need some crushed berries for another batch of punch," Marilee said. She was talking to Emily, but she was staring at Joe.

"I'm keeping you from your other guests." He frowned down into his empty cup. "Thanks for the fresh air," he said as he squeezed past Marilee and disappeared inside.

Emily watched him go and concentrated on breathing again. "Berries? You know where the extra berries are. What was that all about?" she asked.

"What was that all about? What was this—" Marilee waved her hand at the spot where Joe had been standing "—all about?"

Emily rubbed her hands over her arms, trying to get warm again. "What do you mean?"

"You know very well what I mean. You. Joe. Getting to know each other better."

"I thought you thought that would be a good idea."

"That was before I saw the idea put into practice. I didn't know two people could look so hot just staring at each other. I didn't know I could get so hot just staring at them staring." She fanned her fingers in front of her face. "Too much staring. Too much hot stuff. Time for a time out."

Emily shivered. "Time to go back in. I'm freezing."

"Good. Cooling things down sounds like a plan."

"Don't worry," said Emily. "Nothing's going to happen."

"Now you've got me worried."

Emily pushed past her to go in. "Some chaperone you are."

"Not a chaperone. Just an interested bystander." Marilee followed her into the kitchen and leaned against the refrigerator while Emily got the berries. "Very interested."

"Well, the interesting part's over for the evening. Lesson learned."

"That's it?" Marilee frowned. "No review session?"

"Pay attention, class. Don't play with matches." Emily fanned her face and smiled. "Hot stuff."

JOE ACCEPTED another cup of punch from a grad student with a scraggly goatee and a Norman Mailer fixation. He paid just enough attention to make just enough of a response to a rambling review of the literary highlights and scanned the room for Emily.

That was interest he'd seen in her silvery blue eyes. Big-time interest. A definite physical attraction, with no reservations. There had been no short-term doubts or long-term worries out there on that back porch. The body language was doing all the talking, loud and clear. Lots of leaning in, and parting lips, and fluttering eyelashes. All that soft, warm, pliant stuff women were so good at.

There she was, dumping the berries into the punch.

He willed her to look up, to check the crowd, to look at him. To match his heat with a searing glance of her own. *Yeah, that's the way, sweetheart,* he thought when her eyes drifted toward his, and met, and held, before she slipped away. *I could feel that one down to my toes.*

God. He was reviewing each moment as if he were fourteen again. Chalking up each move, reliving each sensation. Looking for the score.

No. No scoring. Not with Em.

What was he thinking? He wasn't thinking—that was the problem. He was feeling...wow, was he ever feeling. He felt great.

Big problem.

He tossed back the rest of his punch and used his empty cup as an excuse to duck out on the Mailer fan and head toward the buffet for a refill. Time to cool off, calm down and wise up.

He still didn't understand why he'd come. He hadn't planned on it, really, not even when he'd asked Linda for Emily's address. He'd rolled out of bed this morning and dressed for his early morning run, and instead he'd wound up shopping for a costume. Not wanting to disappoint Emily was a flimsy excuse, but he'd clung to it as if it were a life preserver, and floated with it all the way to her front door.

All he'd been feeling out on that porch was a simple, shallow, physical response to the situation. Bound to happen. After all, they were two single

people of the opposite sex, working in close prox-
imity, engaged in stimulating discussions and
sharing common goals on a daily basis. Two
healthy adults thrust into that kind of a situation
had to size up the possibilities and decide what to
do about them.

Damn, that was some pretty impressive rationalizing. But he could almost feel his philosophical underpinnings starting to crumble. Their possibilities—his
and Emily's—didn't include the possibility of acting
on an attraction. That possibility was supposed to be
smothered before it took its first breath, before he
backed her into a corner with an ugly power play.

He frowned down at the crackers and cheese. Even
if things didn't get ugly, they'd get messy. And he'd be
taking some big risks, too. If she claimed any kind of
sexual harassment, his career would probably be over.

Probably? Kyle would shove him out the door so fast
Stenquist would never get the skid marks off the floor.

Emily swung through the kitchen door, a plate of
those little quiche squares in her hand. Before she
could squeeze the food into the pile on the buffet, the
bookworm plucked one off the tray and played his
opening line. She laughed at whatever he'd said, but
her eyes were searching the room. Searching, searching...for Joe's. He knew it, when she found him. He
felt it, down to his bones, in the smile that skimmed
along the corners of her mouth, the smile that seared
through his skin to simmer in his veins. She cast one

more smoking glance over her shoulder as she disappeared into the kitchen.

He was looking forward to going down in flames.

Had he been this needy at fourteen? This tempted by the sizzle and snap of one woman? If so, the cerebral trauma must have obliterated the memory.

Speaking of cerebral…he and Emily were both legal adults, capable of mutual consent, capable of sidestepping the entire power play issue. Flimsy, and a bit shaky on the ethics, but manageable. Teachers and students had affairs all the time. That's why universities were constantly writing guidelines and ripping them up again. Heck, even the experts couldn't decide what to do when romance got in the way of reality.

Romance. No reality, no possibility there. Not with him.

And what in the world would someone as fresh and lovely as Em see in him? Here he was, stumbling aimlessly along in his rut, and she had her whole future ahead of her.

Just like Rosaria.

Rosaria. Joe's eyes squeezed shut against the memory, but the breath whooshed out of him at the emotional sucker punch.

There was no way he could start a relationship with another idealistic young woman. He'd been the death of one already.

The party was over. He set down his drink and headed for the door.

USUALLY MATT DIDN'T mind spending a Sunday afternoon on a Garden Project assignment. It got him out of the house, out of the way of his mom's determined slide into her evening stupor. But today, since it was the day after Halloween, only four people had shown up. And none of them was in a talkative mood.

Except for Mrs. Grimble, but she didn't count. It was her lawn that was getting raked clear of maple leaves, and her roses that were getting weeded. Mrs. Grimble was always in the mood to talk. She was at it right now, bent over her cane to whisper some bit of gossip to Lindsay.

He pretended not to notice, just like he'd been pretending not to notice her since that day she hadn't waited for him in the hall.

Beside him, Wiz piled leaves into a wheelbarrow with a grim set to his jaw. He looked kind of raw and worn out, as if he had a doozy of a hangover. And he hadn't once glanced toward the spot where Ms. Sullivan was kneeling to plant spring bulbs, her figure nicely outlined in a pair of snug jeans. It wasn't like Wiz not to steal a chance to enjoy the scenery.

"Matt, dear," Mrs. Grimble called. "Could you help us in the backyard for a few minutes, please?"

He followed Mrs. Grimble and Lindsay through the side gate. "I wish I could get the rest of these apples for applesauce," Mrs. Grimble said, waving her cane at the two overgrown trees in a corner of her yard. "But they're too high."

Matt left to collect a ladder and a cobwebby basket from the garage. When he returned, Lindsay waited alone beneath one of the trees. He lowered the ladder against a scarred spot on the trunk and tested his weight on the lowest rung. It slipped and tilted against another branch.

"You hold the ladder, I'll climb," said Lindsay.

"I should do the climbing. You hold the ladder."

"You're stronger," she said. And then she stepped forward and reached out to slowly brush her hand over the front of his jacket, knocking away a speck of leaf. "You should hold it."

He looked down at her face. She was standing so close he could see the tiny freckles scattered over her cheeks like miniature constellations. So close he could tell she smelled like cider and roses. Something inside him broke loose, and a warm flood of sensation swept through him.

He raised his hand, in a weird and heart-thudding kind of slow motion, and rested his fingers against her jaw, rubbing his thumb over a smear of dirt on her cheek. Her skin was amazing, delicate and soft. So soft. "All right."

He grasped the ladder and straightened it, and then moved to one side to hold it steady so she could start up. She stepped onto the first rung, and then she waited for him to reach around her for the other side. She turned in his arms and rested a hand on his shoulder.

He tipped his face up, and her lips were just a couple of inches from his. He tried not to notice, but he lost control somehow, and his eyes wandered down to her mouth.

"Hold on tight," she whispered.

He dragged his gaze back up to her eyes. They were a dark, clear brown, like the pitcher of cold tea Mrs. Grimble kept in her refrigerator. "I will," he said.

She stared at him for a while, he wasn't sure how long, and then she glanced down at his lips, too. His breath backed up in his chest, and the blood roared in his ears, and he froze, waiting for her to make a move, wanting to make one of his own, needing to breathe or swallow, to lean in or back away.

And then the corners of her mouth turned up in a teasing kind of grin, and she turned and clambered up, and he settled his weight against the ladder.

Man, the scenery was fantastic.

CHAPTER TEN

FOUR DAYS LATER, Emily sat in her observation spot and scribbled her frustrations into her journal. She knew she'd rip out the pages when the bell rang, but she had to do something, even if that something was destined for the trash. The alternative was screaming and tossing her briefcase out the window.

The students around her hunched over their desks, scratching out responses to a Current Events essay assignment. The room was redolent with damp fabrics and the undertone of mildew, and filled with muted sounds—shifting bodies, a pinging radiator and pelting rain that streaked the tall windows and distorted the world outside.

She stared down at her notes and sighed. There were some sound physiological reasons that human beings were programmed for fight-or-flight. Anything else messed with a person's sanity. This pussyfoot game she'd been playing with Joe since the party was starting to mess with hers. It was time to either face the facts or run for cover.

She'd been trying to keep up a brave front, but after

several mornings of sitting and smiling and pretending nothing was wrong, she felt as surly as Joe had been acting. What a pair the two of them were: pleasant and polite on the outside, snarling and snapping on the inside. She didn't know whether to blame it on what had happened—or hadn't happened—out on her porch, or on his abrupt departure, or on something else she wasn't aware of. Whatever had caused it, this tension between them wouldn't go away until they decided what to do about it.

Okay. Time to face the facts. She flipped past the latest list of names beginning with *P* to a fresh page, and then drew a few columns in an attempt to outline her emotions and put her options in order. Short-term goals, long-term goals. An analysis and an agenda. Life and love might not be completely manageable, but she could give it her best shot.

Factor number one: this sexual pull of Joe's was stronger than she'd expected—and why hadn't she seen that coming? He did have quite a reputation, after all. And that same reputation indicated that he wasn't looking for any kind of relationship, let alone a commitment.

Which led to factor number two: the commitment issue. Even if she and Joe were able to agree on some kind of arrangement, he'd be hauling a lot of baggage—a checkered past with far too many women in it, and most likely some pretty low expectations for what a relationship should be.

She hadn't even begun to factor in the ideological hurdles. They just didn't look at things the same way. Heck, they didn't look at life in the same way. How in the world could she develop a meaningful relationship with someone so fundamentally different than herself?

Reality alert: there could never be a relationship.

Of course not, she sighed. Fundamental differences aside, Joe was a good man. A generous and caring man, and an honest one. He would never consider indulging in a relationship outside the classroom, not with his student teacher.

She had no business considering one, either. And she shouldn't tempt him with the possibility, not if she cared for him.

She stared down at her notes, ashamed of what she saw. What a selfish list, filled with items and angst that affected only her. Joe would be risking much more than his emotions if a relationship developed between them—he'd be risking his job.

She pulled the page from her notebook and crumpled it into a tiny ball. There was only one relationship she needed to plan and manage—the student-teacher one.

Decided. Done deal. So why did she still feel so undecided? And so completely undone?

JOE SWIVELED in his chair after the bell rang, creaking back and forth as his students handed in their essays and disappeared. Emily loitered in the back of his room, packing her case as if the fate of the free world hung on where she put her black felt pen.

"How do you think they did?" she asked.

"I have no idea." He knew he was snarling, but he didn't care. He tossed a news magazine down on his desk and scrubbed his hands over his face. "They never do as well as I think they're going to."

She gathered her things and walked up the aisle to stand in front of his desk. "Why is that?"

He frowned at her. He was in no mood for a deconstruction of educational assessment methods and bell-shaped curves. "How the hell would I know?"

She smiled sweetly and crossed her arms beneath her breasts. "Because you've been reviewing the information with them. Because you wrote the question. Because you're their teacher."

"Pretty smart, aren't you?"

She uncrossed her arms and put her hands on his desk, leaning over him. "How the hell would you know?"

The way she tossed his words back at him made something crack and ease up inside. He'd been holding himself tight, wound like a spring for the past few days. He uncoiled and reached for the stack of essays. "Here," he said, tossing them toward her. "Educate me. Go ahead and score these."

"Oh, Joe," she said, shaking her head. "I don't know how you can bear to part with these. Aren't you dying to know how Sara Belton feels about the Palestinian situation?"

Yes, he was. Sort of. And wasn't that strange. He ignored the twinge of—conscience? regret?—and linked his fingers behind his head as he leaned back. His chair complained with a squawk.

"Hmm," she said, flipping through the papers. "I suppose you're right. Doesn't look like anything all that exciting." She paused to read a bit of one of the essays. "Although it looks like something finally got Jeremy to make an effort."

"Something did all right. The end of the quarter. If he doesn't make grades, he doesn't play ball." He held out his hand for the paper, curious to see what Jeremy had written, in spite of his flip remark. "Let me see if he pulled it off."

"No, that's okay. I'll handle it."

She tapped the test papers into a neat pile. Slowly, methodically, on all four sides. Even for her standards, too obsessively neat.

A delaying tactic.

"Is there anything else you want to discuss?" she asked.

He could guess what she had in mind. He'd been avoiding any real contact with her ever since he'd walked out her door, and he still wasn't ready to deal with the situation. "No. You?"

She chewed on her lower lip. "Nothing right now."

He raised an eyebrow and waited for her to give in

and start talking. She opened her mouth to say something, but bit it back.

Cowards, both of them.

"Well," she said, and scooped up the test papers. "I'd better get going. I'll have these corrected for class tomorrow."

"No hurry. I know you're busy."

"No, it's okay. I can do it." She turned to gather her things.

Suddenly, he didn't want her to go. He rose from his seat. "Em. Wait."

"Yes?"

Damn. Wanting her to stay meant starting a conversation. "I noticed Todd Sommers is behaving himself."

"Honey Chil'?" Emily's stiff stance relaxed. "I sure lucked out with that."

"There are worse fates for a guy than having all the girls on campus call him Honey." He shoved his hands into his pockets. "I enjoyed your party."

He watched the emotions skid across her features: pleasure, pain, confusion. "You did?"

"Yes."

"I couldn't be sure," she said. "You left so early."

"I should have said goodbye. And thanked you. For inviting me."

"You're welcome." She hefted the strap over her shoulder.

Their polite words echoed in the silence between them. The bell rang, signaling the end of break.

Emily blinked and stepped back. "I'd better go."

"Yes, you'd better," he said. He gave her a non-committal smile. "See you tomorrow."

She nodded, and then turned and walked out the door.

He lowered himself to his chair with a sigh of relief. They'd managed to get through that okay. Everything was going to be all right.

Like hell it was.

THANKSGIVING WAS all about being grateful. And family—it was all about that, too. So, in a tidy and circular sum, Thanksgiving was all about being grateful for family.

Emily reminded herself of those simple facts on Thanksgiving morning as she disconnected her cell phone and dropped it into her purse before her mother could come up with any more arguments against Emily braving a trip through the thin layer of freezing rain and unseasonal snow flurries. She pulled on her gloves and snatched her scarf off the hat rack on her way out the door.

The front porch was like a sheet of glass. A lucky trajectory across the landing and some fancy footwork down the front steps kept her upright.

"Okay, so it's a little slick," she admitted as she gunned the engine and set the defroster for a full-throated roar. "But I can do this," she muttered as she hopped out to scrape frozen snow pellets from the windshield. "Piece of cake," she added as she turned into the empty stretch of road in front of her house.

She bumped over the crossing near the deserted industrial park, twisted the radio tuner until soft jazz filled the cab, and settled back for the drive to Seattle. "What does she think I am, an imbecile?"

Emily got her answer a half mile later, when the dash lit up like a red-light district and the truck slipped into a brakeless coma, steam roiling around the hood as it drifted to a stop, tipped along a ditch at the side of the road. She pulled her cell phone from her purse and watched the battery flatline, and then studied the frozen view beyond the windows of the cooling car. Traffic along this stretch of road on a holiday morning seemed to be nonexistent.

She stared down at the slim heeled pumps that weren't fit for the icy hike back to her house and sighed. "Imbecile alert."

JOE EJECTED the Coltrane CD and tossed it on the passenger seat of his car. He wasn't in the mood for music. He wasn't in the mood for a trip into Seattle, either, but the alternative was staying at home and staring at his walls for four days. Last night's freeze had put the chill on his plans to shake the dust off his bike, trek into the wilderness, feast on jerky and stare at the trees. Now he faced a weekend in a hotel room and a trek to a gallery to stare at some art.

And he'd feast in the hotel dining room, where no

one would give a damn about Joseph P. Wisniewski or why he was eating all by himself on Thanksgiving. Isolation and anonymity could be such blessings during the holidays.

Rationalizing B.S., all of it. Thanksgiving meant family, and for him, family meant Anna. He'd called her a week ago, fishing for an invitation to flop in her San Francisco flat, hoping to fill his belly with her peppery politics and spicy moussaka. But she was picketing in D.C. this week.

He'd had a couple of offers of turkey with all the trimmings—and not just the edible type—from a couple of ex-lovers. But lately he'd lost his appetites. Ever since that damn Halloween party, Emily was the only item of interest on the menu.

He'd stopped resenting her and his feelings for her. Now he just resented his situation. He was stuck in a deeper rut than usual, a rut that left him itchy as hell. But he figured being stuck in the mud was better than scratching his itch and getting stuck in the line at the employment office.

The old highway loop was empty this morning. Most people were sleeping in or settling in for the day. Getting the turkeys in the oven and putting the finishing touches on the table settings. Greeting grandparents and refereeing fights between cousins. Ah, the blessings of domesticity. Everyone complained about it, and then turned around and tried to foist it on people who didn't have it.

"Gotta git yerself a wife, Joe," Samuel Taggart had insisted when Joe had driven out past the industrial park to drop off a frozen pumpkin pie early that morning. As he always did, Samuel had pulled out a dented flask and offered Joe some of the Jack Daniel's he kept handy. And Joe obliged the old man with a taste of the whiskey and some companionable grunts about women and the fuss they made over the holidays. Samuel considered himself something of an expert on the subject of wives, since he'd had four. But none of his exes wanted his company for Thanksgiving.

Joe wasn't much of a substitute, but he was all the company some of the elderly members of the Garden Project were likely to see this holiday weekend. With Lindsay Wellek's assistance, he'd set up a light visitation schedule, but he didn't feel right leaving for the weekend without checking up on some of the elderly who lived beyond the town center.

Up ahead, a truck rested at a crazy angle across the shoulder of the road, one front tire dipped off the edge. He took his foot off the gas and coasted closer, wondering if the driver had hit some black ice and ended up in a ditch, wondering if whoever was in that truck was hurt or stranded.

Wait. He knew that truck. It was Emily's.

"Emily." Panic and pain ripped through him, violent and visceral. "God, Emily!"

CHAPTER ELEVEN

HE SKIDDED on an icy patch, stumbled out of his car, and scrambled across the road on limbs gone rubbery with fear.

Fighting for footing on the slick shoulder, he smacked a shin against the wheel well of her truck as he tried to wrench the driver's side door open. The window was fogged from the inside, and he couldn't see her. Couldn't see the blood, or the pale skin, or...

The window opened a crack. "Joe?"

She seemed coherent. Not pale, not suffering. He wrapped his fingers around the top of the glass, trying to shove it down. He wanted to get his hands on her, to pull her into his arms. To check every inch of her and make sure she was all right. She had to be all right.

Tatters of steam floated past his face. The slow hiss from the front of the truck finally registered. Engine trouble. Not an accident.

"Are you all right?" he asked.

She lowered the window the rest of the way. "Yes."

"Oh." His vision cleared, and his heart rate decelerated to something in three figures. An adrenaline tidal wave ebbed to the soles of his boots. He was worried that the rest of him was going to ebb into a puddle, too. "Okay."

He collapsed against the side of her truck and took a deep, calming breath. At least, that was what he tried for. What came out was a cross between a moan and a wheeze. "What's going on here?" he asked.

She flopped back in her seat and folded her arms across her chest. "I'm stuck."

He closed his eyes and groaned. "God."

"I know," she said. "I just hate it when this happens."

He opened one eye. "How often does this happen?"

"Getting stuck?" She scrunched up her nose, probably to help her think. Considering the situation—that she was trapped in the middle of a deserted road, stuck in freezing temperatures, with no obvious plan for getting herself unstuck, with holiday rapists and murderers prowling the back roads of Washington State looking for turkeys like her—she needed all the help she could get with thinking. "Exactly like this?" she asked. "Never."

Joe wasn't going to waste his time trying to untangle her response. Keeping his sanity was more important than decoding Emily's syntax. "Waiting for someone?"

"Not really."

He shoved himself upright. "You were just going to sit here like this all day?"

"I was going to walk back to my house."

"That's over two miles from here!" He rubbed one hand over his face and concentrated on keeping his voice calm. "Don't you have a phone?"

She winced. "The battery's dead."

He shook his head.

"I know, I know," she said.

"If you knew, you knew, your phone would be working."

"So glad you could stop by and nag," she said. "Please come again, any time."

He narrowed his eyes at her, and she scowled right back. "Better take a look under the hood," he muttered and started toward the front of the truck.

"You're going to look under the hood?"

"Unless you had something else in mind?"

"No." She opened her door, hopped out and followed him. "That's probably the place to start."

He stood there for a moment, checking her over from head to toe. Then he cradled her face in his hands, needing to touch her, needing to feel for himself that she was safe and whole. "Are you sure you're all right?"

Her eyes widened and darkened, and her lashes fluttered down to spread feathery crescents against her cheeks. And then she jerked her head back. "Yes!"

He yanked his hands away and buried them in his pockets, deep and fisted shut, so he would keep them off her. It was frightening to realize how very difficult it was, at that moment, to keep his hands off her, to keep his arms from tugging her up against him, to keep his fingers from brushing through her hair and his mouth from closing over hers in frustration and desire and relief. To keep from wrapping himself around her, and searching for the sensation of her heart beating beneath his, and breathing in her scent, and believing that if he could keep her close he could keep her safe. "Sorry," he said.

"No—it's just…" She glanced down at her shoes, and then up to stare at some spot past his shoulder. "Your hands were cold."

"Sorry." Thank God for cold hands.

"It's okay." She peeked up at him, and then squinted past him at the fascinating something in the distance. "Well…"

"So…you're not hurt."

"Just my pride." Another quick glance and a tight smile. "It's a little bruised."

"Good." He picked his way to the front of the truck and lifted the hood. "You scared the hell out of me."

She leaned over and peered at the engine, and then up at him. "I did?"

He slipped the support rod into its slot to hold up the hood. "Yeah."

"Sorry about that."

He bent over the engine to find where the steam was coming from, glad to have something besides Emily to focus on at the moment. "The water pump is probably out. You've got a leak right here, see?"

She looked where he pointed and made a noncommittal noise.

"When was the last time you had this checked?"

"When I bought it, right before school started."

"Mmm." He stared down through the steam. "I could put a new one in for you, but it would take most of the day. And we'd need to get the part. I doubt anything's open."

Emily didn't say anything. She was too busy staring up at him. It was that damn puppy stare.

Joe shook his head. "Don't look at me like that. I hate it when women look at me like that."

"Like what?"

"Like there's a leaky faucet in my future." He glanced around for something to wipe his hands on, and settled for his jeans. "What happened right before the truck quit?"

"A red light started flashing on the dash, and then lots of steam came out of the hood."

"Was the steam white or black?"

Emily sighed and crossed her arms. "Steam is white. Smoke is black."

"So. I'm dealing with an expert on car problems."

"Go ahead." She waved her little wave. "Laugh at the stereotypical helpless female, stranded on the side of the road, waiting for a man to come along and bail her out."

"I'm not laughing."

"No. You're not." She frowned and rubbed at her

nose. "Sorry, Joe. I'm mad at myself and taking it out on you."

"It's an old truck. Things are bound to go wrong."

"Which means I should be better prepared for emergencies. Especially when I'm starting out on a long drive. Especially when I'm headed to my parents' place."

"You're taking all the fun out of my lecture."

"You wouldn't be telling me anything I haven't been telling myself for the last fifteen minutes." She poked at a lump in the ditch with the toe of her shoe. Her useless-for-hiking-through-the-ice-and-mud shoe. "I had plenty of time to think while I was sitting here," she said.

He knew her well enough to know there was more. "And?"

"My mom called right before I left." She scuffed at the lump again. "To tell me to be careful."

"Oops."

"Double oops. With the turkey timer ticking."

"Your family's expecting you?"

"Yeah. It's going to be tough now to make it for the appetizers."

"I'll take you."

Joe watched his words float away in a warm puff on the frigid air and wished he could call them back. Playing the Good Samaritan would involve sitting in a small, enclosed space with Emily for that long drive she'd mentioned. And at the end of the road would be a house full of her relatives. He'd probably have to stay for a few minutes, making polite chitchat with rabid reactionaries.

"You don't have to do this," she said.

He looked down at her pink-cheeked face wrapped in misery and a fuzzy scarf, and felt his heart flop over like a well-hooked trout giving up the fight. Yeah, right. Like he'd ever had any choices where she was concerned.

"You can use my cell to call Ron's Garage." He removed the rod and let the hood slam shut. "And then you can call your folks while we wait for a tow."

"I was headed into Seattle, Joe."

He shrugged and walked back to her door. "Do you have any bags in there?"

"I'm sure this is going to be way out of your way."

"No problem." He opened the truck and hauled an overnight bag across the seat. "Anything else you need?"

"No. That's it."

Joe headed for his car. No way was he letting her out of his sight until he delivered her, safe and sound, into the care of her family.

Emily closed up her truck and picked her way across the road. "I can't ask you to take me all the way into Seattle. I feel awful about this."

"You didn't ask. I offered." He opened the passenger door and gestured for her to get in. "I was going there myself."

"Really?" She ducked into his car. "I didn't know you had relatives in Seattle."

He reached past her to grab a small phone book out of his dash box. "I don't."

"Friends, then."

He didn't answer, but handed her his phone, closed her door, and then circled to the driver's side to settle in and wait for Emily to make her calls.

"Ron says he can be here in about twenty minutes," she said as she handed him his cell. She rummaged through her purse and pulled out a neatly folded sheet of paper. "Might as well put the time to good use."

Joe glanced down as she carefully unfolded the paper and smoothed it over her lap. When he saw the list, he groaned.

"Maybe it's something preppy," she said. "Palmer. Parker. Percival. Porter. Preston…."

THE HOUR-LONG DRIVE into Seattle with Joe was an enjoyable surprise. The tension between them seemed to dissolve with each mile, and he never once tried to smother a topic with one of his moody, muttered responses. She told him about her university coursework, and he told her about his summer motorcycle tour of Alaska. They compared notes on their travels and discussed the merits of Italian versus Greek cuisine. She discovered he liked to cook; he discovered she liked to collect recipes and think about cooking.

They spent most of the time talking about their families. He asked lots of questions about Jack, his former student, and she pressed him for stories about Anna, his fascinating aunt. His affection for her was evident in the way his face softened and his voice dipped into an even lower rumble as he spoke of her. Emily thought it was sweet that he still phoned Anna at least once a month, though she kept her opinion to herself.

Eventually, the pleasant interlude drew to an end as they approached her parents' neighborhood. She could feel the tension—her own, at any rate—begin to wind back through her. It was one thing to discuss her family in the abstract; it was another to deal with them in person.

All her shortcomings would seem highlighted in contrast with Jack's success. All her poor choices would be exemplified by her tardy arrival and her lack of transportation for the trip back to Issimish. Her mom would probably slip her some family heirloom to lend a little permanence to her temporary housing, and her dad would probably slip her a check to pad her dwindling savings account.

And to break up the tedium of the prodigal daughter routine, today she'd brought a guest—a man her brother still idolized, a man her mother thought was a hunk, a man her father used to call a commie pinko nutcase. A man who made her blush and sigh, a man who could pull from her any number of flushed and adoring responses she wouldn't be able to hide from the people who knew her best. She usually didn't have a drink before dinner, but the next few minutes might convince her to make an exception.

All too soon, she stood with Joe before her parents' front door, trying not to fidget. "You're going to have to come in for a few minutes," she said as she tugged at a jacket snap. "Just for a little while," she emphasized.

"I know."

"I'm sorry."

"Don't be," he said with a shrug. "I always liked your parents."

"They liked you, too."

"Don't sound so surprised," he said. "I'm a likable guy."

She stared up at him, searching for any traces of put-upon irony in his expression, but there was nothing but unadulterated amusement in his reassuring grin. Somehow, the idea that he was enjoying the situation didn't reassure her at all.

The door swung open to reveal Kay in an ivory wool dress, ivory-tinted pearls, an ivory linen apron and a coordinating dusting of off-white flour along one side of her jaw. "Well, hello!" she said. "I'm so relieved you two made it in one piece."

She gave Emily a loud smack on one cheek, and then hesitated the merest of moments before going up on her toes to peck at Joe, too. "Come in, come in! It's absolutely freezing out there!"

She waved them through the door and shuddered in sympathy, taking Emily's coat and hanging it in the entry closet as she rambled on in her soft Louisiana tones. "Why don't you take your things to your room, Emily, dear, while I take Joe's coat? Here, Joe, I'm sure you'll be much more comfortable without that heavy jacket."

Emily rubbed at the faint smudge on Kay's jaw and tried to explain that Joe wasn't going to be staying, but she was flattened by the Southern Steamroller.

"I cleared extra room in the guest closet for you, dear. And just wait until you see the hand towels I found for the guest bath. They were in an antique linens boutique." Kay held out her hands, patiently waiting for Joe to hand over his coat. "Can you imagine, an entire shop just for old linens? My goodness. Whatever will they think of next?"

Joe shrugged out of his jacket and handed it over, much to Emily's dismay.

"I'm going to have to take you to see it, dear. You, too, Joe, if you'd like, although I can't imagine a man like you would be all that interested in poking through a collection of vintage fabrics. Maybe tomorrow afternoon we can find time for a little shopping. I know shopping during the holidays can be absolutely exhausting, but it does add to the festive mood. Don't you think so, Joe?"

Kay looked up at him so expectantly that Emily knew he'd never find the backbone to disagree.

"Now, tell us what you'd like to drink," Kay said. "Juice? Wine? Something a little stronger?"

"Wine would be fine," he said. "Thanks."

"There's a bottle of Chardonnay circulating in the den, and Jack just opened a Burgundy, if you'd prefer. It's going to need to breathe for a while, first, I'm afraid."

"Chardonnay," said Emily, at the same moment Joe said he'd wait for the Burgundy. She rolled her eyes at the ceiling and fled down the hallway toward her room.

KAY SLIPPED HER ARM though Joe's and led him deeper into Sullivan territory, babbling about some incomprehensible difficulty she'd encountered while preparing the pecan stuffing. Not that he was to worry, she reassured him with a pat on his arm—dinner would be served as scheduled.

Joe felt as if he were moving through an alternate universe, a world of lace-filtered light and clustered mementos, scented with the aromas of roasting fowl and spiced desserts. Through a doorway he glimpsed Jack Senior sprawled in a leather recliner, and his son loafing on a nearby sofa, the two of them sharing a laugh at something on the television screen.

A nice family scene. There it was again—that warm and fuzzy feeling. He wasn't as rattled as he should have been by the quick spurt of longing for a place in the tableau. So he decided he might linger a bit over his wine, if only to remind himself that he didn't want or need any of it.

Both Jacks rose to greet him with identical squared-off stances. Joe noted the silver glints in the father's blond buzz cut and the genuine affection in the welcoming grin. "Been a while, Joe."

"Good to see you, Jack." And it was.

He turned and nodded at his former student. "I hear you've got a family of your own now."

"Susan's out in the kitchen." Jack Junior extended his hand in welcome. "She'll want to meet you before you go."

"Oh, heavens," said Kay with a dismissive wave. "There's plenty of time for that. He's not heading back out into that weather anytime soon. Settle in, Joe. Put your feet up and relax for a spell."

She herded him toward a deeply tufted chair. "Jack, dear, you pour Joe a glass of wine. The Burgundy, when it's ready."

She tipped up on her toes and kissed her husband on the cheek. "And behave yourself," she warned in a voice of honeyed steel.

Jack Senior waited until Kay floated out the door. "Yes, sir," he said with a smile, and then he followed orders, pouring an excellent vintage and serving up apolitical small talk. Susan—a seven months' mound beneath her soft knit dress—appeared with a tray of cheeses and crackers and settled on the arm of Jack Junior's chair to visit. With the television tuned to football and the conversation limited to pleasantries, Joe began to hope he could negotiate the Sullivan minefield without dismemberment.

Then Emily entered the room, and he knew his first misstep would definitely be his last. If her daggered looks were any indication, his lounging and lingering had landed him on her personal shit list.

He wished he could figure out why his presence here made her so tense. The fact that he couldn't gave him one more reason to go. He rose and made his farewells, and then followed Emily into the next room. Kay was adding a place setting to a table lush with layers of linens and plates.

"Mom, what are you doing?"

"Making a place for our guest." She set a stack of flowery plates on a gold-toned charger and threaded a pleated napkin through a gold-sprayed vine. "You simply must stay for dinner, Joe."

Emily started to protest, but Kay cut her off. "It's the least we can do to thank him for coming to your rescue. There's plenty to eat, of course. And just look at my table now—it's ever so much more attractive now that things aren't so lopsided. You wouldn't want us to be ungrateful and unbalanced on Thanksgiving, would you, Joe?"

He stared at the table. It looked like something on the cover of one of those magazines at the grocery store, with fat roses spilling out of a big bowl vase, and crystal and silver winking in candlelight, and fancy pieces of china arranged on rich tapestry squares. Six place settings spread before six tall, sat-in-seated mahogany chairs ringing a massive mahogany table. Anyone who messed with any of it probably deserved to be shot.

"I'm sure he's made other plans." Emily turned to him, baring her teeth in something that almost passed for a smile. "Haven't you, Joe?"

If the aromas drifting in from the kitchen were any hint, he'd be walking away from culinary heaven. "Sort of."

"Plans change." Kay waved away Joe's. "You're here now, and we're going to sit down to dinner in just a few minutes. Why—your glass is empty. I do hope Emily hasn't been neglecting you." Kay shot her daughter a brilliant smile, and then turned and slipped out of the room, putting an end to any further discussion.

Emily glared up at him.

"What?" he whispered.

"I thought you had other plans."

"You heard your mother. Plans change."

"Not yours," she whispered.

"My plans haven't been my plans since the day you showed up in my classroom."

"That has nothing to do with this."

It had everything to do with everything, but she was the last person who needed to know it.

She snatched a wine bottle from the buffet. "You don't have to stay, you know. She's just being polite."

"I know that kind of polite. There's nothing polite about it." He held out his glass for Emily's miserly refill. "That wasn't a request, that was an order. A little trick military wives develop for dealing with their live-in officers."

"But you didn't want to stay in the first place." She set the bottle down and winced at the clunk. "The longer you wait, the harder it's going to be to escape. I don't want you to get stuck."

"I know you don't. And believe me, you're pretty scary. But she's scarier."

"And why is that?"

"Probably because she's had more years to practice." He sipped his wine and weighed the consequences of pissing off the woman he had to work with every day versus pissing off a woman he might never see again. He knew what logic dictated; he knew where his loyalties should lie; he knew what he should do. And yet he couldn't make himself do it. The smells coming from the kitchen were too enticing, the table setting too inviting, the situation too intriguing.

To hell with logic and loyalties and pissing people off. It was Thanksgiving, and he was as entitled as the next person to enjoying a family dinner—even if the family he was going to enjoy it with wasn't his own. A mere technicality.

He finished his wine and reached for the bottle. She moved it behind her back. "Why do you want to stay?" she asked.

He reached around her, trying to get to the wine. His face came within inches of hers.

Big mistake.

And then he compounded it by glancing down and noticing the way her mouth opened in a little gasp, and her eyes went wide and dark, and her breath caught on the same sharp-toothed trap that had already snagged his.

Oh, shit. He'd wanted to kiss her before. Just to see what she'd feel like, what he'd feel like. What they'd feel like together. A scientific experiment in lust, nothing more.

But he'd never needed to kiss her before.

This was crazy. He was just feeling a little worked up after seeing her truck tipped off the side of the road. Shock, that was what it was. That would explain the electrical current snapping between them like a high-voltage wire on steroids.

He told himself he didn't really need to kiss her. Not in her parents' house, not with Kay slaving over her dinner in the kitchen and Jack Senior struggling through his best behavior in the den. Not when he was her mentor. Not when his job depended on not kissing her. Surely the instinct for self-preservation was stronger than this irrational urge.

But then Emily's gaze dropped to his mouth, her lashes sweeping low along her flushed cheeks, and he knew he was going to do it anyway.

Just this once.

"Emily?" Kay yodeled from the kitchen.

Just not right now.

Emily's head snapped back. Her expression morphed from dazed to mulish in less than a second, setting a new speed record for a woman's scorn.

"Here, have some more," she said in a sweetly lethal voice as she shoved the wine bottle at him. "Have all you want. Just remember, you'll want to keep your wits about you for the dinner conversation with Jack Senior. I'm sure it will be absolutely fascinating."

CHAPTER TWELVE

EMILY WAS NO LONGER enthralled, entranced or impressed by the image of The Great and Powerful Wiz sharing a meal with Jack Senior. Instead, she was enduring the boring reality, sitting in her spot at the Sullivan dining room table, rubbing one foot against the other and trying not to roll her eyes while she listened to Joe's dinner conversation. She'd given up hope of any debates arriving at the table before the dessert.

She was almost disappointed no blood had been drawn, no curses had been shouted. Not one red splotch had appeared on her father's face, and not a single vein had throbbed in his forehead. Instead, he'd spent most of his time listening to Joe discuss sports with Jack Junior, or stock investments with Susan, or herb gardens with Kay.

In fact, there didn't seem to be any subject their Honored Guest couldn't discuss with someone at the table in a relaxed and expansive way. He was amazingly talkative—downright charming, in fact. It was enough to ruin her appetite for some of her favorite dishes, and her temper failed to improve even after a third glass of wine.

He was up to something. He'd deflected Jack Junior's crack about her truck. And he'd glossed over the details when her dad questioned him about how he'd found her at the side of the road. It was almost as if he were acting as her champion, defending her from her own family.

And when he wasn't playing her knight in shining armor, he was playing up her accomplishments at school. Like right now, the way he was bragging about her fund-raising efforts.

"She's helped raise more money than ever for the Garden Project," he said.

"She has?" asked Jack Junior.

"Yes, she has." Joe sent one of his looks across the table, the kind that curled her toes and made her stomach feel like a washer on the spin cycle. She leaned back into her chair, afraid the table would start vibrating.

Whatever he was up to, she wished he'd knock it off.

Kay cleared her throat. "Can I pass you anything, Joe? More potatoes? Stuffing?"

"No, thanks." He nodded at the tomato aspic trembling near Jack Senior's water goblet. "But there's something I missed. Could you pass that, please?"

No one moved. Emily could hear the grandfather clock in the entry tick off three seconds before Jack Junior lifted the small platter and passed it across the table to Susan. She hesitated a moment before placing it in Joe's outstretched hand. Jack Senior's fork was frozen in midair, a sliver of turkey dangling inches from his lips. Kay whispered, "Oh, my lord," and then snatched up her napkin to cover a strangled cough.

"How's that gravy boat doing?" Emily asked. "Almost empty? Well, I'll just fill it up." She almost knocked her chair over in her haste to scramble from the table. "Mom? I'll bet you need to get the coffee started right about now."

"I suppose I do." Kay placed her napkin on the table but didn't rise. She waited as Joe scooped up a mound of red goo with a fussy silver spoon and slid it onto his plate. "Although I surely don't want to miss a moment of the dinner conversation."

Emily looked around at the stunned, silent faces watching Joe spoon aspic into his mouth. "I think there might be a brief lull in the proceedings." She circled the table and grasped the back of Kay's chair. "And you've already caught the highlights."

"Well, then," Kay said, rising with as much dignity as she could manage as her chair was tugged out from beneath her. "If y'all will excuse us, we'll be right back."

The moment the kitchen door swung shut behind them, Emily spun to face her mother, who collapsed against a counter, her shoulders shaking with bottled-up laughter. "What was that all about?" she whispered.

Kay crossed her hands over her chest and took

several deep breaths before she whispered back, "Whatever do you mean?"

"You know very well what I mean. That 'oh, my Lord' business. The man is entitled to a little gelatin if he wants it. It's on the table, for crying out loud. I'm sure he assumed it was edible."

"Of course Great-Grandmother Ellen's aspic is edible." Kay swiped at the tears in her eyes. "It's just…it's just…" She bent at the waist as another spasm of giggles broke through. "Oh, my."

Emily fought back a grin. Joe hadn't known the aspic was something of a traditional holiday decoration, just like the centerpiece—and no one ate the roses, did they? She emptied a saucepan of gravy into the pretty china boat and set it aside. "Mom. Get a grip."

"This has nothing to do with aspic," said Kay, "and you know it."

"I know nothing of the sort."

"It's Ginny Krubek, all over again."

"What in heaven's name are you talking about?"

"Ginny Krubek." Kay tied her apron around her waist and began to measure coffee into two French roast dispensers. "Joe Wisniewski has made a perverse habit of seeking out and finding the most inappropriate women to become involved with—and then going right ahead and becoming involved with them. You are, at the moment, the most inappropriate woman in his life, so of course he's powerfully attracted."

Kay's theory stunned Emily. Stunned and stung. Why hadn't she figured this out for herself?

Worse yet, why did it hurt so much? She should be relieved that Joe's meaningful glances were nothing more than some kind of abnormal behavior pattern. It should make it that much easier to ignore them.

She grabbed the kettle, dropped it in the sink and slapped at the faucet handle before wrapping her fingers around the sink's edge. She squeezed her eyes shut. This was what she'd feared, why she didn't want Joe joining her family at their table. She couldn't hide her mistakes from her family. Couldn't hide the latest mess she was making of her current career choice, couldn't hide the latest disaster looming in her personal life.

"Okay." She turned off the tap and shrugged away from the sink. "You may have a point."

"I wish it were that simple," said Kay. She took the kettle and set it on the stove to boil. "He never looked at Ginny Krubek the way he looks at you."

"What do you mean?"

"There's something more than an inappropriate attraction going on here, I think."

"No." Emily shook her head. "Now you're reading too much into things."

"It was the aspic," said Kay. "It was merely a symbolic gesture, I'm sure. But it was a truly lovely token of affection."

Insanity alert. Her mother had entered the chrysalis of an antique linen shop and emerged as Blanche DuBois. "The man spoons up tomato goo and you see that as proof of tender feelings?"

"It was part and parcel with the way he's been talking about you and gazing at you all evening long." Kay sighed a happy little sigh. "Taken all together, it's a lovely picture of a man who's trying to please the woman he cares for. Who's trying hard to humor her father and butter up her mother."

Emily swallowed past her panic. "He's just being polite."

"There's polite, and there's pleasant, and then there's a deep and compelling desire to please. It seems to me that sampling a tomato aspic that no one else would touch might just fall into the third category." Kay reached up to twist a strand of Emily's hair into place. "I do believe he's courting you, Emily. You, and all of us, too."

"That's impossible." Emily batted away the strand of hair Kay's fussing had loosened. "He barely tolerates me most of the time."

Kay laughed. "I'm sure it seems that way. It's part of every man's self-defense techniques. Remember how Sammy Spanner used to cover your shins with bruises when you were both in the second grade? He was so sweet on you, and he simply didn't know how else to show it."

"Well, Joe keeps his sandals to himself. Besides, I'm not his type."

"No. You're not. And that was the biggest part of the initial attraction for him, I'm sure."

"You're not making sense." Emily flopped into one of the chairs at the tiny kitchen table. "None of this makes any sense."

"It never makes sense when opposites attract. It only makes things more interesting." She turned to deal with the screeching kettle. "You're different than the women he usually spends time with. I think that means something."

"I'm certainly no Ginny Krubek, but I don't think that means anything at all." It couldn't mean anything. Not anything real or lasting. "*If* there were anything at all to be thinking about in the first place. Which there most definitely is not."

Kay poured hot water into the two coffee dispensers. "With Ginny, it was a definite lusting-after-her look. He didn't look at her the way he looks at you. This is more than simple attraction." Kay set a timer and leaned back against the butcher block island. "And the reason I'm bringing it up at all, Em, is that you look at him in just the same way."

"I'm not looking at him any way at all." Emily swiped a crumb off the tabletop. "And if I do, what you're seeing on my face is pure terror that he and Dad are going to start in on each other."

Kay glanced at the timer and sighed. "Things have been a little tense this afternoon."

"I knew it. I knew I wasn't the only one who could

see through that cozy act out there. It was all I could do to choke down my turkey."

"Let's give them credit for trying, at least."

"It's probably because of Jack Junior and all their old history," Emily said.

"I don't think your brother has anything to do with it. I think it has to do with the fact that Joe wants to jump your bones, and your father isn't too happy about the idea."

"Mom!" Emily winced and lowered her voice. "Where do you get this stuff?"

"A mother just knows these things."

"I meant the part about jumping bones."

"Don't you think your father still wants to jump mine? I recognize the look." Kay crossed her arms. "Joe's giving you the look."

The timer binged. "Time to serve the coffee," said Kay. She collected the dispensers and swung through the door.

Emily slunk back to the dining room table with the gravy boat, afraid to look Joe in the eyes. She snatched up her fork for a halfhearted stab at the vegetables still on her plate.

"What are your plans for tomorrow, Em?" Susan asked as she offered to fill Joe's coffee cup. "Shopping?"

"Yeah." Emily shot Kay a warning look, and then concentrated on abusing her carrots. "I just love that holiday craziness."

"Need a lift?" asked Susan.

"I'll take you," said Joe.

Emily's fork clattered to her plate. "Excuse me," she muttered.

"I can give you a lift," he repeated.

"No, I heard what you said, I'm just—" Clumsy. Mortified. Terrified. "Thank you, Joe. I'm sure it won't be necessary."

"I know it's not necessary. I just thought it might work out, for both of us. You don't have a car, and I was hoping you could help me find something for my aunt. Her birthday's coming up."

Emily stared at the Honored Guest across the table. His answering grin could have been lifted from a Boy Scout recruitment poster.

"How convenient," said Kay. She raised one eyebrow and nodded at Jack Senior in a signal that could have been picked up in Poughkeepsie without a satellite transmission. Subtlety had never been part of Kay's repertoire. "That's so very kind of you, Joe."

Jack Senior raised his coffee, but paused in midsip when he caught Kay's combination nod and flutter. His mouth thinned in a tight frown. And then he set his cup back, oh so carefully, in its saucer. "So, Joe," he said. "What do you think about this latest flap over federal funding for the arts?"

Emily closed her eyes and slumped back against her chair with a groan.

EMILY AVOIDED looking Joe in the eye the next day as he drove them to the mall. She continued to prevent eye contact by studying the holiday decorations. She even managed to evade meeting his eyes while suggesting various aunt-appropriate purchases. And now she had a twitch in her left eye, because in spite of all her efforts at avoidance, she was all too aware of the tall, silent man attached to her side like an elongated shadow.

He wasn't shopping. He wasn't talking. He wasn't teasing, or picking an argument, or doing much of anything except being extremely patient, and extremely polite, and extremely agreeable, and giving her a headache. So she started plotting a way to get out of her promise to visit an art gallery with him after lunch, though it made her feel ungrateful. He obviously wanted some companionship over the holiday weekend, and he certainly deserved it. She just wished he hadn't decided to get it by adopting the Sullivans.

Right now, though, she'd had enough of the holiday spirit and the holiday crowds. She told Joe it was time to head back to the car.

"Finished already?" he asked.

"Finished with the mall."

"Oh." He glanced down at her one small bag, which held a baby-themed photo frame for Susan and Jack's nursery. "Okay."

They changed direction, heading toward an exit.

Emily paused at the door. "You're sure there isn't anything you want to go back and check on? For your aunt?"

"No," he said agreeably as he politely opened the door for her.

"Well, then." She pulled on her jacket. "We'll have to look somewhere else."

Her head was pounding from the stress of the silences that fell between them. This was so strange. She'd never been uncomfortable with Joe before. Yesterday, in his car, they'd chatted nonstop for over an hour. An hour in which she had felt connected with him, somehow. It seemed like a lifetime ago.

Damn that aspic.

They stepped outside into a world that had turned dark and sullen, and the first fat raindrops hit as they sprinted for the car. Emily stopped to open her umbrella as Joe fumbled for his keys.

"It's a little early for lunch," she said.

He leaned down to open her door. "Is it?"

"Maybe you should just take me back to my parents'. Okay?"

He paused with his fingers over the handle and his face too close to hers.

"Joe?"

His gaze lowered to her mouth. Something about the way he was staring at it made her insides all hot and bubbly, the way cheese foamed and slid over the edges of a slice of leftover pizza in the microwave.

Yep—things were definitely heating up and shifting around in there.

Now her heart was pounding in sync with her head, and the heat was spreading through her body. Maybe she needed something to eat, after all. Maybe she wouldn't be feeling this way if she had taken her mother's advice and eaten a healthy breakfast before the shopping trip. Maybe they should get moving, fast, and find a place where they could sit on opposite sides of a wide table with plenty of things between them they could stuff into their mouths so they wouldn't have to talk, or think, or feel.

"Joe?" she whispered.

His eyes flicked back up to hers, twin tractor beams guiding her deeper, deeper into twin black holes. She wasn't aware that either of them had moved, but suddenly her umbrella tipped back, and her bag plopped on the pavement at her feet, and his hands pulled her close, and his face tilted toward hers, and she realized he was actually, finally, going to kiss her. And then his mouth closed over hers, and everything else—umbrellas, hands, time, headaches, heartbeats, reality—ceased to exist.

Later, she would remember that this was a really bad idea. Later, she would panic because they were standing in the parking lot of a major shopping center where any Caldwell High passersby would have an excellent view of the new chairman of the social studies department indulging in a hot lip lock—not to mention a full body press against the car—with his student teacher. Later she would worry about the fact that he was crushing her to him as if he wanted to eat her alive, and that she was gobbling him up right back.

But right now she was too busy sampling all the sensations of his lips and teeth and tongue, and absorbing all the dark and yearning and reckless and tender flavors, and memorizing the texture of his hair as she gripped it with clawing fingers, and wondering whose moan she thought she'd heard just a second ago. But mostly she was concentrating very hard on sucking air in and forcing it out so she wouldn't collapse on her rubber chicken legs. Because she wanted this moment to spin out forever. She wanted to go on and on feeling his busy hands trace her shape through her bulky clothes, and his long arms wrap clear around her, and his warm, ragged breath puff against her ear and her throat and her forehead. She needed to go on feeling, in every tingling corner of her body, that he wanted her every bit as much as she wanted him at this moment. She wanted to go on feeling swamped, and devoured, and set free, and soaring, soaring so high she thought she'd burst.

Desire—yes, yes, she could taste it in the way his tongue licked along her lower lip, a lush sweep of dazzling promise. And, oh, there was a hint of tenderness in a nuzzle across her nose, right before he dipped his knees to snatch her up closer, closer against him so he could assault her mouth all over again. He thrilled her and humbled her, he sent her spinning and flung her dreaming, floating away on murmurs and caresses. He was everything, everything, and she was nothing but his in this silvery moment. She shuddered and fell in surrender.

"God." He set her feet back on the ground and rested his forehead against hers, gasping like a marathoner at the finish line. His fingers came up to cup her face, and they trembled against her cheeks. *"God."*

"Joe—"

He shook his head, and dropped his hands to her shoulders. "Get in the car."

"I—"

"Get in the car." He leaned past her and opened the door, and then he swept up her bag and crushed it into her hands before shoving her inside.

Time, and heartbeats, and reality were still warped in some strange, alternate universe. Everything else seemed clearer, somehow, thrown into harsh relief against her white-hot awareness. The dampness of her jacket where it twisted behind her back, the stray drips that fell from her hair and tickled their way down her neck. The rustle of her shopping bag as she settled it against her feet, the tang of the air freshener strip that swayed below the rearview mirror. The lingering warmth of Joe's lips against her own, the tide of panic vising her chest. No. No, no, no.

Oh, please, no. Misery washed through her,

pushing every other sensation into a cold, hazy background. It couldn't be. Those kisses didn't just happen. And nothing like them could ever happen again. She already mourned the loss.

But the worst part was trying to decide which mental health option—denial, shock treatment, lobotomy—would strip away all those sensations and emotions ping-ponging around inside, or trap them and shove them into a calm and rational box. Which method was going to hurt the least in the long run.

What was it that people said about not being able to appreciate the highs without experiencing the lows? Well, the principle could work in reverse, Emily supposed. Now she had the ecstasy of Joe's kisses to remember through all the rotten things life might dish out. Like the way she was feeling right now. Cold, damp, empty, and…what was she sitting on? She reached beneath her soggy jacket and felt her parents' house key poking through a pocket.

Cold, damp, empty and punctured. Maybe she should shove the key back and give it another chance to do her in. Bleeding to death seemed one of her better options at the moment, although Joe probably wouldn't appreciate the mess she'd make of his upholstery. At least she wouldn't have to face him in class next week. And he wouldn't have to deal with her.

But first, they had to make it through the next awkward, awful minutes. And then through the ride back to her parents' house, trapped together in this small, confined space. She squeezed her eyes shut, searching inside her damp, punctured shell for enough fortitude to get her through the coming tortures, and then opened them again to see Joe at the driver's side of the car, wrestling her umbrella into a sloppy bundle.

He stood for a long moment, staring at the handle on the door, rain trickling down his hair to drip over his face. And then he looked through the window, through the spatters of kamikaze droplets and the snaking rivulets that bled from them, and found her eyes. And it started, all over again. The tractor beam tug, the nuclear meltdown, the emotional annihilation. "No," she whispered. "Oh, please, no."

CHAPTER THIRTEEN

JOE OPENED THE DOOR, slid into his seat and dragged Emily against him again. He didn't know why he was scraping his mouth against her soft, ripe lips, or running his hands through those wet, silky curls. He simply felt that if he didn't do these things, if he didn't do them right now, he would die. A seizure, or spontaneous combustion, or nuclear detonation. Whatever it was, it wouldn't be pretty.

Her soft whimper brought him to his senses. He didn't let her go, but he tried to give her a little more room to breathe. She needed to breathe. He didn't want her to pass out, because then he'd have to wait for her to regain consciousness before he could slip his tongue into her mouth again. And again and again…

The selfishness of that thought finally brought him to a state of full consciousness. Well, relative consciousness, anyway. He wasn't too sure he would ever regain a state of complete normalcy, at least not while Emily was in the immediate vicinity, looking like, and smelling like, and feeling like she did.

Finally. He *knew* what she felt like. Tossing rational thought into the air like confetti, he sank into another kiss, just to hold amazing fact, just to feel all those soft curves against him for a little while longer. Or a lot longer. Whichever came last.

He. Knew. What. She. Felt. Like. *No.* He shoved her away and backed against the car door. "This is insane."

She nodded, her face flushed, her eyes wide and dark, dark blue. Full of panic. And passion. He wasn't sure which was worse. "Yes, absolutely," she said. "Insane."

"This did not happen. I mean, it did happen, but it's not going to happen again."

"You're right." She bit down on her lower lip. He really wished she would stop doing things that drew his attention to that part of her anatomy. "You're absolutely right."

"Are you sure?"

She nodded again, and then shifted to stare out the windshield. "Yes."

She was agreeing with him. This was worse than he'd expected. "No argument for the sake of argument?"

"No. No arguments. Not even a discussion." She turned away from him to tug her seat belt across her chest. Right across those dual handfuls of luscious, moldable flesh. "I'm ready to go now."

He started the car, pulled out of the parking space and headed through the lot. Small, normal, everyday movements. This was good. He could do this. He could handle these little activities, could start with clenching his fingers around the steering wheel and pressing his foot on the accelerator and then move up to more complicated activities like carrying on a coherent conversation while walking. One step at a time. One sentence at a time. Sort of like making this smooth turn around another row of parked cars, with the sound of Emily's breathing filling his ears, and her perfume tickling his nose and the jean-clad length of her legs in his peripheral vision.

"The hell with this." He jerked into another parking spot, ripped the key out of the ignition and turned to find Emily fighting her way out of her seat belt.

"Here. Let me help you with that." And, as long as his hands were in the general vicinity, they might as well help her undo her jacket, too. And find their way inside her sweater.

Heat, scent, soft, soft skin. Heaven. Taste—he needed another taste. Now. He aimed for and missed her lips as they strained toward each other, but right now, just about every target was delicious. Her chin, her earlobe, her chin again. Hell, even that snap on her jacket had a sort of kinky appeal.

If he hadn't known he was in trouble before, the business with the jacket snap exploded like a flare. What in hell was wrong with him? This was his student teacher. Emily Sullivan, the thorn in his side with the smart mouth and the half-baked ideas. And the snotty attitude that had nearly spoiled his Thanksgiving dinner.

She laughed as he hauled her into his lap. He had to kiss her, thoroughly, once—no, twice—before he could pull back and scold them both. "This is no laughing matter."

"Yes, it is."

"Oh, so now I get an argument."

"Is that what you want to do right now?" She nibbled a little line of kisses down his throat. "Argue?"

"God, no." He settled low in his seat, wanting to pull her down, down, deep under with him. There was that rush, that rocket blast of the first dizzying contact of lip to lip. And there was that sizzle within the soft, silky pleasure of her mouth. He traced the outline of her lips with his tongue, inhaled her breath, sipped her contented sigh and swallowed it whole. He cradled her in his arms and brushed her hair back from her face, marveling at the miracle in the arrangement of this amazing feminine skin over these particularly lovely bones. Emily's skin, Emily's bones. *Em.*

He brushed a knuckle over her nose and she wrinkled it in a frown. "We've ruined everything, haven't we?" she asked.

"No. Not everything." He bent to kiss her again, taking care to be very, very gentle with her. With this. He felt as fragile as the moment.

"But a lot of the important parts," she said.

"Short-term? Yeah." He took a deep breath, let it out in a resigned gust. "It's blown sky-high."

She straightened a bit to face him. "I don't suppose there's any way to salvage some of it? Short-term?"

Joe tapped one hand on the steering wheel. "We're two intelligent, responsible adults. There's got to be a way to work things out."

She closed her eyes and sighed a deep sigh before crawling back into her seat. "I was hoping one of us would say that out loud. I'm glad you were the first."

He reached across her to buckle her belt, used the chivalry bit to sneak another satisfying, stimulating kiss, and then started the car and backed out of the space. "All we've got to do is agree to a plan and stick to it."

"Okay."

He knew there was more to it than that, but the rational part of his brain seemed to have shut down for the duration. The section in charge of making excuses was now in full operation.

Neither of them said anything as Joe guided the car out of the lot. He drove aimlessly through the city streets, avoiding freeway on-ramps and the general direction of the Sullivan place. "Okay," he said after a turn into a quiet residential neighborhood. "Here's the thing. There probably shouldn't be any more physical contact. Nothing at all. Not until the end of your internship at Caldwell. Nothing until after finals, grades, everything."

"Right. Definitely. Makes absolute sense," she agreed.

He drove another block, thinking about how far away the end of the term seemed, and how close Emily was right now, and pulled to the curb beneath a shadowy fir. This time, her seat belt was off before he shut down the engine, and she was wrapped in his arms a second later. "Starting tomorrow," he managed to add just before her mouth closed over his.

For a long time, he simply focused on the sensation of her mouth—that mobile, sassy, teasing, talkative mouth. A mouth that was turning out to be as inventive and generous with kisses as it was with words. He had never craved this part of the sexual dance before, considering it just a warm-up to the main event. But now, with Emily, he reveled in the intimacy of shared breath and the affection of a tight embrace. He coasted in neutral, drawing out the pleasure, delaying the moment he'd shift into gear and head toward the finish line.

It stunned him to realize he didn't need to. He could taste a world of possibilities on her lips. Heaven help him.

Heaven help them both.

"The thing is," he said later, leaning out the window a bit as he drove because the defroster hadn't quite finished erasing the steam from the windshield. "I think we have to admit that all this…this heat we're generating didn't just come out of nowhere. It's been there all along." He glanced at her. "Hasn't it?"

"Yes." She turned to him and smiled. "Yes, it has."

He took her hand and squeezed it, and then brought it to his lips. Warm, and smooth, and fragrant, just as he knew it would be. He couldn't get enough of her, of touching her. It was the most incredible thing—touching her—and what was even more incredible was that right now he didn't care if he couldn't explain why it was so incredible. "I think we'd both be fooling ourselves," he said, "not to acknowledge, up front, that an attraction exists, and deal with it. Rather than pretending it's not there."

"It's there, all right." She untangled her hand from his and brushed her fingers down his cheek. The gentle stroke punched right through to his heart.

"But acknowledging it is one thing," she said. "Dealing with it is another. And I think you were right. Waiting until the end of the term to deal with this is absolutely the best, the wisest thing to do."

He turned into a busy avenue and concentrated on changing lanes in the holiday traffic, on practicing abstinence with temptation so close. A taut silence stretched for one mile, and then another. "Is that what you want to do?" he asked at last. "Wait?"

Emily squinted at the view beyond the windshield. "I just think it's the intelligent thing to do. The responsible thing to do."

He continued down the avenue, stealing glances at her profile, trying to catch her looking at him. Willing her to look at him, to make eye contact. He couldn't believe she could mean what she had just said. Didn't she feel what he was feeling right now—feelings that weren't going to wait in cold storage for weeks?

They stopped at an oversize intersection, and Emily unbuckled her seat belt. "This is a really long signal," she murmured right before she pounced on him.

He pulled her close, exulting in the fact that the craving wasn't completely one-sided. He took a moment to reacquaint himself with her lips before treating himself to a sample of the spot behind her ear. It tasted even better than everything else.

Everything else—Lord, he wanted to taste that, too. Now. This afternoon. Or tonight. Maybe he could settle for sometime before the end of the Thanksgiving holiday. No way was he going to make it to the end of the semester. "Let's go to my hotel," he said as he nibbled on her earlobe. "Or we could head up the coast. Or—"

The blat of a horn sent them scrambling. Joe rolled ahead, the taste of her still on his lips, the scent of her wafting around him, driving him crazy with desire. He had trouble focusing on anything other than one image: Emily, in his bed. With those crazy blond curls spilled over his pillow, her long legs wrapped around his, her eyes navy blue with pleasure. He squeezed his own eyes shut tight, and redoubled his efforts to see nothing but the road and the bumper ahead when he reopened them. "Think about it, Em. I'll bet we could find a place where no one could find us, where no one would know us."

"I don't…I wouldn't know where."

He cursed silently at the uncertainty in her voice, and coasted around the next corner to stop along a quiet residential street. Emily sat very still, except for the fingers that twisted a ring on her hand. He sank back and closed his eyes. "God. I'm sorry, Em. One kiss and I start planning an affair."

"Joe—"

"No," he said. "You didn't deserve that. You don't deserve any of it." He rubbed a hand over his face, wishing he could rub away the shame and guilt that were seeping in to smother this fragile joy in thick layers of muck. "You're not—" Not like the other women in his life. The women he'd made a habit of meeting at the coast, or in Seattle for the weekend, or at a discreet but convenient distance from Issimish.

"I know."

"No, you don't." He reined in the temper that flowed from his self-disgust. "You don't know—" The kind of man who would suggest what he'd just suggested. "You're not the kind of woman who'd want to sneak around. Or hide what she's feeling from the people she knows."

"Just what is it that I'm supposed to be feeling here, Joe?" Emily smiled a sad little smile, one that didn't wrinkle her nose or light up her eyes. It hurt his heart—broke off a piece of it—to know he was responsible for the low wattage. "I don't think either one of us is ready to answer that question."

"Em—"

She held up a hand to stop him from saying whatever it was he'd been about to blurt out. "And besides," she continued, "what makes you think that whatever it is either one of us might be feeling is such a big secret? Or that we can keep hiding it?"

"God." He closed his eyes again and let his head fall against the back of his seat. "Has anyone said anything to you?"

"Linda."

Joe snorted. "Figures. She's been threatening me, too."

"Threatening?"

"Probably because she knew I'd be clumsy. Like I was a couple of minutes ago." He rolled his head on his seat to face her. "I *was* clumsy. I *am* clumsy. I don't want to hurt you, Em."

"I know that."

He sighed, feeling old and weary. "You don't know me as well as you think you do."

"Isn't that what dates are for?" She shifted so her face was closer to his. "So people can get to know each other better?"

"I don't want to date you, Em. I want to get you naked."

"Now *that* was clumsy." But her smile brightened.

He wrapped a hand around the back of her neck

and pulled her down for a long, deep kiss. "I'm much better at show than tell."

"Yes, you are." She pulled away. "Mom guessed, too."

"Kay?"

"Last night, during dinner. When we went into the kitchen to get the coffee, she said she thought it was…well, interesting, the way you look at me."

"Interesting."

"Those weren't her exact words." She shifted to face front and stare out the window again.

"Never mind. I can imagine." He groaned. "What about Jack Senior?"

"He caught on, too. After Mom pointed out a few things."

"God." He scrubbed at his face again. "I'll bet they were thrilled to see me back on their doorstep today."

Her chin came up a bit. "They're just going to have to have a little more faith in me."

"So they know you're attracted to me, too."

She shrugged. "They must. Or they wouldn't have brought up the subject."

"What a mess." He shook his head with a hollow laugh.

Emily tugged at her jacket and straightened in her seat. "Maybe this is just too much of a mess to deal with right now. Maybe we shouldn't make plans, for the end of the term or otherwise. Maybe we shouldn't deal with this at all." She took a deep breath and faced him. "Maybe I should ask for a new assignment, at another school."

At last, the one thing he'd been hoping for since the moment he'd met her. Now it was the last thing he wanted. "What?"

"You heard me. I could ask for a transfer."

"It's too late for that now."

He started the engine to buy himself time and shoved at the gearshift because he couldn't shove aside the hurt and the anger. "Why does this idea sound like something that didn't just pop into your head a moment ago?"

She looked away from him, out her window.

"Em? Had you been considering asking for a transfer? Before this?"

She nodded.

"Why?" He had a good idea of what she'd say, but he wanted to hear it.

"So I wouldn't have to watch every move I make, and everything I say. So I wouldn't have to be around you, all day long, wanting to touch you and knowing I can't. I wouldn't have to sit in your classroom every day, hanging on every word you say, watching every move you make, and wondering if anyone is going to notice that I'm attracted to you. That I—that I care about you."

His insides turned to mush as he pulled away from the curb. How could anyone be elated and nauseated at the same time? He wasn't going to be able to get lunch down his throat, but he could move mountains if she asked him to. He could even ask the next question. "Do you? Do you care about me?"

"Yes."

"Good." That was easy. It was the rest of his life that was going to be impossible. "Because I care about you, too. A lot."

The words were incredibly insipid. They didn't convey half of what he was feeling. But he felt pretty fantastic for having said them. Especially when he stole a glance at her face.

"Oh, Joe," she whispered.

Her smile got all sort of screwed up. Not just scrunched, but sort of twisted around the edges.

He panicked. "You're not going to cry, are you?"

"I don't think so."

"Good." He leaned over and kissed her, hard and fast, to ward off any tears. "Want to go get something to eat?" Nausea was easier to deal with than a weepy female.

She sniffed, just once, and nodded. "Okay," she said.

What a trouper.

"Tell you what," he said. "Let's spend the rest of the day like we said we would. Shop for gifts, go to the art gallery. Enjoy each other's company. Get to know each other a little better. What the heck, we could live dangerously and call it a date."

He turned a corner and aimed for the city center. "How about we ignore all of this other stuff for, say, another twenty-four hours? Let ourselves sleep on it, think it through?"

"I guess so, for now." When she glanced at him her eyebrows were gathered in one long frown line. "But we really do have to talk about this, Joe. The sooner the better."

He sighed. "I didn't think you'd go for an indefinite postponement."

She plucked at one of the snaps on her jacket. "What do you think might happen, Joe? With us?"

"With us?"

She laughed a halfhearted laugh. "Just for the sake of argument."

With us. He stretched and looped an arm over her shoulders. "Come here, Em."

She scooted over as far as she could and leaned her head against his shoulder. It felt so good, so right. How could anything that felt like this be so wrong? But it *was* wrong. Wrong, and foolish, and potentially dangerous for them both. Until the end of the term.

The end of the term. It sounded so final. Like the end of the road. And he knew that was coming, too, up around some corner. It had to. They were too different, wanted too many different things from life. He couldn't let her go on thinking in terms like *us,* even though the idea of being part of Emily's *us* filled him with that nice warm and fuzzy feeling.

It would be so much easier, so much smarter to end it here. Now. At the end of their one day together.

Before they were tempted to risk an affair. He closed his eyes and kissed the top of her head in silent farewell to all that might have been.

"So," he said. "Where are we heading now?"

She rubbed her cheek against his shoulder with a sigh. "I have no idea."

TWENTY-FOUR HOURS LATER, Emily suffered through a nearly silent trip home in Joe's car. Back to Issimish, back to reality. Cold, brittle reality. She knew it was time for their talk, but she couldn't for the life of her think of an opening line.

Joe pulled into her driveway in a smooth curve that brought them close to her front porch and stopped beside her troublesome truck, which was waiting right where Bert at the Service Stop had promised it would be. He hesitated, and then his fingers slid down the steering wheel to shift into park. He didn't turn off the ignition.

"Let me get your bag," he said in a growl of a voice.

"That's okay, I can get it."

"Here, then." He twisted back, hauled it through the gap between their seats and set it between them.

Emily cleared her throat. It was so tight she knew her words would come out sounding as strangled as she felt. "Would you like to come in for—"

"Not a good idea."

"—a drink," she finished limply. "Or, well, hmm. Never mind." She wrapped her fingers around the handle on her bag. "You'll be at your own place in a few minutes, anyway."

"Right."

"Well." She slipped her fingers through the door handle. "Thanks for the ride. For both of them."

"Mmm-hmm."

She wanted to say something, anything, to end this awkwardness before Monday morning. Now, before it sprouted fangs and slithered between them to coil and crush the life out of whatever it was that was trying to sprout between them. But nothing came to mind.

When she shifted to begin her escape, Joe's hand fell over hers on the suitcase. "Em."

"Yes?" She hated the desperation in her voice.

He took a deep breath and let it slowly escape. His fingers slipped between hers, hard and callused and warm, a simple contact with undertones of passion and fulfillment and overtones of doubt and disaster. And then the harmony of their twined fingers changed in key, the merest change in pressure from a reassuring squeeze to a tug full of longing, and she was leaning, falling, straining toward him over the suitcase barrier, her lips within inches of his, where she stopped, and he stopped, and breathing stopped.

"Em."

"Yes?"

"This is not a good idea."

"I know."

He closed the gap between them and pressed a

sweet, lingering kiss to her forehead. "So do us both a favor and get out of my car before I change my mind."

She pulled away and waited for her pulse to stop hammering. "Will this get any easier, do you think? At school, I mean?"

"Probably. Familiar surroundings and all. Clearer boundaries. Dozens of teenage chaperones."

She imagined him lecturing in that deep rumble of a voice, one lean hip cocked against his desk and his shirtsleeves rolled back to expose sinewy forearms, sunlight streaming through the windows to tease sable highlights from his black hair, and irony twisting one side of his mouth in the suggestion of a grin. Heat and longing surged through her. "Right."

"Yeah. Right."

She could tell he didn't believe it any more than she did. "Well." She gave his fingers one last squeeze before pulling her hand from his, grabbing her suitcase and swinging out of the car. "See you Monday morning," she said, leaning down to look in the window. "Bright and early."

He slouched back against his seat and grunted. "Early, anyway."

The grumbling was familiar, the closed car door a definite boundary. She stood on the gravel and watched him drive away.

They couldn't both continue to live in this state of hot and cold, up and down, on and off. It wasn't smart, it wasn't fair, and it wasn't sane. She trudged up the steps to her front porch and pushed her key into the lock. The way she saw it, she had three choices: put in for a transfer, tough it out on Planet Platonic, or jump into a risky affair.

It was time to take another look at the short-term and long-term aspects, from every angle. She had forty-eight hours to make up her mind—give or take a few weeks.

CHAPTER FOURTEEN

MONDAY MORNING Emily dressed for effect. After buffing her pale cheeks with a swipe of blush and rubbing some concealer over the dark circles under her eyes, she chose her flirtiest black skirt, strappiest black heels and the soft, baby-blue sweater with the V-shaped neckline that hinted at cleavage farther south. Just to make Joe think twice about what he'd be missing until the end of the term—if he had decided to wait that long.

Then she changed her mind. Again.

She coiled her hair in a tight little bun at the base of her neck and stepped into her long gray skirt—the one that fell to her ankles without a leg-revealing slit. She pulled an oversize gray sweater over her head and rolled back the cuffs, shoving at the sleeves to keep them out of her way. Then she slipped on a thigh-length black vest and her high-top black boots.

"Great," she muttered after checking out the top half of her ensemble in her bathroom mirror and then climbing up on the toilet seat to view the bottom half. "The *Dr. Zhivago* look."

Minus the sexy fur hat, of course. It must have been the fur hat that did it for Julie Christie. That and the pouty lower lip. It couldn't have been all those long, loose layers that kept Omar Shariff lusting after her.

Not that Joe was lusting after her in the same way Omar had lusted after Julie. Even with the one "get you naked" remark he'd made. That was probably nothing more than Joe's verbal routine with women he'd been nibbling on. Just a slip of the tongue.

Do not go there, she ordered herself. *Get your mind off slips of the tongue, and all other tongue slippage and slidage, inage and outage.* Think U.S. Supreme Court. Think NATO. Think essay questions, and essay answers, and the paper on Vygotsky due in Ed Psych on Wednesday night, and whether the truck is fully recovered and can get to school without any problems. Think of how this retro Siberian prison garb is going to turn sweaty and itchy by the middle of first period. Sackcloth and ashes for holiday sins.

She tried to turn off her thoughts as she tickled and teased her temperamental truck to her space in the faculty parking lot. She focused on rescuing Joe's notes from the condemned mail in his box and exchanging postholiday chat with the staff. On falling back into the safe and familiar routine of greeting students and taking roll. On staying within the boundaries of her observation post.

On keeping her cool when Joe walked into his classroom, a rough and rumpled romantic dream of a man.

And if his greeting seemed gruffer than usual, well, that was probably because he looked like he might be coming down with a cold or the flu or something. A little gray, a bit strained, a touch distracted. More lined around the mouth, more smudged beneath the eyes.

The end of American History arrived on schedule, and after that, the end of Current Events. The bell rang, the last student emergency was dealt with, and the classroom emptied for break. And then it was just the two of them, breathing the same radiator-scorched air and grasping for the same conversational straws.

Joe cleared his throat. "Your truck working okay?"

"Okay so far. There were a couple of bad moments, but we made it."

He hung back behind his desk. "You going to be able to get to the university all right tonight?"

"Oh, yes." She flipped a hand at him. "You don't have to worry."

He grunted and turned to swipe at his chalkboard.

Emily waited to see if there was going to be any more scintillating small talk, and then gave up and concentrated on the reassuring routine of packing her notes into her organizer, her organizer and pens into her bag, and her bag into her backpack. Feeling much more put together, and after surviving a brief skirmish between the toe of her boot and the hem of her skirt, she managed to extract herself from her observation post. Then all she had to do was tug her vest into place, sling her pack over her shoulder and pass within kissing range of Joe for the first time since those tense moments in her driveway two days ago.

One of her pack straps tangled in her baggy knit sleeve. *Don't panic,* she willed herself. *You can do this. You can get everything untangled, hold everything together for just a few more moments. Then you can make your escape and find someplace quiet and discreet to explode before you have to start twisting yourself into tomorrow's stick of dynamite.*

"Wait," Joe said. He ambled down the aisle and grasped her thickly rolled cuff. "You might flash a little wrist if you're not careful."

He held her sleeve in place while she tugged the strap over her shoulder. "I might be tempted to rip off your clothes," he said, "and attack the clothes underneath."

Emily huffed a stray curl out of one eye. "Guess I overdid the layered look."

"It's the thought that counts."

She shrugged and wriggled and adjusted until things were tolerable for the short hike to the faculty room. "You weren't supposed to notice."

Joe slipped his hands into his pockets. "I always noticed," he said in a soft and ragged voice. "Every little thing. Every damn day."

Some women got flowers and candy. She got scowls and growls. But she wouldn't have traded the emotions that moved through her at that moment for all the romance in the world. "I'm not sure you should have. That you should now."

"I have to. That's the assignment. You observe me. I observe you observing me." He started to lift his hands out of his pockets, and then shoved them deeper. "That's the trouble."

"We'll get through this, though." She smiled what she hoped was a confident smile. "One day down. Almost. I need to check with you about the handout for Thursday."

"Yeah. Right." He hesitated a moment, and then walked back to his desk. "Here are some notes. You want to flesh it out and add some study questions?"

"Sure. I'll have a copy ready for you to check by tomorrow."

He followed her to the door. "You're sure your truck is going to make it?"

"Yes. Absolutely. And if not, I can handle it."

"If it acts up, call." He pulled a slip of paper from his pocket, stared at it for a moment and then handed it to her. She glanced down at his home and cell phone numbers.

"I can come and get you," he said. "Any time."

"You don't have to take care of me, Joe."

A tiny muscle throbbed along his jaw, and then it smoothed out again. She wondered if he was angry. She didn't think so, but it was hard to tell. He was doing a terrifyingly terrific job of holding everything inside. "I know," he said.

She glanced back down at the numbers scribbled across one of Linda's memo slips and focused on this small, tenuous connection. "Thanks. I appreciate it." Then she moved past him and headed toward the door.

"Emily."

"Yes?"

"Call. If you need to. It's no trouble."

"Okay."

"Or if you just want to talk." He looked down and shuffled his feet into a slightly different arrangement on the floor. "About anything."

"All right." She wondered if she should give him her cell phone number, too. He could probably get it from Linda.

And then, when she pictured Joe asking Linda for her private cell number, and Linda's reaction, she pulled her backpack off her shoulder and pawed through it for her notebook and pen.

He took her number and shoved it into one of his pockets. "Thanks."

Neither of them moved. An awkward pause stretched between them. Emily was afraid she'd snap in the silence. "We should have traded contact info weeks ago."

He shrugged. "I guess so."

Another silence. "Well," she began, but then couldn't think of a way to finish.

The second bell rang, jarring them both.

"Better go," she said.

"Mmm," he grunted.

And that was that. She was free to leave, to walk out the classroom door and chalk up another day of classroom observation and interaction. Another day of seeing, and talking to, and being with Joe. Her first day of not touching him. Her first day of purgatory.

She turned to go, but paused for one last glance over her shoulder. He stood his ground, his expression guarded. But then his eyes fell to her lips, and his face softened with such sweet longing that her breath caught in her chest. She watched, unable to move, as he let her in, just for a moment, to see his frustration and his desire, before he shut things down with a frown.

And when his frown twisted into a grimace of wry bemusement, she realized she'd seen that very same expression on his face every day they'd been together. He'd been struggling with this, dealing with the irony of this situation, fighting his attraction to her from the very beginning.

She didn't think she'd ever wanted to put her arms around him, to pull him close to her body and to her heart any more than she did at that moment. Instead, she swallowed and focused on one of the wooden buttons on his shirtfront. "Will this get any easier, do you think?"

"No."

She shut her eyes. "I didn't think so, either."

EMILY WRESTLED a mangled paper out of Arnold's mechanical grip and wished for the hundredth time she had the nerve to march right back up to Joe's room, shut his classroom door behind her and kiss the stuffing out of him.

The jam light continued its monotonous blink. Just not her day, she decided. In spite of her assurances to Joe earlier, her pickup had coughed all the way to school, and she was worried she might not get home, let alone to campus. His taxi service offer was incredibly sweet and generous, but there were times, like today, she headed to the university before lunch, and he couldn't leave school to rescue her in the middle of the day.

She pried open the copier's front panel and flipped all the handles, poking gingerly though black plastic while trying to ignore the bright yellow stickers warning her of possible electrocution or dismemberment. There was the culprit—a tiny scrap of paper wrapped around a gear.

She reached in, wriggling her shoulders to slide her prickly sweater fabric back and forth over an itchy spot. This sweater-vest combo made poison oak rash seem like a good trade. She couldn't imagine being trapped in her fashion disaster for the rest of the day, but the extra time necessary for the detour home to change clothes would cut into her lunch date with her study group.

Arnold wasn't cooperating with her schedule. So many irritations, so little time.

"Just the person I wanted to see." Kyle's voice slid over her from behind.

Emily shut her eyes and swallowed a sigh. Never count your irritations before they hatched.

"Hello, Kyle." She closed the panel, hit the Start button, and watched the copier grind out two pages before jamming again. "What is it you need to see me about?"

"I thought it might be a good time to touch those bases."

Was it just her, or did Kyle creep out everyone else when he said the things he said in that oily voice? Emily used her struggle with the copier as an excuse to keep her back to him, lifting the top half of the machine and leaning down to search the works around the drum. When she pulled out another shredded paper, her elbow collided with Kyle's belt buckle.

She spun around to face him and waited for him to back off. Hoped he'd back off. He didn't move, and she raised the papers between them like a shield. He had her trapped against the machine.

His lips spread in a smear of a smile. "Is that copier acting up again?"

"It doesn't like making double-sided copies."

"Let's give it some time to cool down." He pulled the stack of papers out of her hand and set them on the counter behind her. His tie fell forward and slid across her breasts. She sincerely hoped he wouldn't choose that moment to smooth it back into place.

He paused, his face much, much too close to hers. "I hope this isn't an awkward time for you."

Everything in her was screaming to get away, tensed to run at the first opening. She forced herself to relax enough to respond in a calm, level tone. "Actually, I'm in a bit of a hurry. I have to get to the university."

"Ah, yes. You have such a busy schedule." He stepped back, far enough for her to collect her things without bumping into him again. "It might be easier if we arranged a meeting that would work around both your school schedules. Maybe later in the day, closer to the university. Something more convenient for you. We could meet over coffee, perhaps. My treat."

"That's a very generous offer, Kyle. But I couldn't possibly accept."

"Anything's possible, Emily. Think about it."

He stepped back, giving her a little more room to breathe, but not quite enough room to escape without brushing up against him. "We really should find some quiet, relaxed time to get to know each other better. I'm prepared to go the extra mile if that's what it takes."

"I don't think that will be necessary." Forget the copies, forget the booby-trapped escape hatch—she was getting out of here. She slid past him, flinching when her skirt rubbed against his trouser leg. She reached for her backpack and tipped it off the counter.

The paper scrap with Joe's phone numbers shook loose and fell to the floor.

Kyle picked it up and glanced down at Joe's scrawl before handing it to her. His smile compressed in a tight line.

"Thank you." Emily took the paper and crammed it back inside her pack. "Let me check my schedule. I'm sure we can find some time to meet, here, in your office."

"You've got me at a bit of a disadvantage. I'll need to check my calendar, too." He closed his hand over hers and stilled her jerky efforts to close her pack. "Relax, Emily. We can discuss this later, after you've had a little more time to consider." He slid his hand slowly over hers, smoothed down his tie, and left.

She made it as far as the faculty lounge, where she collapsed in a low vinyl chair, breathing deeply and waiting for the shakes to subside.

"Emily? Got a minute?"

Emily looked up into the woebegone face of Coach Dornley. "Let me guess," she said. "You haven't been able to find anyone else to coach the JV girls' basketball team, right?"

CHAPTER FIFTEEN

"TELL ME you didn't say 'yes.'"

Emily took a big sip of her vodka-and-cranberry cocktail to avoid answering Marilee's question. She was hitting the hard stuff tonight. There wasn't enough Chardonnay in the university pub to wash the scum from her crummy day.

"You said 'yes,' didn't you? You're actually committed to coaching an athletic team. On top of everything else." Marilee shoved her gin and tonic aside and glared at Emily. "Wiz is going to kill you."

"No, he won't." She desperately hoped he wouldn't. He wouldn't be too happy about this latest development, but he wouldn't do anything violent. She couldn't picture him doing anything that would involve expending so much energy. "I'll distract him with Kyle's latest move."

"Your principal?"

"Yeah." Emily took another dose of her drink. "He basically hit on me this morning."

"*No.*" Marilee shifted closer. "Really?"

"Yep." Emily tugged at the neck of her nubby

sweater. "But he's going to have to stand in line, because first I'm going to have an affair with Joe."

"What?"

"An affair."

"I heard you." Marilee emptied her glass and signaled for refills. "Since when are you having an affair with your master teacher?"

"Since he asked me."

"And I thought I had an interesting day. Okay, wait a minute." Marilee held up a hand. "Hold everything. Let's back up a bit."

She scooted her stool closer to Emily's and glanced over her shoulder to see who was within eavesdropping range. "Wiz asked you to have an affair?"

"While we were necking in his car. The day after Thanksgiving."

"Oh. My. God." She studied Emily's face. Slowly, Marilee's frown tipped up into a smile. "That good, huh?"

"Oh. My. God," said Emily.

"Details, Em. Details."

Emily laughed. "I know this is a complete and total disaster. I know we should both be committed, or fired, or something, but I'm telling you, I'm flying so high every time I think about how it felt—how he felt—I don't care how hard I crash."

"It's going to be awfully hard, Em. Probably fatal."

"I know." She shook her head at the bartender's offer of a second round. "Or maybe I don't, not really.

I've never been in this kind of trouble before. All my life, I've tried so hard to be the good girl, to do everything I was supposed to do. Sure, I've made mistakes, but nothing really big, you know?"

"You don't need to make up for it all at once," said Marilee. "This is so typical. Even when it comes to making a mess, you're such an overachiever."

"I didn't set out to do it. It just happened."

"Love usually does."

"No." Emily waved her hand, wiping away the possibility. It made absolutely no sense. She couldn't begin to wrap her mind around it. Which meant it wasn't going to happen. Hadn't happened. Couldn't happen.

"It's not love," she said. Just saying the words out loud made her feel more certain she was right. "I'd know if it was."

"And this is because you've been in love…how many times?"

Emily shrugged. "Never."

Marilee lifted one eyebrow with a wise and superior smirk. "Ah, an expert."

"You don't have to be an expert. You just have to know it. And I know I'm not in love with Joe."

"Let me get this straight. You're *not* going to risk everything—this internship, your professional reputation, your career—for someone who's worth it. Someone you care for. Instead, you're going to risk all those things for someone you have a temporary case of lust for. Someone you just want to sleep with for a little while."

Emily stared down into her drink. "You make me sound awful."

"No, not awful. Just confused. That's what happens when you keep trying to ignore the facts."

Marilee leaned in closer and put her hand over Emily's wrist. "I was there at that Halloween party," she said. "I know what I saw. Two people who can make the world go away when they look at each other."

"It's called chemistry. Attraction." Emily drifted for a moment, remembering the way Joe had looked at the party. The way he had looked at her. "A pretty intense attraction, but that's all it is—an attraction."

"An attraction."

"Right."

"Whatever you say." Marilee shrugged and picked up her drink, watching Emily over the rim of the glass. "Okay, back to the part about the principal hitting on you. But don't think I'm going to totally ignore the affair topic. We're not finished with that one."

"Didn't think we were." Emily wiped at the counter with one of the tiny square napkins.

"So, how did this hitting happen? Details, details."

She listened to Emily's tale, and then set her glass on the bar with a clink. "Creep."

Emily narrowed her eyes. "With a capital *K*."

"Are you going to tell Wiz?"

"Do you think I should?"

Marilee hesitated. "Yes."

"You don't sound too sure."

"Yeah, I'm sure. In fact, I think you should distract him with the principal story before he kills you over the basketball deal."

Emily stared down into her drink and wondered how things had reached this point. Sure, she'd hinted and teased and nudged Joe into taking more interest in his classes and finding more enjoyment in his Garden Project, but she didn't know if she could push him into an involvement with a team sport. Maybe she didn't know him as well as she thought, and she was afraid to push him too far, too fast. Or maybe she knew him too well, and she was making excuses for him because he wasn't here to make them for himself. Maybe those kisses—and the aftermath—had confused her more than she realized.

Marilee crossed her arms on the bar and leaned in close again. "Now, before we move on to that bit about the affair, tell me about this necking in the car."

THE NEXT MORNING, Joe negotiated his way through an icy crust on the ground and political lunacy on the car radio. There was a time, not so long ago, he would have let things like sooty slush and slate gray skies dull his outlook on the rest of the day. But not today. Today he'd decided to be cautiously optimistic. Nearly positive.

He turned off his engine and wondered if he was

coming down with something more serious than a change in his attitude toward an early retirement. If he quit teaching, he'd miss out on mornings like this, mornings that gave his life a purpose. He'd already tried to come up with some reason to ditch this new outlook on life during his morning run, but he'd ended up with zip.

Zip—except for his craving for contact with Emily.

He headed into the school office with some promising lesson plans tucked under his arm, looking for validations for his upbeat attitude. Like the mail piled neatly in his box, filled with possibilities. Or the morning bulletin item about an achievement award for a deserving student. And Linda—hardworking Linda—motioning him over to the counter. She probably had some good news for him. He smiled. "Good morning."

She shot him one of her looks, the one that mixed disgust for the world in general with loathing for the latest mishap in particular. "That's what you think."

"As a matter of fact, I do." He set his folders on the counter and flipped through a cable television guide for teachers. Fascinating stuff. "It's a beautiful day."

"Not in this neighborhood, Mr. Rogers." Linda checked over her shoulder before leaning in close. "You've got trouble."

"What happened?"

"Nothing," she said. "Yet."

"What's going to happen?"

"You're going to pound Kyle into a little pile of dust."

"You know I don't believe in violence."

"Prepare to be converted." Linda tossed another glance toward Kyle's office door. "He's been bothering Emily. Big-time."

Anger and adrenaline pumped through Joe so fast he thought he might erupt through the roof and come down somewhere in the next state. "Tell me. Everything."

"I was heading into the workroom yesterday. Emily was in there making copies, and Kyle was in there putting the make on her. I heard him ask her to meet him for coffee. And he was issuing the invitation from uncomfortably close quarters. The poor thing looked a little green around the gills when she came out. I thought I was going to lose my breakfast, and I didn't have to deal with the up-close and personal version."

"I'll take care of it."

"Dust, Joe. Powder-fine particles."

"Where is he?"

"Off campus. Scrounging up some sponsors for winter sports and his new hot tub."

Joe shoved his fists into his pockets. "I'd better talk to Emily first."

"That's not all you need to talk to her about." Linda looked a little green around the gills herself.

He ground his teeth. "What else?"

"Dornley hit on her right after Kyle."

"Basketball?"

"Bingo."

At least his outlook was still positive. He was positive heads were going to roll, right after he grabbed them and bashed them together. "Thanks, Linda."

He started out the door. Linda called after him, "Take it easy on that girl, Joe."

"I will."

"Joe?" She sounded a little desperate. "I mean it."

"So do I. Kid gloves, I swear." Smacked right across that pert little butt.

He skipped his usual detour to the faculty lounge and climbed the stairs to the classroom, lava roiling through his veins. He needed to calm down before he said something he might regret. Or do something that might require paramedics and lawyers to undo.

Emily was alone in the classroom, dug in deep in her observation post. It didn't take more than a second to register the misery in her eyes and the blue-gray smudges underneath. And one second more for sympathy to cool him down. A notch.

"Hi," she said, with a brilliantly fake smile.

He set his mail down on his desk and pinched the bridge of his nose. Pinching was supposed to stop the headache brewing behind his eyes, but he didn't think it was going to work. "Anything you want to tell me?"

She nodded and stared down at her fingers, which were wrapped in a death grip around her pen. "Just to confirm what you've probably already heard."

"About basketball."

"Yes." She set the pen down, carefully and precisely aligning it with the crease in the center of her observation notebook. "I can handle it, Wiz. I've got a schedule all worked out. Most of the regular season practices will fall after finals at the university, and the first tournament is set for right before Christmas vacation."

"Sounds like you've got everything under control." She didn't have a clue.

He moved down the aisle to stand over her desk. "Anything else you want to tell me?"

Her gaze searched his face for a few seconds. He watched her struggle, watched indecision flicker across her features before she pressed her lips together in a stubborn line. "No."

No. She wasn't going to tell him about Kyle. He didn't know why her decision knocked him to the cold, hard ground. This was exactly what he'd wanted from the first—not to get involved. Now that he was getting what he wanted, he didn't want it any more.

"Okay," he said, even though it felt like nothing was. "Okay?"

He sucked in a deep breath and let it out. Breathe in, breathe out. Walk, talk, block. All he had to do was hang in for a few more hours, drive home, climb the steps to his apartment and grab the half-empty bottle of Jamieson to rinse away the sorry dregs of optimism.

That, and pound Kyle into powder-fine particles of dust. "Yeah, okay."

EMILY DASHED OUT at break, and Joe headed down to the main office. Linda tilted her head toward Kyle's door. "He's in there."

"Okay." Joe slipped his hands into his pockets and weighed the satisfaction of what he was considering against a prison term for assault and battery.

He stalked down the short hall. "Dust," Linda called from behind him.

"Joe, come in." Kyle jumped out of his seat and motioned Joe toward one of the two chairs facing the big desk. "How's it going?"

"That depends." Joe reached behind him and shut the door, just shy of a slam.

Kyle's smile faded. "I take it this something serious?"

"Sexual harassment usually is."

Kyle flinched. Joe figured he was shuffling through several scenarios for Trouble, and How to Avoid It.

"You're right, Joe. This is serious. Please, have a seat."

"I'll stand. This won't take long."

He stepped closer to Kyle. Too close, invading his space, squaring off in slow motion. He noted, with nasty satisfaction, the spasmodic jerk of Kyle's hand over his tie. "Stay away from Emily," Joe said in a soft voice.

"What are you suggesting?"

"I'm not suggesting anything except that you should stay away from Emily Sullivan."

"Did she say anything?"

"She didn't have to. And she doesn't know I'm here. I'm the one making the suggestion."

"Are you threatening me?"

Joe smiled. He straightened to his full height and leaned in, just a bit, so Kyle had to lean back. "Do you feel threatened, Kyle?"

Kyle stepped back and puffed up. "No."

"Then I guess I didn't threaten you." He turned and opened the door. "I'm glad we understand each other. Good communication is important in a working relationship."

ON FRIDAY AFTERNOON, Matt set his calculus text on the highest bleacher bench and leaned back against the gym wall. He couldn't concentrate on the homework assignment beside him, not with the chaos on the basketball court below.

There was a possibility that this year's junior varsity girls' squad had even less talent than last year's, and that was going to make the entire season a come-from-behind proposition. Rumor had it that two of the freshmen players weren't on speaking terms with two of the sophomores, and that made it tough to get the girls to pull together as a team and work out the kinks. But in addition to the dismal possibilities and the troublesome rumors, it was an obvious fact—at least from where he was sitting—that the coach didn't have a clue what she was doing.

Oh, she knew how to play. That was also obvious. That was one of the reasons Matt was here, after all. Enjoying the scenery. Watching Ms. Sullivan, all decked out in her slightly sloppy sweats, her hair escaping its clip to riot around her face. Dodging defenders on her way down court, lifting off the ground and laying in shot after shot, smooth and light and effortless as thistledown.

That was the problem. No defense. Even after Ms. Sullivan's detailed explanation of a clever, complicated setup. And that was another problem. It was too clever, too complicated, too detailed. She spent way too much time explaining when the team should be practicing.

Too many problems added up to disaster. Matt didn't need calculus to tell him that.

Just like he didn't need fancy equations to figure out he had a serious case on Lindsay Wellek. He only had to figure out what to do about it.

He watched her jog down the court, her cheeks pretty pink patches against that milky white skin. Her tank top revealed slender arms, and a clip held her hair in a kind of a twist on top of her head. She should wear her hair that way to school sometime. He'd like to sit in class and stare at the back of her neck.

He'd read somewhere that the Japanese thought

women's napes were sexy. He could see why. He thought the back of Lindsay's neck looked pretty good. And her legs—they were definitely sexy. He'd never realized how long they were, or how her knees stuck out in those cute knobs when she stood still, or how her thighs kind of bowed out in interesting curves.

He lifted his hand in an almost wave when Lindsay glanced up at him. She'd done that a couple of times during practice. It made him hot inside, and sort of tight through the chest. He liked the feeling. He planned on staying a little longer, to see if she'd look up at him again and wave back. He'd offer her a lift home, and find a private spot somewhere to park, and pull her close for one of those long, deep, lingering kisses they'd been sharing lately.

Ms. Sullivan's whistle blew, jolting him out of his daydream. He was spending way too much time lately dwelling on Lindsay's kisses, reliving them, letting the sensations roll through him again, plotting for more, thinking of how much better the next batch would be. Wondering how to move things along to the next step....

What he should be doing was figuring out a way to help the team. Lindsay was upset about the way things were going, and he wanted to fix it. He'd do just about anything to make her happy.

The bleacher bench rattled beneath him. Matt looked down the row and watched Wiz climb the last few steps up the aisle and pause at the top.

Amazing. Here he'd been thinking about how to solve the team's problems, and the solution had simply walked in the door. Of course, it would take some skillful maneuvering and manipulating to get Wiz to do it. But Matt was pretty sure he knew which buttons to push.

Wiz frowned at another bungled attempt at a relay screen on the court below. "How's it going?" he asked.

"In general?" Matt asked. "Or down there?"

"In general."

Matt shrugged. "Better than down there."

"That's not saying much."

Ms. Sullivan had called the girls into another huddle. They spent a lot of time huddling.

"Nothing much new," Matt said.

Wiz grunted. He picked his way along the narrow plank and then settled down next to Matt, his ankles crossed over the bench below.

"So, what are you going to do about it?" Matt asked.

"About the lack of news in your life?"

"About the mess down there."

"It's not my mess," said Wiz.

"That's convenient."

"No," said Wiz. "That's the truth."

"It's kind of your responsibility."

"No. It's not."

"You can tell yourself that all you want," Matt said, "but you're stuck with it, whether you want it or not."

Wiz rubbed at his pants leg. "I'm not the one who said I'd coach."

"Maybe not. But you'll still have to deal with the fallout."

"There's nothing nuclear about a junior varsity girls' basketball team at a minuscule high school in an out-of-the-way town." Wiz frowned at another botched play down below.

"Tell that to their parents when they start losing every game on the schedule," said Matt.

"I'm not the one who's going to have to deal with it."

"Nope." Matt leaned in a little and grinned. "You'll just have to deal with the fallout."

Wiz turned his head and leveled a neutral stare at him. "Ms. Sullivan can handle it. She's the responsible adult in this scenario."

"The responsible adult who sits in your classroom every day, working with you. Working *very* closely with you. Helping you with all your lessons and paperwork."

"I take it there's a point you're trying to make."

"I don't think I need to make it," said Matt. "I think the fact that you're here means it's already been made." Heck, Wiz had probably been on a rescue mission when he walked in the door.

"Smart-ass."

"I hope you phrased that differently in your recommendation to Berkeley."

Two girls went for the same pass and collided. The ball shot up into the bleachers on the opposite side of the gym.

"So," said Matt. "When are you going to talk to her?"

"Tonight. After practice."

"How do you think she'll take it?"

"Oh, pretty well, I imagine." Wiz rubbed at his face, and Matt knew he was expecting trouble. "Especially since she tried to talk me into this coaching spot weeks ago."

"Maybe she was hoping you'd bail her out all along."

Wiz grunted. He watched for a while longer, and then rolled up out of his slouch and leaned forward with his chin in his hands. "So, I guess I'm here to rescue the fair maidens. Why are you here?"

"It's that fair maidens thing."

"Enjoying the scenery?"

"Yeah."

"Any tree in particular?"

"Lindsay Wellek," said Matt.

"Hmm."

"Nice limbs."

Wiz raised one eyebrow. "You know I can't comment on the landscaping."

Matt shrugged. He could tell from Wiz's response that he approved. "It's cool."

Down on the court, Ms. Sullivan blew her whistle. Practice was over.

"The winter formal is coming up," said Wiz.

"I know."

Wiz stood and slipped his hands into his pockets. "Just making sure."

"No problem." Matt smiled. "Lookin' forward to it."

Wiz smiled back. A crooked, knowing grin, man to man.

Matt grabbed his math book and tossed it into his pack. "See you, Wiz."

"Yeah."

Matt started down the row, and then turned and jerked his chin toward where Ms. Sullivan stood, writing something on a clipboard. "Good luck."

Wiz grunted. "It's cool."

CHAPTER SIXTEEN

EMILY WAITED, bouncing the ball near the free throw line as Joe stepped onto the court. She'd been aware of him since the moment he'd come into the gym—his long-legged climb up the bleachers, his casual grace as he slid into his seat, his dark eyes roaming over the court. Roaming over her. She tried to ignore him, to avoid glancing up at the top of the stands, where he sprawled next to Matt. She waited for him to leave, hoping he'd clear out with the players and the parents who came to collect them. But he stayed until the bitter end, until it was just the two of them in the empty, echoing space.

He paused at one side of the key. "Stop looking at me like you're afraid I'll take a bite out of you."

She huffed the hair out of her eyes. "I'd like to see you try."

"I might like to see that, myself."

She smiled, but couldn't keep it up for long. "I'm not going to ask what you think."

"I didn't expect you would. You're much better at knowing what I think—or at least what you think I should think—than I am."

She brought the ball up to her chest and fired it at him. "You think you're so smart."

He caught it and spun it around in his hands. "But not smart enough."

He dropped the ball and snatched it back up a couple of times, and then started a slow, rolling dribble, pacing under the basket in his Birkenstocks. It seemed that the ball became a part of him, something as natural as the next breath he drew, even as he kept his laser-beam stare focused on her.

"Seems like I'm always a step or two behind these days," he said.

"Is that why you're here?" she asked. "To try to catch up?"

He paused, and then resumed his pacing. The sound of the ball hitting the boards echoed off the walls. *Blam, blam, blam.* "Maybe. Besides, you wanted me to come."

"I don't recall issuing an invitation." She winced the moment the words flew out. She hated sounding petty. She hated sounding defensive. Heck, she hated *feeling* defensive, but it seemed she was doomed to feel that way for the rest of the season.

He spun and took a shot at the basket as if it were a moment's impulse. *Swish.*

"Why do you want to make this so hard on both of us?" His tone was friendly, and conversational, and made her feel very small.

"Sorry," she said.

Joe snatched up the ball and bounced an easy pass at her. She caught it, took aim on a step, and made the shot. The practiced flow of the motion, the familiar crouch and arch, the power behind the release helped settle her down. The ball hit a little to the side of the hoop, but jounced through.

"I'm glad you're here," she said as he reached out to snag the rebound. "I'd like your input."

"I'm not going to evaluate this, Em."

"That's good. Because I'd probably fail."

He jogged to the side, twisted suddenly, and let the ball fly. *Swish.* "Why are you selling yourself short?"

"I'm not," she said. "I'm trying to be honest."

He scooped up the ball and twisted, passing it to her with a little more force. "Why don't you try for fair, instead?"

She caught the ball and balanced it against her hip. "Fair? You mean, cut myself some slack because I've never done this before?"

"Maybe. If you think that's fair." He shrugged and moved toward her, his hands flexed at his sides and his weight shifted over the toes of his sandals.

She took the ball in both hands and held it out of reach. "I don't need you to make excuses for me, Joe."

She was expecting some tricky moves from an ex-college player, but it still stunned her when he knocked the ball away. Shuffling Joe Wisniewski could move like lightning when he wanted to.

"No one needs to do anything for you." He

jogged to the three-point line and spun, sending the ball up in a perfect arc. *Swish.* "No one can do anything for you. You never let them. You're perfectly capable of doing it all yourself. Everything. Including beating yourself up before anyone else can throw the first punch."

"That's not true."

He dashed under the backboard and swept up the ball with one of his oversize hands. *Blam, blam.* "Is this the 'trying to be honest' part?"

"You don't know what you're talking about."

"The hell I don't. That's exactly what you do."

Emily gasped. She'd never heard Joe use this tone of voice, not with anyone. It was still soft, it was still gentle, but there was a flash of heat and a lot of steel beneath the mild-mannered delivery.

She didn't know what to say. She stood, shocked into silence, and watched him dance through a simple, graceful layup. It hurt, more than she'd ever thought he could hurt her, to hear him say those things. It hurt because any criticism always stung. It hurt because what he thought of her mattered so much.

It hurt because he was right.

But mostly, it hurt because he knew her so much better than she'd given him credit for. She'd sold him short, too. She'd been so arrogant, thinking she could help Joe solve his problems—here he was, trying to help her solve hers.

Joe scooped up the ball and stood, turning it

around in his hands. He glanced at her, and then focused on the ball as he spoke. "Anyone who's ever been on the receiving end of one of your decisions to make a change for the better knows you have no problem making up your mind and sticking to it."

He looked up again, and when his eyes met hers, she could see what it was costing him to say these things, and that he knew what it was doing to her to hear them. But he thought enough of her, cared enough about her, was brave enough and honest enough and decent enough, to say it all anyway.

Even through her shame and guilt, she felt as if her heart might leap out to him, right across the court. Her throat closed up so tight she couldn't speak.

"You know what your problem is?" he asked. "You're insecure. You're one of the most insecure people I've ever met. And that's an insult to the love and support you've been given all these years. Look at all the people who love you, Em, who think you're pretty damn special. They're probably as baffled as I am by your inability to settle down and choose just one thing in this life to work on, because you've got all the potential you need to do just about anything you choose, and to do it well. Instead, you fly around, trying to fix everyone else's lives, because you're too afraid to fix your own."

He wrapped his long fingers around the ball and squeezed. "Maybe some people's lives do need fixing, but it's up to them to choose. It's up to them to make their own mistakes." A grin teased the corner of his mouth. "And to learn how to fix them."

He still had the ability to inspire, and she, with all her observing and all her analyzing, had missed it. She'd been flying around, just like he said, trying to fix his life to suit her image of what it should be, and she'd failed to see what was right in front of her: the genius behind Joe's quiet, personal one-on-one interactions with his students. Anyone could prepare and deliver a splashy lesson in front of a classroom, but it took a master teacher, and a special person, to offer direction in life's lessons behind the scenes.

She nodded, forcing a tiny smile back at him.

"Yeah, well..." he said, and then he cleared his throat. "I guess what I'm trying to say is, I wish you'd stop flying around and just apply yourself. To one thing. Maybe, when you do, it could be a way to say 'thank you' to everyone who's been putting up with you."

She swallowed. Her head was buzzing, and her eyes were hot with the strain of staying dry and focused on his. "I guess I'll start with this," she said. "With you. Thank you, Joe."

He shrugged. "You're welcome."

He turned and made another shot at the hoop. It missed by several inches. They both stood and watched the ball ricochet off the bleachers and bounce back toward them.

"So." Emily rubbed her damp palms against her sweatpants. "I really would like your input. On basketball, I mean," she added. "I think I've had about all I can handle when it comes to your advice on life in general."

"Yeah. Advice is pretty easy to ladle out." He snagged the ball when it rolled within range. "It's a lot harder to suck it up."

"Well, I'm ready to start sucking." She felt her cheeks flash red-hot. "I mean—"

He waggled his eyebrows. "God, I love it when you talk dirty."

She laughed. "I didn't mean—"

"Oh, sweetheart, don't disappoint me now." He tossed the ball over his shoulder and came at her, his long legs and quick moves cutting off her escape routes until she'd run out of running room and the hands she'd thrown up to stop him were spread against his chest. She could feel the strong, solid wall of muscle through his shirt, and the steady thud of his heartbeat beneath her palms. His breath brushed the curls on her forehead, and the familiar scents of soap and Joe seeped into her.

He covered her hands with his own. "Why didn't you tell me about Kyle?" he asked.

She tried to pull away, but his long, dark fingers curled around hers and held her in place.

"I want to deal with it on my own," she said.

"I'm your master teacher. I want—I need to know what you're dealing with."

"Okay." She looked up at him, but it wasn't her

master teacher who was looking back. It was a man who wanted to protect the woman he cared for, a man who wouldn't let another man start poaching on his territory.

"He's made a few remarks," she said. "On the surface, there's nothing wrong, but it's the way he says them. He makes me…uncomfortable."

Joe's fingers tightened around hers, but she shook her head before he could speak. "I want to handle it, Joe."

A tiny muscle rippled along his jaw, but he nodded. "Okay."

"Thanks. And I'll tell you if he approaches me again."

"Okay."

He dropped her hands, but didn't move back. "It's all right to ask for help if you need it. With anything. I won't think any less of you."

"Thanks."

"If you don't let me help, you don't let me do my job."

"It's not your job to deal with Kyle," she said.

"Or with basketball?"

Emily sighed. "Or with basketball."

"Dornley asked me first."

"Were you ever going to say yes?"

He paused. "No."

She tossed up her hands. "So?"

"So, maybe I want to say yes now."

"Now that I'm blowing it, you mean."

"I'm not bailing you out. And I already said I wasn't here to pass judgment."

"Why are you here, Joe?"

He glanced around the court, and shifted from one foot to the other before he looked back at her. "If you won't let me help, Em, it's like you won't let me in. You're like this machine, this completely independent and capable entity, moving through my life, and interacting with me, but not letting me *in*."

He sucked in a deep breath. "And it just hit me that I was treating you exactly the same way, at first. Not letting you in."

She smiled. "No kidding. You were trying your darnedest to keep me as far away as you possibly could."

His breath gusted out in a humorless laugh. "You don't know the half of it. I'm sorry, Em."

"No problem." She crossed her arms. "So. You want in?"

He frowned, and she could read the confusion and regret in his eyes. "I think I do," he said. "The thing is, I care about you, about what you do and what happens to you, and I don't know what to do about it."

"Oh." She reached up and cupped her hand over his cheek. Under her palm his skin was warm and scratchy with late-afternoon whiskers. Elation and panic and desire welled up inside her, a hot brew that threatened to spill over in some embarrassing way, like tears. "That's a wonderful, awful thing to say."

He hesitated, and then lifted his hand to cover hers. "I need you to help me figure this out."

"Okay," she said. "I'll try."

"Good." He grinned. "We're both going to need all the help we can get."

"Right." She smiled back. It was impossible not to smile back when his boyish grin flashed over those rugged features. He quite simply took her breath away.

"So," he said. "This is the part where you're supposed to say, 'Wiz, will you please help me coach basketball?'"

She laughed. "Wiz, will you please help me coach basketball?"

"Why, thank you for asking, Ms. Sullivan. I'd be delighted. See how easy that was?"

He took a step closer. "And now, this is the part where you're supposed to say, 'Wiz, about that sucking—'"

"No sucking, Joe."

"Damn. I mean, damn right. No team of mine is going to suck."

She raised her chin. "Your team?"

"No, ma'am. My mistake. Your team."

"Just so we know where we stand," she said, slapping her hands on her hips. Standing toe-to-toe with him like this, arguing with him, teasing with him, made her feel like she could fix any problem that might come her way. "I'm in charge."

He smiled. "There was never any doubt about it."

STUDY GROUPS AND EXAM PREPS, lesson plans and paperwork, shopping and socializing, strategy sessions and practices—Emily's days and nights during the next week were crowded with everything but sleep. That was almost a blessing, because her nights were filled with dreams of Joe. As she tossed in her bed, alone and afire in the long, dark hours, her subconscious tortured her with fantasies she'd repressed during the day.

She felt as if she were surfing an avalanche, trying to keep her balance so she wouldn't get buried. Christmas vacation was hurtling toward her at light speed, bringing with it the end of the university term and a break in her responsibilities. And bringing her one step closer to a possible resolution of her relationship with Joe. *If* there was going to be a relationship past that of student and master teacher.

But first she had to survive the annual preseason basketball tournament.

She was a little apprehensive about her team's chances, but eager for this first test of Joe's coaching contribution: It's the basics, stupid. He tried to cast his advice in a historical perspective by comparing it with Clinton's campaign strategy, but the girls and Emily chose to ignore the analogy.

At least the team could take advantage of Caldwell's traditional underdog status. All losses were expected and accepted because Caldwell was such a small school. All victories were major upsets.

And now, on a clear and frigid Saturday night, near

the end of the fourth quarter of the tournament's championship game, with a capacity crowd crammed to the tops of the bleachers and the edges of the court, it looked like the Caldwell JV girls were about to enjoy one of those major upsets. Really major. Historic. If victories in an occasional game were treasured, winning a tournament was a miracle. In the final moments, Emily could hardly watch, let alone breathe.

With four seconds left on the clock, and the score tied, and the parents in the stands ready to riot, Lindsay spun around with the basketball hugged to her chest and signaled for the last time-out.

Emily waved them over, and Joe bent down to wrap their team in one of his oversize hugs. "You're killing me here. You know that, don't you?"

Jody giggled, and the tension in the circle eased a bit. Emily glanced at her assistant coach and caught a none-too-subtle wink. Behind them, the home crowd stomped in the stands and chanted something that sounded suspiciously like death before dishonor. She hoped it wouldn't come to that. "What do you think, Wiz?"

"I think we can do this." He paused to meet the eyes of each player in the circle. "If we stay calm. I'm not going to give you some fancy play here. You all know what to do. It's the same simple stuff we've been working on in practice, remember? Make a good pass to the person who's open. Get a good shot off. When you see the opportunity to screen for somebody who's open, take it. You've been doing it for the last three games, and all night tonight, and it's working, right?"

"Right," they agreed.

"No one knows what's going to happen," he said. "But whatever happens, I'm not going to remember the final play. Well, maybe," he admitted, to another round of giggles. "But I'm sure going to remember this moment, right now, with all of us together and your parents up there yelling their hearts out."

The ref blew his whistle.

Joe hugged them all a little harder. "Anybody can win. Anybody can lose. But not everybody can have what we've got right now, tonight. It's a pretty good feeling."

"It's the best, Wiz," Tina agreed. The thin, warm arms draped around Emily's shoulders squeezed tight, and she got one last glimpse of five smiling, sweaty faces before the team jogged back out to the court.

She lifted her fingers to her lips, and her eyes stung with tears. Joe had done it. He'd fired them up, and given them the confidence they needed wrapped in a lesson about life. She blinked her vision clear so she could watch him prowling the edge of the court, a long, lean man with dark, rugged looks, vibrating with energy in his every move. A leader, a warrior, a poet. This was The Wiz of legend, and he was a beautiful sight.

And then the ref handed Suze the ball, and she

lobbed it in to Jody, who sprinted down the court before firing off a pass to Tina when Heather set a screen, and Tina shot it down to Lindsay under the hoop, and it was up, and in, and the buzzer sounded, and the crowd went wild.

The tidal wave of bodies that poured from the bleachers and surged onto the court caught Emily in its mass and propelled her to its center. Hugging, screaming, crying players and parents milled around her, grabbing her for brutal, bouncing hugs or slapping her on the back. She fought for air, fought for footing, fought against the choking, happy sobs that threatened to explode from her with every embrace.

Only one thing, only one person mattered, and she fought to find him in the crush. She had to be with him, had to touch him, had to wrap her arms around him and feel him wrap his arms around her. Nothing—not the elation, not the joy—none of it would be complete without Joe, because he was the other half of all she was feeling.

There, for an instant, his shaggy black hair bobbed above the sea of heads like a beacon, and she shoved a weaving course through the forest of bodies. She lost sight of him when Mr. Howard tugged her close to shout in her ear, and again when Tina's mom grabbed her arm for a lopsided embrace.

And then someone plucked her off the floor and tossed her up and around like a rag doll, and she fell against a solid chest and into a pair of long arms that closed around her the way she liked best—and she was home. She wrapped her arms around Joe's neck and her legs around his waist, and in that moment, as his big hands cradled her back and his breath puffed warm against her throat, she knew that she'd been wrong about everything. He wasn't the missing half of her emotional equation. He was its sum, its center, its completion.

She was in love with him.

She threw her head back and laughed. "We did it!" she shouted.

"They did it!" he shouted back. And then he wound the fingers of one of those big hands through the curls at the back of her head and crushed her mouth to his. Just for a second, just for a heartbeat, to the delight of the team and the amusement of their parents and the entertainment of the bystanders.

It probably looked harmless, just another wild and crazy part of the celebration, the assistant coach laying a quick one on his lady boss in the midst of all that excitement. But it wasn't harmless. There was too much frustration, too much intensity, too much heat in that brief kiss. Too much promise.

She pulled back to look at his face. Way too much promise.

"God," he said. He twisted his fingers, gathering a tighter hold on her hair, and staggered her with the dazed happiness and desperate hunger she read in his features. She drank it in, and stored it up, and wished with all her heart he didn't have to let her go. But he did.

She had to let him go, too.

Someone bumped into her from behind, and she dropped her legs. Another jostle, and she slipped to the floor. "Joe," she said. It was the only thing she could think of, but it was everything.

"Yes," he answered. *"Yes."* He released her then, to pull Suze into a bear hug, and he stared at her over the top of Suze's head. She saw in his eyes that he understood the topic under silent consideration: a follow-up on their Thanksgiving kisses. A follow-through on the weeks of slow-motion foreplay. "Tonight," he said.

Heat flowed through her, and a yearning so powerful it tipped her dangerously toward acceptance. She stepped back, away from him, and drifted on the tide of families and fans toward the locker room exit.

CHAPTER SEVENTEEN

JOE ACCEPTED Al Wiltse's invitation to a celebration dinner at his pizzeria. The girls shoved two long center tables together and piled onto the bench seats in a noisy clump, jostling for space and food. Their parents sipped beers and sodas and beamed at them from more comfortable booths around the edges of the restaurant. Lindsay pulled Matt down next to her, and Emily plowed her way into the middle of the pack, reliving details of the triumph and joining in the giddy girl talk.

Joe settled down in a slightly quieter spot near one end of the team table and looked around, amused to be a part of such a normal, family-style scene. Usually by this time on a weekend he'd be stretched out on his sofa with a bottle of wine or stretched over some woman with his legs tangled in hers. It was strange to feel so relaxed in these slightly exotic surroundings, to feel almost at home amid the noise and confusion.

He stared at the faces of his players and their parents, and he realized he was looking at them differently now—as if they were refracted through a prism, as if their personalities had become part of their facial features. He knew so many bits and pieces about the people behind those faces that his impressions had shifted, in the past couple of weeks, from vague tolerance to active liking. He actually felt a connection to a group of relative strangers.

This wasn't his style, not his preferred way of going through life or dealing with people. This wasn't something he'd seen coming, not anything he'd wanted to happen. This was Emily's doing. She'd questioned and challenged him, and prodded and dragged him into deeper lessons and bigger projects, into more interactions with his students and more involvement with the school community.

He'd shut it all down, and shut it all away before she'd bounced into his life. He'd sought peace and solitude, but all he'd found in the quiet, lonely places was himself, and it turned out he wasn't all that happy with his own company. He was finding much more pleasure in this elbowing, chattering, laughing mob of people—and wasn't that a surprise.

There had been a lot of surprises in his life lately, thanks to his student teacher. She'd turned his life upside down. And now she was busy turning him inside out.

He watched her snag a slice of mushroom-and-olive pizza and slowly bite into it as sauce oozed. She teased the slice away, stretching the cheese, and then brought it back for another nip. Her tongue slipped out to catch each gooey strand and licked the sauce from her lips. She smiled at him as she chewed, and then reached for her soda and puckered her lips around the straw.

He wondered if she was intentionally driving him insane.

He sipped his beer and watched her. He watched her as she stripped the toppings from a sliver of crust and agreed that Lori had improved her free throws. He watched as she sucked sauce from her fingertips and argued with Matt about a ref's call. He watched as the last few slices disappeared into foil wraps, as the last player finished reliving the last play, as the last parent thanked her for all her hard work. And then he followed her across the dim parking lot, his boots crunching over gravel and his breath spouting clouds that mingled with hers in the chilled night air.

She climbed into her truck, and he waited while she rolled down the driver's side window. He stepped close to the opening, and she shrank back a bit. So he waited, again, waited until she was aware there was no one watching, waited until she shifted a few tantalizing inches toward him. Neon rainbows from the sign over the restaurant door slid across her forehead, and dipped into the hollows at the base of her throat, and filled her eyes with fireworks. Her familiar scent wafted up to him, and he inhaled the floral and female essence like a drug.

His thoughts chased each other in a vicious spiral. She was so special, so beautiful, and that's why he wanted her so much. He'd hurt her if he acted on that desire, but if he didn't act, she'd never know how he felt, because he didn't have the words to tell her. He could only show her.

If he tried to show her, he'd risk ruining the fragile magic of this friendship they shared, but he wanted to show her they could share so much more, be so much more together. He wanted her to know how much he wanted that, how much he wanted her... wanted her...wanted her....

"Follow me," he said.

EMILY FOLLOWED HIM into the heart of town, into an alley just off Main Street. She bounced in behind him, bobbing through potholes until she came to a stop, inches from the peeling paint at the rear entrance to Dixon's Hardware. Her truck's motor rumbled and the defroster hummed as she watched him climb out of his car. He jogged up a narrow flight of stairs to duck under a stingy porch light and disappear into a slant-roofed apartment.

His apartment. She'd heard he lived somewhere in the middle of town, but she wouldn't have imagined him tucked into an alley access walk-up. Were teachers' salaries at Caldwell that low? He did travel during the summers; maybe that was where his money went. It certainly didn't go into housing.

What a sad, lonely little place. Hidden away, a touch run-down at the heels. Just like Joe, she realized. Suddenly, his careless, shabby place made sense.

He hadn't invited her in; she wasn't sure she should stay. Before another thought formed, she twisted the key in the ignition, and the truck's engine coughed and died. She sat in the dark, and the cold, and replayed a lecture gone hollow and dry with repetition. *He's your master teacher. He's writing your internship evaluation. He's secretive, and difficult, and your ideological opposite. He's bad news.*

He's not the man for you.

He reemerged dressed in sweats and jogged down the steps to climb in through the passenger door of her truck. The edge of a condom packet poked out of his pocket. "Let's go," he said.

This—whatever it was—it had all seemed to make so much more sense back on the court, with the adrenaline surging and the crowd shoving, or in the pizza parlor, with bright lights and yeasty smells and plenty of laughter to scatter her doubts and delay the inevitable. Now that the inevitable was here, it seemed so…inevitable. Emily hesitated, sinking back against the familiar lumps in the bench seat.

She thought she knew the destination he had in mind, but she needed to make sure. "To my place?"

"Yeah." He glanced at her, his eyes glinting like obsidian from the shadows. "Okay?"

Okay? Her choice, her decision. He wouldn't

make it easy on her, wouldn't touch her, wouldn't seduce her. And he couldn't know he already had.

He'd been seducing her since that first day in his classroom. He'd seduced her with his reluctant wit and his disarming patience, with his gentle lectures and his laser beam stare, with the brush of a fingertip over her shoulder in her truck and the slide of a leg against hers in a dance, with his spoonfuls of Great-Grandmother's aspic and his pacing on the edge of a basketball court. With his kisses and his yearning glances, and with the need for her that broke over her in waves and drenched her with desire.

She wanted to show him what she felt for him, now, while her heart was full of him, while they shared this bond of victory and accomplishment and school and community. Now, with no reservations, with no somber calculations about the future or the risks they'd both be taking. Now, because after she left Caldwell, there might never be another night like this.

"Okay," she answered.

She pulled out of the alley and drove, slowly, carefully. They traveled without a word over the black ruts of the railroad tracks and glided past skeletal orchards that beckoned with pale, dead arms in the moonlight. The night smelled of stale smoke and tasted of snow clouds threatening to unload. The only sounds were the swish and whine of the truck moving over the pavement. Not particularly romantic, but neither was this chilled, silent drive toward her house. Toward her bed.

She guided the truck over her gravel drive and stopped near her front porch.

"You didn't leave your porch light on," he said.

"The bulb burned out a couple of days ago."

"Then get a new one."

"I will." She pulled the key from the ignition. "I keep forgetting since it's usually still light out when I leave."

"It's not safe."

"I won't trip on the steps," she said.

"That's not what I meant."

She rolled her eyes in exasperation. "This isn't the big city."

"No, it's not." He opened his door and swiveled out of the truck. "Here you don't have any neighbors who could see if something was wrong or hear you call for help."

Emily closed her eyes and wrestled back a surge of nerves. "I know it's extremely irresponsible of me, and I promise I'll do better from now on. Would you like to come in and nag at me where it's warmer?"

Joe slammed his door shut on a mild, muttered curse. Guess she wasn't the only one feeling uneasy.

She climbed down and trudged to her little porch. Joe's tall, broad-shouldered figure seemed to take up all the available space. He sidestepped as she bent to unlock her door, but she brushed against him, and the shock wave of awareness had her fumbling in the dark.

Her little house seemed so much emptier in the sudden, stark glare of the overhead lighting fixture. She blinked a couple of times, wishing for candlelight and potpourri. It was too late now—and a bad idea, anyway—to ask her mother how to decorate for a sexual encounter.

This is The Wiz, she reminded herself from habit as he angled through her door. The much older, more experienced man who taught your older brother when he was in high school. The man who makes a habit of arguing with your father. The subject of your adolescent fantasies. Run while you can, escape before it's too late.

It was already too late. Her world had flip-flopped. Short-term goals, long-term goals, career plans, family expectations—just a few weeks ago these things had been overwhelming priorities competing for her attention, drowning out the whispers of what she felt for Joe.

Now her plans and goals seemed diminished, seemed like pieces of a puzzle she could easily snap into place and set aside, or sweep into a box to hide in a closet. What she felt for Joe overwhelmed it all and consumed her. It flowed over her, and through her, not competing with who she was or what she wanted to accomplish, but buoying her up and taking her wherever she wanted to go.

She watched him prowl with a frown through her front room, and she looked right through to the heart of things, through all the personal history and all the complications of here and now, and all she saw was Joe. A man who was patient and funny, who was kind and tough, who demonstrated his beliefs with quiet actions. A man who had been her friend, her supporter, her teacher. A man who was about to become her lover.

The man she loved.

She took a step closer, needing to close the space between them. She wanted him to pull her close, so that her tangled thoughts and last-minute doubts would vanish with the magic of his touch. If an affair was all she would ever be able to share with him, then she'd hold her nose and jump right in. She'd love him as much as she could, as much as he would allow. She'd show him everything she felt, everything she couldn't put into words.

He cleared his throat. "I've been thinking of this moment, this night, for weeks now. I never pictured it feeling like this."

"What did you picture?" she asked. "Soft lights? Music? A more seductive setting for seduction?"

"I don't need any more seduction." Joe shrugged out of his parka. "I've had about four months of seduction, not counting that last little bit of foreplay with the mozzarella, and I'm about ready to explode."

"Oh." She smiled, thinking of him being so hot and bothered for so long.

He scrubbed a hand back through his hair, a wry

grin tugging at one corner of his mouth. "I can't believe this. I'm actually nervous."

"Nervous?"

"Maybe not nervous. But…something. I only know that this suddenly seems too big to get a handle on. And I don't know where or when things got out of control."

He slid one hand into his pocket and she heard the faint crinkle of the packet inside. "It doesn't make sense that we're so attracted to each other. And that we can't work together without all this stress and strain. It's not right that you might be wondering whether my…my feelings for you are going to last long enough to ensure a good recommendation, or whether going to bed with me is the only way you'll get the recommendation you want. And it's starting to drive me crazy that I can't get through a lecture without getting hard every time you cross your legs."

"You do?"

"Why do you think I spend so much time leaning back against the edge of my desk?"

She smiled, and when he smiled back his fierce look softened, and she saw how much he wanted her, so much that he was losing his own internal battles. She saw it in those dark eyes, saw the frustration shift to longing. She felt it, too—the rush of heat, the licks of desire, the pulsing of surrender. It was overwhelming, but he was wrong about things being out of control. It was still her choice to make.

"I don't worry about those things, Joe. I've thought about them, sure. But I don't worry about them. Because I trust you."

His mouth twisted in a wry smile. "I'm not sure you should."

"Do you trust me?"

"Yes," he said.

She closed the gap between them and lifted her hand to his face, gazing up at him to let him see her need for him. She tipped up on her toes, and Joe leaned down, and their lips met in a nibbling exploration.

"What about when we argue?" she whispered.

"What about it?" he said as his tongue flicked along the corner of her mouth.

She sighed against his lips. "Don't you like arguing with me?"

"Yeah," he said. He nipped at her earlobe as he slowly lowered her jacket zipper. "It's a hoot."

"Admit it." She leaned her head back so he could kiss a path down her neck as he tugged her wrists out of the sleeves. "Arguing's one of the best things we've got going."

She heard her jacket hit the floor behind her as his mouth closed over hers. "Okay," he whispered against her lips, "I admit it. I like to argue with you."

"In fact," she said as she tugged up the hem of his sweatshirt, "arguing's probably your favorite thing to do with me."

"Not after tonight," he said as he yanked his top

over his head and tossed it near her jacket. "Dropping down to second place."

Oh. His chest was amazing. Teenage fantasies couldn't have conjured this golden slide of flesh over muscle and bone, and womanly imagining couldn't have provided all the wonderful details of crisp black hair sprinkled between...*oh.*

"Why, Mr. Wisniewski," she said as she trailed her fingers along his collarbone and traced them over the swells of his wide, curving chest, stopping just short of the dark nipples. He trembled, and she told herself she'd have to pay special attention to these particular spots later and make him tremble again. "You're a hunk."

CHAPTER EIGHTEEN

"A HUNK?" he asked. She could always make him laugh. He should have known that having sex with Emily would be fun, as well as a workout for his philosophical underpinnings.

He didn't think it could be possible to want her more than he had with that first touch of her shoulder in her truck, or that dance on her porch, or those Thanksgiving weekend kisses. But he wanted her more than he'd ever thought it would be possible to want a woman, and all because of that last sassy crack.

He'd never been big on romantic gestures—or romance of any kind—but something tender and thrilling swept through him, and he scooped her up into his arms and carried her down the short hallway to her room.

He was desperate for her, and in a hurry with it. Should he lay her on the bed and undress her there, where she'd be ready for him? Or should he let her slide down his front as he lowered her to the floor, and strip her more efficiently as she stood? The matter was decided when he tripped over the edge of an area rug and they tumbled to the bed.

She lifted her arms to circle his neck, her eyes shining in the moonlight that streamed through a bare window. "Kiss me," she whispered.

On the other hand, there was a lot to be said for taking it slow and easy. Plans scattered as he stretched over her, sinking into her sweet lips and her welcoming curves. Slow, he thought, as he brushed his hands through her soft, soft hair. Easy, he thought, as his fingertips skimmed the smooth, smooth skin of her cheeks.

Kissing her was beyond wonderful. Even knowing that he would soon be doing a whole lot more than kissing her didn't detract from the pleasure he found in sipping her sighs from her lips.

The only problem with kissing was that he couldn't look at her while he did it. And he wanted to see her. All of her.

He shifted to his side and watched her face as he traced a line from the tip of her nose to the knob of her knee, enjoying detours around the hills and valleys, into the shadows at her throat, and the curve of her shoulder, and the mound of her breast, and the dip of her waist, and the swell of her hip, and the warm line of her thigh. He watched her eyes flutter closed, and her body arch toward his, and knew he had never seen anything as erotic as Emily Sullivan.

She was pure passion packaged in a buttoned-up Henley, trim slacks and lace-up boots.

He worked his way through the buttons at her neck with clumsy fingers, and then tugged at her shirt where it was tucked into her pants. He clamped down, hard, on the urge to rip her clothes off and dive right in. He couldn't remember ever—no, never—being so tempted to skip his opening moves. He took a measure of pride in his skill with women, in his efforts to give them pleasure while he took his. He wanted to bring Emily a great deal of pleasure, since she meant a great deal to him.

So why was he fumbling his finesse?

He was thinking too much, that was why. Thinking about who this was, and what this meant. He squeezed his eyes shut and ordered himself to focus on how this felt.

Like nothing he'd ever felt before—because of who this was, and what this meant.

He gazed down at her face and watched her lips turn up in a shy smile before they softened for his kiss, and affection for her flooded in to mix with the craving and wash everything else away.

Clothes slid from bodies with strokes and sighs. As each layer disappeared, he marveled at what was revealed. There was nothing subtle about the body that lay beside his. Yes, it was soft and curvy and feminine in all the right places, but it was also strong, and vital, and sexy as hell. Sex with Emily was going to be like sipping expensive champagne: plenty of fizz mixed in with the tang.

And plenty of nerves bubbling beneath the desire. He shifted to his side. "Tell me what you're thinking."

She closed her eyes. "I was remembering when I almost got my first kiss. You know—not the wispy or smacky kind you get from a close male relative. The kind you get from some tall, solid high school senior when you're only a freshman."

Okay. As an ice breaker, this had been one of his dumbest moves ever. There was no stopping her now. She was on a roll.

"In the dark," she continued. "On a date. On the beach, for instance. Late at night, with the wind blowing your hair and your hair getting in your mouth and you're thinking, gee, what if he tries to kiss me at the exact moment my hair blows across my face and—"

He leaned down and kissed her. He couldn't help it. She was asking for it. She let out a little *mph* of surprise, and then softened beneath him, taking him in. He deepened the kiss, lingering over the satiny texture of her lips and the moist heat of her mouth.

And pictured someone else kissing her, too. "All right," he said as he pulled back. "What was his name?"

"Whose name?"

"The guy on the beach. The junior who took you to a deserted beach in the middle of the night when you were only a freshman in high school."

"He was a senior." She reached up and tucked his hair behind his ear. "And it wasn't a completely deserted beach, and it wasn't the middle of the night. We were double dating and I made it home in plenty of time for curfew."

"Double dating? There was another couple?" The pictures in his mind were crowding out everything else. "Where were they? Necking on the sand dune next door?"

"Probably." She shifted closer to him, rubbing her leg over his. "It was too dark to see."

"So it was also too dark to see if some creep was out there planning to attack a bunch of distracted teens at an orgy."

"Joe. It wasn't an orgy. Nothing happened. I made it home, safe and sound. And still unkissed."

"But you kissed the guy later, right? This three-years-older-than-you high school guy. After he risked your life at the beach."

"Aarghh!" She shoved at his shoulder, laughing. "You sound like my father."

Joe rolled to his back and stared at the ceiling. "Well, that certainly puts a damper on things."

She rose over him, a grinning goddess with moonlit skin and tousled curls, and brushed her fingertips down, down, from the base of his throat to a ticklish spot above his navel. "How much of a damper?"

He flinched as she circled his navel with her nail. He knew it was pink, and polished, and the thought of it roaming farther south was driving him crazy. "Not too much, as it turns out."

"I didn't mean to get sidetracked. But I always babble when I'm nervous. I suppose I talk a lot all the time, but especially when I'm nervous. Like the time—"

Joe pulled her head down until her mouth was a breath away from his. "Shut up, Em."

"Oh." She blinked. "He didn't say that."

"Who?"

"The senior on the beach."

"We're not going to start with that again, are we?"

"Not if you don't want to."

Joe held her close as he rolled, until he was sprawled over her and could take her face in his hands. "The wind isn't blowing." He caught her lower lip between his teeth before kissing a meandering path down her chin, down her throat. "Your hair is perfect. Like it always is. All soft and tumbled over the pillow, just like I've imagined." He brushed his fingers through the strands, spreading them across the linen as he slid one leg over hers. "Your lips are soft, too. Soft and warm and delicious. They're sort of spicy, like the pizza."

"Pizza?" she whispered.

"It was the best I could do on short notice. Poetry takes a little preparation." He lifted his head from where he was nibbling at her shoulder. "I could go back to describing your hair. I wasn't getting any complaints about that."

Her eyes drifted closed. "Are you babbling, Joe?"

"That's the game plan. At least we're making some progress now that I'm doing the talking."

She sighed, and he licked along the delicate line of her collarbone. She had the most amazing hollows at the base of her throat, and he intended to sample each one. Starting right now.

"Joe?"

"Mmm-hmm?"

"You're so much smarter than that guy at the beach."

"That's why I'm the one who's here right now doing this." He nuzzled his face into the valley between her breasts. "And this." He drew one perfect nipple into his mouth and slowly ran his tongue over the tip. He raised his head and said, "That guy at the beach is probably still stuck in the sand wondering how he missed out on his chance to make the big move."

He lowered his mouth to her other breast, but paused. "He did miss out, right?"

Emily ran her fingers through his hair. "Jealous?"

"I don't think I can fit jealousy into the schedule tonight. I've had enough to handle with all the other obstacles on the course. I can't concentrate on my big move if I have to worry about the other guys' moves, too."

She arched up against him and wrapped her arms around his neck, and he followed her as she sank back down against the sheet. He dipped a hand between her legs and began to tease her with a lazy rhythm, driving them both near the edge.

She gasped and shifted beneath him. So hot, so close. "You don't have to worry about the other guys' moves," she whispered. "Your moves are just fine."

"Thank you," he said as he lowered his mouth to hers.

EMILY DRIFTED on his kiss, awash in a sea of sensation. The only sounds were their murmurs. The only tastes flowed from their lips. The only scents rose from their bodies.

She loved his kisses, with their delicious contrasts: fiery and tender, overpowering and cherishing, all at the same time. How gently he cradled her head as his tongue plundered her mouth, how softly he threaded his fingers through her hair while he ravished her throat. Her heart stumbled with the sweetness.

She loved his touch, with its tantalizing counterpoints: teasing and demanding, sliding and stroking. How hesitantly his fingertips brushed over her, as insubstantial as butterfly wings. How possessively his palms shaped her, searing her with urgency.

So much of him was revealed in his touch, so much more than she had imagined he would let her see. Moments of shy surprise mingled with maddening patience, drawing her out and driving her higher. Movements ripe with passion were tempered with delicate caresses, spearing through her and shredding her control. So much of what was inside him was there in the spasm of his breath, in the tremor of a fingertip, in the pressure of his lips, in the arch of his back. So much hunger.

His mouth, his hands—he was everywhere, and everything. Everything. Her body, her mind, her heart all flowed out to him, and returned to her, sensitized by his touch, too exquisite to bear. She writhed from a pleasure that bordered on pain.

"You once accused me of being predictable," he whispered, his voice a ragged rasp in her ear.

She struggled toward him, lifted her hips toward him, could feel him hot and rigid against her, so close, so close.

"Is this predictable, Emily?" He shifted over her and pressed against her, moved against her, branding her with his heat and trembling against her with his restraint, until she thought she might explode with anticipation.

"Is this?" he asked as he slid into her and swallowed her gasp with a lingering kiss.

"Or this?" he whispered at her ear as he surged into her, in long, deep, powerful strokes that drove her, breathless, toward bliss.

Somehow she found the strength to lift her hands, to frame his face, to meet his eyes. To let him see what the moment meant to her. "No, Joe. I could never have predicted this."

They moved together, and smiled together, and sighed together, and loved, together.

JOE GROANED when Emily's arm landed across his face for the fourth time that night. No, it was morning, he saw when he squinted through the one eye that wasn't full of elbow. His first night with Emily. Maybe his last. It all depended on what happened when she woke up and found him in her bed.

He wasn't sure why he cared, anyway. It wasn't like a night with Emily meant a fellow could get any sleep. She hogged the mattress and stole the covers. She was a thrasher and a snorer. The only thing that made the cold and the bruises worthwhile was all the interesting stuff she talked about in her sleep. Not to mention the even more interesting things that happened when he prodded her awake enough to move over. Awake enough to stop snoring. Awake enough to slip into another round of sex.

He wasn't sure he could survive too many more nights like the last one, but he sure as hell wanted to give it a try. The sex had been incredible.

And wasn't that a surprise.

It wasn't like she was gymnastic, or inventive, or had the libido of a sailor on shore leave. He'd even laughed in bed before—in fact, he'd already done everything the two of them had done, and more besides. Plenty more. He just couldn't remember enjoying sex in general with anyone as much as he'd enjoyed sex in particular with Emily.

There was probably a perfectly logical explanation for the level of lust he was feeling, a lust that was crowding out the usual morning urge to make his escape. He was just too tired—and too aroused—to think of it at the moment.

She muttered something about raisins in the cereal and pulled her arm back to rub at her nose. Joe shifted to his side and rested his head in his hand, looking down at her. God, she was pretty. He'd noticed how pretty that first moment he saw her in Kyle's office, looking prim and proper and tasty enough to gulp right down. He'd been trying not to notice ever since. But now he was in her bed, and he could notice all he wanted.

She still looked good enough to eat. And somehow, even in her sleep, all prim and proper. She also looked warm and inviting. And clever and funny and generous. She was so much more than a collection of pleasing features. Her mouth could turn stubborn, or spread in a dazzling smile, or babble nonsense. Her nose could tilt up, or scrunch up, or stick into all the wrong places. Her eyes could tear up, or squint in concentration, or go all soft and dreamy.

Any minute now she was going to open those eyes and see him there. Would she be embarrassed? Smug? Annoyed? Ready for some good morning sex?

The correct answer to the multiple choice question: all of the above. "Good morning," he said.

She cleared her throat. "Good morning."

He leaned down and kissed her, before either of them could say something to regret later. She pulled him close, before either of them could change their minds. Joe's last coherent thought before diving into another round of sensual oblivion was that good morning had never felt so good.

EMILY WATCHED Joe frown down at the interior of her refrigerator an hour later and tried to decide between pinching herself at her good fortune or panicking at her folly. She hadn't imagined the awkwardness of the morning after. If she had, her daydreams would have included sunlight streaming through the kitchen window, the scent of bacon frying, and a stimulating political debate over whatever topics the Sunday paper had to offer—not this gray winter chill seeping through the house, an embarrassingly empty larder and a moody man who seemed to prefer to start the day in silence.

She'd also neglected to imagine all these worries about the morning after the morning after. She thought she knew Joe well enough to trust that he'd be careful and generous, that he'd never knowingly hurt her. But could she give him what he might need from a relationship? She wasn't even sure what those needs might be. She'd given more thought to last night's basketball game plan than she'd given to her immediate emotional future, and to Joe's, and the fact mortified her.

Where were her lists of short-term and long-term

goals, her charts and her files and her organizer, when she needed them most?

At least one minor mystery had been solved: no tattoo. Patsy Velasco had been lying.

"You said there was breakfast food here," he said. "I don't see anything."

Emily nudged him aside and reached for a little white box. "See this? This could be breakfast."

"What is it?"

"Chow mein."

He looked uncertain. "Doesn't look like there's enough for two."

"There's some leftover pizza in here, too." She pointed to a foil-wrapped package.

"We didn't bring any home with us last night."

"It's from Thursday."

He pulled her away from the refrigerator and shut the door. "I appreciate the multicultural approach to dining," he said, "but I think we should come up with another idea."

She leaned back against the counter and folded her arms across her chest. Her thick terry-cloth robe gapped open, and she reached up to scrunch it closed. "Such as?"

"Hmm?" He was staring at her fisted collar.

"Breakfast, Joe." She yawned. "I need some food. And then I need some sleep."

"I can feed you." He grabbed the belt of her robe and tugged her up against him. "At my place."

"Your place?"

"Yeah. I'll jog home, and you can come by later. Folks around here are used to seeing me running in the morning. And there's no reason why you wouldn't park your truck in front of a Main Street shop on a Sunday morning." He moved her hand out of the way and tickled his knuckles down her throat. "I've got eggs and cheese at my place."

"The inner sanctum?" She leaned forward and whispered, "Will I be struck down?"

"Not if you mind your manners," he said. "And your mouth."

"Don't worry. I'll behave."

"Let's not be hasty."

"Okay." She turned to go, but he still had her belt, holding her in place. "I have to take a shower," she said.

"Fine."

"Joe." She tried to tug away. "You've got my robe."

"Yeah." He lifted one eyebrow. "Is that a problem?"

She called his bluff and walked out of the kitchen, leaving him with handfuls of terry cloth. When she looked back over her shoulder, the grin on his face was worth every goose bump.

CHAPTER NINETEEN

THAT EVENING, Joe listened patiently as Emily outlined the terms of their new relationship: no physical contact of any sort at school or school functions. No play time at basketball practices or games. She assured him she felt no professional pressure, and that these boundaries were not based on any perceived or potential exploitation of their working relationship—that they were merely common sense.

He watched her pace the length of his kitchen as she wrestled with the organizational details of an affair, her hair a curling riot around cheeks still flushed from a bout of shower sex. Then he swept her off her feet and carried her back to his bed, planning on some negotiations of his own. It didn't take much persuading to add an option clause to the contract: they could indulge in discreet mutual rewards for good behavior on the weekdays.

On Tuesday morning, at a meeting in his classroom during his third period prep, the agreement broke down. Everything seemed to be going as planned until they got into an argument about France.

It was her sassy mouth that did him in. That and the way she crossed her arms under her breasts and twisted her mouth to one side in disgust. He couldn't help reaching out and hauling her up against him. "It makes me hot when you argue with me," he said. "Tell me I'm an idiot again, but this time stick your tongue in my ear."

"Joe! Someone will see us." But her arms were already circling his waist.

He nibbled his way up her neck, and the tiny gold hoop in her earlobe danced over his tongue. He smelled talcum and honeysuckle as he nuzzled raspy wool and warm female flesh. The sharp intake of her breath made the spot between his shoulder blades tingle and the space beneath his ribs tighten.

She was driving him wild. She was annoying and argumentative—and delicious—and she'd scored some solid political points, damn it. He hated when she pulled that off. But burying his face in her silky curls went a long way toward softening the blow. He reveled in the scent of her shampoo, the warmth of her scalp, the feel of her wrapped in his arms.

God. There it was again. That sneaking suspicion that he was in love with her.

It was the only logical explanation. Here he was, holding the opposite of everything he'd ever thought he wanted in a woman, and he never wanted to let her go.

"I HOPE YOU KNOW what you're doing."

Emily glanced over her shoulder at Linda,

standing in the doorway, and then turned to close the copier feed tray. She wanted to finish Friday's chores as quickly as possible, and then head home to change before tonight's practice basketball game. After the game, the weekend was hers—hers and Joe's. Well, there was some studying to do for the final exam in Methodology, and chaperone duty at the winter formal on Saturday night, but after that, she could relax and enjoy an intimate Sunday with Joe. Just the two of them.

Filled with anticipation, she pressed Start and hoped for the best. "Arnold and I have been getting along just fine ever since I threatened to break one of his little green handles."

"I was talking about a different male." Linda took a sip of the coffee she carried into the workroom before setting the mug on the counter. "The one you work with. Although breaking body parts might be one way to deal with the situation."

"What situation?"

"You. Joe."

Emily pasted an innocent smile on her face and turned to face Linda. "Me? Joe?"

Linda's eyes narrowed. "Joe, Tarzan. You, Jane. Don't make me do the jungle call."

Emily brightened her smile. "I think you have the wrong idea."

"No way. I've seen the socks."

Emily collected her handouts from the tray. "Socks?"

"Joe's," Linda said. She crossed her arms over her chest and blocked Emily's escape route. "New socks sticking out of those grubby sandals."

"Socks?"

"A dead giveaway. With some men, it's flowers and candy. With Joe, it's socks. New ones. A spiffy new image for a spiffy new relationship. And, if I'm not mistaken, freshly pressed shirts. Neatly trimmed hair. This morning, I think I caught a whiff of cologne," she said. "It made me want to gag."

Emily tapped the papers on the counter, neatening the edges. "You have a problem with good grooming?"

"I have a problem with courting on campus."

Emily sighed and set the papers down. "It's not what you think."

"Oh?" Linda leaned forward and lowered her voice. "And what do you think I think?"

Trapped. "You're really good at this," said Emily. "I should be taking notes."

"Flattery will get you absolutely nowhere." Linda picked up her mug. "Spill it. But skip the lurid details. I have to work with you people."

"Well…" Emily had no idea where to start, what to say. "I think you might think that Joe and I have developed a…a special friendship. Because we work so well together," she added. "And we have. We do."

"Mmm-hmm." Linda stood her ground and took another sip.

"But there's no candy and flowers here. None.

Nothing like that. As for the socks, I have no idea what you're talking about. And maybe the rest of it is...well, he is interacting with the parents more. With coaching and all. And he's department chair now."

"It's not the new title I'm thinking of," said Linda. "Or the increase in parent interaction. I'm thinking it's the close and personal interaction with his student teacher. It's the 'special friendship.'"

She set down her mug. "You know, with Joe, there won't be any candy and flowers. Just a world of pain."

Emily swallowed the nasty taste of panic that trickled into her throat. She crossed her arms and leaned against the counter for support. "So, this is where the old friend gives the new friend a bit of advice."

"My advice? My gut reaction to this whole mess?" Linda reached out and squeezed her arm. "Go for it. Go for it all. And take him with you. Please. You deserve each other. And I mean that in the nicest possible way."

"I care about him," she told Linda. "I do. A great deal."

"I know, hon. I know exactly what you mean, and what you're not admitting. And the socks are proof he cares about you, right back. At least," Linda added with a frown, "in the only way he knows how."

Emily lowered her hands to grip the counter edges. "Is this the pain part?"

Linda sighed and toyed with the mug's handle. "There's something there. Something dark, buried down deep. Sure, he's lightened up considerably lately. Getting a chance at a fresh start with a fresh young thing like you—and getting away with it—heck, that's bound to put some spring in anyone's Birkenstocks. But I don't know if he's ready to let himself go. Really go. And then you're going to get hurt. And then he's going to be hurting for having hurt you. And, like I said, I just hope you know what you're doing."

"Of course I don't know what I'm doing. I've never done this before." Irony alert. *The joke's on me. I'm in love with Joseph P. Wisniewski. I'm in love with the man, and I don't even know his middle name.*

Emily shoved her hands into her hair and pushed it back from her face. "I've always run away before I got into anything this deep. Anything. Any problem, any job, any person, anything."

She had too much at risk to run now—her life, her love. Everything would be okay, everything would work out. She knew it. She could feel it, could feel it in Joe, too. He couldn't make love to her with such sweetness if he was still struggling with something dark and damaging. She knew him, better than Linda did.

She relaxed her fingers, and her curls bounced back around her eyes. "I'm not running this time. I can't. I won't. It's… complicated."

Linda stared at her for a long, steady moment. "Okay."

"Okay?"

"Okay. That's what he needs. Someone who's going to stick. No matter what. 'Cause I think there's a shitload of trouble headed his way."

"We're being careful."

Linda rolled her eyes.

"We are," Emily insisted. She hesitated. "Aren't we?"

"Some things you just can't hide," Linda said. "But no one's going to give you too much grief for making cow eyes at each other. No, there's something else. Something fishy going on with Kyle and the school board."

Fishy. Kyle. Ugh. "What is it?"

"My sources aren't clear on that yet. One thing for sure, though, Kyle would be in a twist if he thinks Joe's making headway where he's not." Linda lifted her mug and took another sip, grimacing at the cooled coffee. "But if jealousy's the motive behind this, that's lower than even I gave Kyle credit for."

Emily held up her hands. "You've lost me."

"Kyle's been making some noise about Joe's teaching. His dress, his habits, his political views. Whether he's an 'appropriate' choice for the position of department chair. It's an easy sell—Joe's reputation in this town has always been a little edgy."

"Joe didn't want to be department chair. He still doesn't want it."

"Not appropriate for department chair, not appropriate to teach. It's not such a big leap." Linda shrugged. "It's all political, it's all personal. Joe knows that. He knows what it'll mean if people find out you and he have a 'special friendship.'"

"Then they won't find out."

"Hon, everyone finds out everything here, sooner or later."

Linda reached past her to dump the coffee down the drain. "Kyle's never liked Joe. Never, not from day one. He can't make Joe squirm, and he lives to make people squirm."

She glanced over her shoulder at Emily. "He hasn't been bothering you lately, has he?"

"No. I haven't seen much of him."

"Hmm. Probably just a temporary reprieve."

Emily shivered. "Ugh."

"Oh, it's more than that." Linda glanced at her watch and stepped toward the door. "I think he's plotting, long range. If he could get rid of Joe, he could hire you in his place. You've been getting rave reviews. You'd be cheaper, easier to manipulate and better looking."

"That's disgusting."

"That's Kyle." Linda paused in the doorway and shook her head. "I sure hope you know what you're doing."

JOE LOVED to run his fingers through Emily's hair. First scraping gently along her warm scalp, and then combing out through the silky length. He hadn't tired yet of watching the pale curls twist and stretch between his fingers before they snapped back to bounce around her face. Every once in a while, one little wisp would land over her eyes or near her nose, and she'd blow it out of her way.

She leaned against his shoulder as he sprawled across her bed, one hand marking her place on a crumpled list of names she'd spread over his chest. She seemed distracted—probably reliving the team's defeat. "You can't win 'em all," he said.

"Why not?" She flashed a halfhearted smile.

"What is it?"

She sighed. "Nothing."

"I know that sigh. That sigh means it's something."

She started to speak, seemed to think better of it, and then sighed again. "I guess it's just…this is so strange."

"What is?"

"Being here with you. Like this."

He started to stiffen and ordered himself to relax. Since their first weekend together, the subject of their working relationship, of what might happen at school, had never come up. "What's so strange about it?"

"Well…it's sort of…" She wrinkled her nose. "Oh, never mind."

"Tell me." He tugged at her hair.

"Promise you won't laugh."

"Okay."

"It's just…no," she said. "It's too embarrassing."

"Oh." He spread his fingers and a tangle of curls escaped. "Okay then. Don't tell me."

Emily pushed the mess out of her face. "Oh, all right."

He smiled. The fastest way to get Emily to talk was to tell her she didn't have to. It wasn't manipulation; it was just plain fun.

"I used to have a…a kind of a crush on you," she said. "When I was a teenager."

"Used to?"

"I got over it," she said with a shrug.

"How could you have a crush on someone you'd never met?"

"Jack Junior talked about you all the time."

"And Jack Senior."

"Yeah, he did. I guess you could say you were something of a legend in the Sullivan household. Besides," she added, "I saw you around town a couple of times on your motorcycle. I thought you were kind of hot."

So, her taste in men had been questionable from the beginning. "Kind of?"

"Like I said, I got over it."

"Hmm."

"That's all? Just 'hmm'?"

"What do you want me to say?"

She frowned. "I shouldn't have to tell you what to say."

Now it was Joe's turn to sigh. "No, you shouldn't.

But I'm a male, which means I'm clueless. I shouldn't have to remind you about males."

"Hmm," said Emily.

"Right."

They smiled at each other. He studied the streaks of silver in her eyes, and the way her lashes curled up at the corners, and the arrangement of freckles on the tip of her nose, and the tiny scar just beneath one corner of her chin. He could have drawn a map of her features from memory, but he never got tired of going over the same territory.

She slid one foot up along his leg and back down again to play with his toes. "Don't be starting something, now," he said.

"Phoenix. Phineas. Uh...Pisces." She drew a circle around his nipple with a pink polished nail. "Poppy. Plato."

"Plato?"

"Plato bothers you and Poppy doesn't?" She frowned. "I'm going to have to start a new category: flora and fauna."

He tossed the paper on the floor and drew her head down beneath his chin. "Em?"

"Hmm?"

"Is it really strange?"

"Not knowing your middle name?"

He closed his eyes and twirled a strand of her hair around a fingertip. "It really bothers you, huh?"

"Mmm-hmm. Especially at times like this."

"Why now?"

"Because." She lifted her head and propped her chin on her hand. "Because when I'm with you like this, I'm not Ms. Sullivan, the student teacher, or Emily, the university student. Or Em, the dutiful daughter, or anyone else. I don't know who I'm supposed to be with you, or if it matters. I don't know which of those names to use for myself, just like I don't know what's behind that *P* in yours. I'm just…I just am. I'm just me. It feels…"

She bit her lip. "It feels free. And safe, somehow, even though I know it shouldn't." She lay her head back down on his chest and wrapped her arms around him as far as she could reach. "It feels good, Joe. So good. So right. And I feel like I've got to pinch myself or something. To tell myself it should feel strange, or wrong, or…I don't know. *Something.* You know?"

He closed his eyes. He knew exactly what she meant. When he was with her like this, he could let go. Let go of the responsibilities, let go of the guilt. Banish the memories and ignore the risks. Just let go of everything he should be thinking and doing and just *be.* Be with Em.

That was all he wanted—to be with Em, just like this. To feel close, to be close, to show her how much he loved her. He rubbed his hand over her back. "Yeah. It feels good."

Her toes scraped along the side of his ankle. He threw a leg over hers to trap her tickling foot, and then shifted to his side. She lifted her hand and traced the side of his face.

"So," he said, "about this crush…"

She laughed and tugged on his ear. "Tell me what the *P* stands for, and I'll—"

He cut off the negotiations with a kiss. One kiss led to another, and Joe let himself go, let himself slide, let himself empty into the nameless woman who filled him up with everything good. With everything…Em.

THE WINTER FORMAL on Saturday night was the worst night of Matt's life.

He jerked the wheel of his mother's car when he felt the tires slew through the mush at the side of the road. He had to be extra careful tonight. Pay attention to the traffic rules. Go the right speed. Speed up a little—there, that's right. Stay in the middle of the road. Middle of the right lane. It was important.

He had to get home in one piece. Drag himself up the stairs to his bed. Real quiet. Don't wake up Walter. Wouldn't want Walter to see him coming in late, smelling of alcohol. One drunk in the family was enough for Walter to deal with. And Walter was an okay guy. "You're okay, Walter," Matt said out loud.

He was a little drunk tonight—but he wasn't a drunk. Not like Mom. Matt rubbed his nose, and then overcorrected when the car started to drift toward the left. Gotta be more careful than that. Gotta be real careful, get home in one piece. Get home and sneak into bed. He could do it. He wasn't going to pass out on the sofa. Not like Mom. He wasn't a drunk like her.

Just a little drunk. But he could still drive.

A wave of dizziness rolled in, and then the nausea, sucking at him like an oily undertow. He pulled over to the right, slow, steady, barely bumping to a stop, barely missing the shallow ditch at the side of the rural stretch of road. A porch light up ahead gave him something to focus on as he waited for things to stop spinning around. He stared at the light, wondering where he'd seen that porch before. It looked familiar, somehow, but he couldn't be sure. Nothing looked the same in the dark as it did in the daylight.

Nothing. Not even Lindsay's sweet face. He remembered the shadows moving across her features, the way she leaned back into the dark. He could see her pale blue dress, but he couldn't see her eyes as she told him she wanted to break up. They were getting too serious about each other, she said, and there was no point. He'd be leaving for college in a few months, maybe as far away as California, and it would just hurt more to say goodbye if things kept moving in the direction they were moving.

"Bullshit," Matt said. "What a crock of bullshit." He shifted against the leather seat, nursing his misery with a dose of anger. If Lindsay wanted to break things off, why didn't she just come out and say so? Why drag the whole college thing into it, make it somehow his fault for leaving? "Hell, it's not like I'm leaving next week. Fall term is months away."

Months he could have spent exploring his first real relationship. He'd had some girlfriends before, but he'd never had an exclusive one, a steady one. Lindsay was special. She valued his opinions and shared his silences. She made him feel sort of powerful and sort of peaceful, all at the same time, like he could do anything, and do it well, because she'd support him.

And then the friendship had heated up. Their first kiss had spun out, and out, a kind of revelation. And later, when she'd let him reach up inside her sweater and touch her, he'd thought he'd burst. Her warm, soft skin had opened up a whole new world—and he wanted more. He wanted that warm skin up next to his, wanted her the way he'd never wanted another girl before.

He missed her so bad the pain gnawed at him, carved him up and opened him wide. He needed to fill the gaping hole. He wanted to fill it with Lindsay, but the open bottle of vodka he'd found in the trunk of his mom's car had him thinking that some other girl would do just as fine.

She'd have to be more honest than Lindsay. Someone he could trust with his feelings. Someone who would appreciate him, no matter what. Someone like Ms. Sullivan.

That was her porch light. Ms. Sullivan's. He sat

there, feeling the cold seep into the idling car, but too lethargic to shiver. She would understand what he was feeling right now. She would listen, would know what to say. She was a mature woman, someone who'd never play Lindsay's games with a guy.

If it weren't so late, he could go talk to her. She'd probably be worried that he'd been drinking. But then she'd make a cup of coffee for him, and they'd sit in her kitchen, discussing things. Important things. Things Lindsay wouldn't be able to discuss. Matt was ready for someone like Ms. Sullivan. He was ready for college girls. Not immature high school liars like Lindsay Wellek.

He sat there a while, letting his imagination run with images of the welcoming glow of Ms. Sullivan's kitchen and the rich smell of coffee. He felt himself drifting, and in some small corner of his mind he knew he should get moving, get home to his own dark, cold house and haul himself into his dark, cold bed. In a few minutes. Just a few minutes more, basking in the light from that yellow bulb over Ms. Sullivan's front porch.

He heard the crunch of gravel before he saw a tall figure jog into the pool of light that spilled over the front porch steps. Matt struggled upright and fumbled for his door handle. He had to warn her, to save her from the prowler. Nausea swamped the fear that spread though him, and a thin coat of sweat spread the chilled night air over his skin. His foot caught on the brake and the door handle slipped from his drink-clumsy hands.

Ms. Sullivan's door opened. There she was, bathed in the cascade of light. It touched her hair with gold, and made her skin look like something from a fairy tale. She gazed up at the man on her porch, and she smiled. A beautiful, radiant smile. A smile that Matt would give anything to see some woman aim in his direction.

She knew this man. She loved him. Matt could see it, even through the windshield and the dark and the vodka. She never took her eyes off him, never stopped smiling that heart-stopping smile as she reached for his hand to pull him into her house.

And as the man passed over the threshold, and the porch light caught him in its yellow nimbus, Matt recognized the man who made Ms. Sullivan smile like that, the man who was welcome in her house so late at night, the man who was probably going to skip the coffee in the kitchen and head straight to her bed: The Wiz.

CHAPTER TWENTY

JOE STARED UP at the shadow play of bare tree limbs dancing across Emily's bedroom ceiling. Beside him in moonlight, she snored lightly. Her soft, round rump was pressed up against his hip, and the sheet draped across his chest smelled like honeysuckle and lovemaking. He knew that if he turned his head he'd see her pale curls and the familiar slope of her shoulder, that he could watch that shoulder rise and fall in a slow, steady rhythm. He listened for the rhythm of her breathing, there in the darkness, and matched his breath to hers.

It was so simple a thing, breathing together like this. It was so simple, really, all of it. He had no idea how he'd arrived at this particular place, which steps had led him into Emily's life and into Emily's bed, which path had brought him here to blend his breath with Emily's in the dark, but he was a part of it all now, and she was a part of him. His life, his bed, and every breath he took. She filled him up. All his empty spaces.

He felt…whole. A complete person, far removed from the dark, ragged fragments and days at the start of the school year. He was able, now, to climb out of the shadows and set himself free. Able to make some long-term decisions, to sign a teaching contract for next year, and all the years after that.

He sighed in contentment. God, he loved to teach. He loved his job, here in this dust mote of a school in this fly speck of a town. Em had given him an "opportunity for a kind of personal and educational renewal," and he would always be grateful to her for the gift. It may have had a steep learning curve, but the best lessons were the tough ones.

She sighed and shifted, brushing a satiny thigh along his knee, murmuring some nonsensical accompaniment to whatever she was dreaming. Even in her sleep, she babbled. One more quirk to treasure.

He closed his eyes and allowed himself to drift on a peaceful current, buoyed by her presence. He craved these times, these feelings. He'd never known life could be so good, so close to perfect. He'd always thought that the moment of sexual climax was supposed to be the closest thing to, well, to heaven of a sort. But he'd been wrong. It was simply a prelude, an overture—a bridge to what he was feeling right now.

He wanted to have it all, and he never wanted it to end. He wanted Emily, like this, forever. It was that simple. He would ask her to marry him.

Now *that* wasn't going to be so simple. He didn't have a ring, and he didn't have much money for one. Hell, he wasn't sure she wanted one in the first place.

And he supposed he should say something to her father first. It might make her upset, but if it was a choice between a scene with Emily or a showdown with Jack Senior, he'd take his chances with Emily.

He could come up with some reason for a weekend trip to Seattle, which could lead to a visit with her parents. Which could be followed by a visit to a jewelry store.

Here he was, thinking in terms of patriarchal bondage rituals and white picket fencing around a single family housing unit. Anna would laugh herself into an early grave, or arrange for an exorcism.

Of course, he had no intention of requiring his wife to deny herself a career and make their home her priority. He was fully prepared to do half the chores, half the child-rearing duties.

Children. Teaching was terrifying enough—but being a father?

Em could help him. With her at his side, he could do anything. Raise a child. Conquer the world. Eat chow mein for breakfast.

He turned his head to look at her in her sleep. Yes, he could be a father. He pictured their children. Miniature people with her eyes, her curls, her spunk. He'd love them, too.

Daydreams, happiness…contentment. For the first time in a long, long time. And a feeling of peace for the first time in years.

God, he loved her. It was getting easier to think it.

He could hardly wait to say it out loud, to tell her. He didn't think it would be too hard. It shouldn't be to hard to propose, not after that. And then she'd say *yes*, and the rest of his life would begin, from that moment.

The phone on her bedside table rang. Emily flung an arm out and knocked her lampshade askew.

His stomach twisted. Bad news. That was the only kind that came at two o'clock in the morning. The phone rang a second time, and she sent her Mickey Mouse alarm clock clattering to the floor.

He lunged across the bed and snatched up the receiver. "Here," he whispered, and shoved it into her flailing hand.

She pulled it down to her ear. "Mmph?" she groaned. "Yes?"

He straightened the shade and flipped the switch. Emily grimaced in the sudden glare and rolled to her back, rubbing at her eyes. "Who? Oh, yes, just a minute." She yawned and waved the receiver in his direction. "It's for you."

He was right: bad news. And he could tell the instant it registered for Emily, too. She hugged the phone to her chest, her eyes wide with shock in a face gone pale. "It's for you."

It's for you. Her voice came to him through a dark, echoing tunnel. A tunnel that yawned between them, lengthening with each heartbeat, obscuring everything, numbing everything—everything but the suffocating pressure around his chest.

The call was for him. Here, at Emily's house, in the middle of the night.

It was over. All of it, over. The stimulating work relationship, the heady friendship, the love affair. He had to get her out, get her away. Get her far, far away, out of range of all the sordid misery that people could spew in so many directions over a situation like this. Get her far, far away from him.

He sat up and pried the receiver from her fingers. Maybe this wasn't the disaster he was expecting. Maybe there was a perfectly innocent, rational reason someone might be looking for him at this number at this time of night. Whatever it was, he would deal with it, would do whatever he had to do. Would live with the consequences of his choices, the way he'd been living for the past ten years. But, God, he didn't want to go back to that lifeless life. To a life without Em.

He took a deep breath and held the phone to his ear. "Yeah?"

"Wiz?" It was Matt. "I'm at the police station."

The light at the end of the tunnel winked out.

EMILY REVVED UP her pace to match Joe's determined stride. He didn't seem to care whether or not she fell a mile behind him in the police station hallway, just as he hadn't seemed to care whether or not she was beside him on the drive into town. He'd accepted her offer to play chauffeur, but he wouldn't talk to her unless she asked him a direct question. And even then, his answers weren't anything she could develop into a conversation.

He was angry. With Matt, with himself, with her. She could see it on his face, read it in his jerky motions and the terse way he spat out the few words he'd managed for the officer at the night desk.

She understood how Joe might be angry with Matt. She understood how he might be blaming himself in some way for the fact that Matt got drunk and plowed into a stop sign. What she couldn't understand was what she had done to deserve the silent treatment.

They rounded another corner, and she shivered beneath the wintry glare of the fluorescent lighting. She hugged her coat over her old sweatshirt and faded jeans, and focused on the floor and Joe's heels, trying not to meet the eyes of the people they passed in the building. She'd never been in a police station before; it wasn't something she cared to experience in vivid detail.

Joe stopped abruptly. "Okay, I'm here," he said.

Emily peered around him to see Matt slumped on a low bench, his eyes closed, his head leaning back against a dull green wall. Above him, a bulletin board held fresh announcements and photos in crisp black and white surrounded by curling papers edging toward yellow. She got an impression of how Joe's classroom decor might look if someone tried to spiff it up, only to quit before the job was finished.

She felt silly for focusing on something so inconsequential as a bulletin board with all the trouble floating around in the air. Air she was breathing in and exhaling, air that smelled of sweat and stale coffee and cigarettes and despair. She wanted to hold her breath and make it all go away, wanted to go back to her little house and her warm bed, to snuggle into Joe's solid side and close her eyes, to make the crisp and curling police bulletins fade away like the tattered edges of a bad dream.

Matt opened his eyes and groaned. Joe leaned down to eye level. "What do you want, Matt? Hmm? You got me down here. Now what did you have in mind?"

"I don't know. I didn't think that far ahead."

Joe leaned in closer. His voice dropped to a whisper. "You know something, buddy? You're full of shit."

He wheeled around, stared at Emily until she moved out of his way, and then crossed to a desk staffed by a clerk who was tapping at a computer keyboard. "Did he call his parents yet?"

"He got one call," the woman responded without looking up. "You were it."

"Can I make a call?"

Without glancing up, she indicated a pay phone at the end of the hall. Joe stalked back over to the bench where Matt had doubled over, holding his head in his hands. "Give me Walt's phone number."

Matt mumbled the number, and Joe headed to the

phone. Emily sat down next to Matt. She put her hand on his shoulder, and he shrugged it off. "Are you hurt?" she asked.

"No."

"How are you feeling?"

"Drunk."

Great. Two monosyllabic males to deal with in one night. And a third on the way, she guessed as Joe stalked back down the hall. She jumped up and hurried toward him, hoping to cut him off at the pass, to get something more than a verbal dismissal out of someone tonight before she exploded with frustration and anxiety. "What's going on?" she asked. "Did you get hold of Matt's parents?"

"Yeah," he answered without a flicker of a glance in her direction.

He tried to move around her, but she sidestepped into his path. "What's going on, Joe?" she asked again.

He shoved his hands into his sweatshirt pockets and lifted his eyes to meet hers. There was nothing there. No anger, no worry, no affection. Nothing. If it weren't for the little tick along his jaw, she wouldn't have known he was upset about anything at all.

"I told you," he said. "Matt wrecked his car and was brought in on a DUI. He used his one call to find me."

"At my place." She took a deep breath. She had to ask the question again. "How did he know you were there?"

"I don't know."

"If he knew you were there, how many other people know? How many people have known all along?"

Joe looked past her to where Matt sat staring at the floor. "There are more important things to deal with right now than the fact that we've been sleeping together." He shoved past her to join Matt on the bench.

Emily stood in the hall until the first bright pain of Joe's slicing remark passed, leaving her feeling cold and small and alone. Then she turned and walked in the opposite direction. "Where's the women's restroom?" she asked the first person she passed.

It was utilitarian. Streamlined and gray and smelling of disinfectant, but it was sanctuary. She knew she had to come out sometime, but not for a while. Not until breakfast, maybe. Or lunch. She'd skipped meals before. At least there were sinks and toilets. That meant a supply of water and other basic necessities.

She stared at her reflection and wondered if she should bother digging through her purse for anything that might make her look a little less like a walking corpse. Not that Joe would notice. He was too busy shutting her out. Walling himself off. Playing the martyr and keeping all the game pieces to himself.

She was just as worried about Matt as he was, damn his selfish hide. She was just as worried about the implications of Matt's decision to dial her number. She was just as much a part of the whole situation. She needed to be just as much a part of the solution.

"So why are you hiding out in here?" she asked the Emily in the mirror. *Because,* the mirror Emily answered back with eyes filling with tears. *Because he never wanted anyone to know he was involved with you. Because he didn't want to be involved with you in the first place. Because this is the end. Because he's going to keep shutting you out and driving you away until you're all shriveled up inside and out. Until you're just as gray and utilitarian and lifeless as this place.*

"Well, hell." She sniffed. "Nothing a little lip gloss and a pep talk won't cure."

She pulled a tiny pot out of her purse and dabbed some pale gloss on her dry lips. Better, she told herself, turning her head to check the way the fluorescent light bounced off her mouth. And tomorrow, everything else would be better, too. Better in awkward bits and jagged pieces, at first, and then better in smoother shapes and familiar patterns.

Okay. She nodded at the Emily in the mirror and took a deep breath. The time for hysterics had passed. She was a bit relieved she'd kept them to a minimum. Now it was time to get out there and deal with whatever needed dealing with.

She could do this. If she worked hard enough, and long enough, she could do anything she set her mind to. Hadn't her parents always told her that? Hadn't Joe taught her that? Besides, she'd always been able to charm or slide her way out of any problem, eventually. She just needed to find out what it was that needed to be done. That was the problem here: no clearly defined goals.

Goals and objectives, she told herself as she shouldered her way out the restroom door. The building blocks of a lesson plan. Life was just one big set of lessons, after all—and there certainly was a lesson to be learned here tonight. Mistakes were the best teachers. She should know—she'd learned plenty from hers. And one thing she'd learned was that a situation like this would resolve itself more neatly if she could break it down into manageable parts and stop letting the big picture overwhelm her.

Even if the big picture looked pretty overwhelming from where she was standing.

Walter Mullins had arrived. And from the expression on his reddened face, and the way his jaw jutted up toward Joe's, and the way his index finger kept poking Joe in the chest, Emily guessed he was as upset with Joe as he was with Matt. Great. This was going to add an interesting touch to the general ambiance of the evening, not to mention Joe's mood.

She approached cautiously, making sure she was out of range of the attack digit. Matt moaned, and Joe asked him if he needed to use the restroom again.

"No," Matt said.

Walt used all ten of his fingers to shove Joe back a half step. "I told you to stay out of my business."

Joe raised his hands, palms out. "I'm not a part of this."

"See that it stays that way," Walt snapped at him. "We don't need you. I can take care of my own."

"I know that, Walt."

Walt clenched his hands in tight fists. "No one gives a damn what you know. Why don't you just get out of here?"

Joe hesitated and looked down at Matt, but Walt shifted to block his view. With one last glance in the boy's direction, Joe turned, took Emily's arm and dragged her to the station entrance and out the door.

The cold night air slapped at her, stinging a little of the surrealism out of the scene. "Do you mind telling me what that was all about back there?" she asked.

"Walt's upset."

She tried to stop, but Joe kept going, tugging her along with him. She staggered a bit, but finally dug in and held her ground, forcing him to turn around and deal with her. She wasn't stumbling through another step until she got some answers in complete, complex sentences with adverbial phrases and descriptive modifiers.

"Walt left 'upset' back home," she said. "What he brought for you was something else entirely."

She waited for a response, but he ignored his conversation cue. "Why was that, Joe? What did I miss?"

He stared up at the stars and worked his jaw a bit, and then he looked down at her, and what she saw on his face sent something colder than the night air moving through her. "Ancient history, Em. Walt's still a little bent out of shape that I slept with his wife."

She wondered if frostbite could penetrate and blacken the heart. "Does Matt know?"

"He's never mentioned it." He released her arm and slid his hands into his sweatshirt pockets. "It was years ago, when Matt was away at summer camp. Before she married Walt. He didn't find out until later, but he didn't take it very well when he did. He knew about her other husbands, but he didn't know about the men in between."

"Men like you."

"Yeah. Men like me. Men who are looking for a one-night stand with a woman who's not feeling too choosy." He shrugged. "I was looking for company, and she was convenient."

He shifted a little closer, leaning down, crowding her. "That's what I do, Em," he said in a soft, cold murmur. "I look for convenient women."

She didn't know what to say. Something sophisticated, perhaps, but that might come off as flip, and she didn't want him to think she might be using sarcasm to mask the hurt. That she might be hemorrhaging inside, her emotions mangled beyond recognition, her dreams seeping away through a hundred little stab wounds. But she needed to say something.

"Was that what I was?" she heard herself ask. She

didn't recognize the wavering tone, but she knew it had to be her voice she'd heard. She was the only one there. "Was I convenient?"

"Right there in my classroom, Monday through Friday. And lately, ready and willing on the weekends." Joe's lips twisted at the corners in a parody of a smile. "Heck, I didn't even have to buy you dinner or a drink to get you in bed the first time."

This wasn't happening. He wasn't saying those things. It was all like something in a movie. A movie cliché, where the victim lies dying on the pavement while sirens scream in the distance, too far away to prevent the worst from happening. Too late to do anything but clean up the mess that's left behind. And the victim on the cold, wet ground always wants to know why. *Why? Why'd you do it, Joe?* "And when a woman's not convenient anymore?"

"There's always a convenient woman."

Ginny, Patsy, Matt's mother, countless others. Older, divorced, troubled, available. And then there was Emily Sullivan. Younger and more naive than the rest, but just another notch on the bedpost. A slightly more interesting item to add to the bad-boy reputation.

And the most stupid woman of them all. All that advice, all those warnings, and still she'd been so sure she was the one who could handle it, the only one who knew the real Joe.

He zipped his sweatshirt up to his neck. "Thanks

for the head start into town. I can jog home from here." He took off down the driveway and disappeared around the corner.

CHAPTER TWENTY-ONE

JOE LEANED FORWARD about three miles later, his hands on his knees, gasping for breath. He should have made the turn to his apartment a few blocks back, but he wasn't ready to face that dark, empty space just yet. He wasn't ready to face anything that had been filled with Emily, that might remind him of the confusion and shock he'd seen on her face in the glare of the station security lights. He didn't want anything reminding him that he was responsible for the pain in her eyes.

But he was fooling himself if he thought he could outrun the dark, empty spaces opening up like gaping wounds inside him.

At least he'd been honest with her. He always looked for convenient women. And he'd never had to look very long or very hard.

He paced the circular glow on the sidewalk cast by a street lamp, remembering the highlights. The thirty-year-old Rainbow Family member who'd initiated him the summer he'd turned fourteen. The freshly divorced activist attorney who'd taught him how to drive and how to make the best use of the backseat. The grad-level floor adviser in his freshman year college dorm.

Older women. Women who knew the score. Women who shared his inclinations to bend the rules and dodge the consequences. Fresh young things didn't interest him, especially if the innocence came wrapped in expectations.

Until Guatemala. Until Rosaria.

Joe started running again, into the night. But he couldn't outrun the memories, the images strobing like the street lamps he passed. Impressions pounded like his feet on the pavement, and emotions pummeled him with each gulp of icy air.

Rosaria, doe-eyed and willow-slim, a shy elf picking her way through sawdust and concrete blocks. Strolling through the marketplace with her maid, a comb slipping loose to let silky hair spill in a black waterfall down her back.

Joe tripped over an uneven paving block and picked up his pace. Sleet knifed down from the inky sky, laying a slick surface on his treacherous course. His breath was a sob, but he raced on, seeking the dark at the end of the road.

Rosaria, aloof in a wine-colored riding habit, trailing her fingers along the edge of his makeshift desk. His fingers reaching out to touch hers.

Meet me tonight at the bell tower…Sí, José…Sí….

"*No.*" Joe staggered to a stop and leaned against

a street lamp. Liquid ice stung his skin and soaked his clothes. The memories jumbled together now, a collage of pain and drugs, of beeping monitors and gut-twisting helplessness. Flashes of a nightmare. Pain exploding in his skull…tumbling down, branches slicing…the shotgun crack of his leg, the crunch and snap of his side…blinding lights, cold white sheets…confusion, pain…so much pain….

Rosaria. Gone.

He willed the dull ache of the memories to sharpen, craved a more brutal punishment than the bite of sleet on his cheek or the frigid iron pressed into his shoulder. But he was numb.

He fell to his knees in the cold, wet, vacant street, wallowing in the guilt, wringing his conscience for every ounce of the misery he deserved. He'd taken one chance, long ago, on love and life with an idealistic young woman. He'd lost that first chance at love.

She'd lost her life.

And now, because he hadn't learned his lesson, because he'd been weak and selfish, he'd taken another chance at love with another idealistic young woman. He was prepared to deal with the loss, but this time he couldn't let his woman lose her chance for the life she'd chosen. He couldn't let Emily's career be tainted at its start, wouldn't let ugly rumors blot out the glowing recommendations.

First, he had to drag himself up and get himself

back home. He had to protect her. Protect her from Kyle and anyone else who might do her harm. Most of all, he had to protect her from himself.

Later, he'd mourn the loss and learn to live with the emptiness. He'd stumbled through hell before and survived.

He could only pray he didn't drag Emily with him through purgatory on the return trip.

EMILY DROVE an aimless, spiraling route through night-blackened country roads. She welcomed the empty stretches that swallowed her and the cold that numbed her. She wished she could shut out the sound of Joe's voice, echoing in a loop that played over the swish of the soggy pavement: *I look for convenient women…. I didn't even have to buy you dinner or a drink to get you in bed the first time….*

She waited for shame to coat the pain, to bury it beneath a layer of remorse. But she wasn't feeling sorry, or cheap, or foolish. What she was feeling was angry. A crystalline, energizing *anger.* And the more she thought about what Joe had said, and the way he'd said it, the angrier she got.

She pounded her fist against the steering wheel. "Why did he pull a stunt like that? Just how stupid does he think I am?" Accelerating around a corner, she slammed the shift stick into a lower gear to prevent another slide into another ditch. "Does he really think I don't know him well enough by now to know that he'd never intentionally hurt someone—anyone—like that?"

She coasted to a stop at a railroad crossing and swiped at the tears scorching messy trails down her cheeks. Okay, so he'd done it. He'd hurt her.

If anyone knew just which of her buttons to push, it was Joseph Whatever-That-Damn-*P*-Stood-For Wisniewski. And that made her angry, all over again. That was why she was crying—because she was angry. Not because she was bruised and shaky and hollowed out. Because she was angry. Angry and frustrated.

"Yeah." She sniffed and wiped at the last of the tears. The very last, she promised. "I'm angry because he's stupid and I'm frustrated and it's all a big mess. But no more." She pounded the steering wheel again. "No more."

She took a deep, shaky, cleansing breath. She needed to figure things out, to mop up the mess before things got worse. There were so many things that could go wrong: her exams, her evaluations, her university credit, the basketball team, her other extracurricular commitments. Her family's reactions to her latest disaster. Joe's job.

For one long moment, she surrendered to the down-the-drain sensation in her gut. It sucked her into the blackness, swamped her and terrified her. So she ground her teeth against the fear and the hurt and clenched her fists around the anger and willed her head to start working out the problems. Step by step, in an organized fashion.

How had Matt known to call Joe at her place? Why had he called Joe instead of Walt? What was he trying to accomplish?

Emily took her foot off the brake and headed down the street through the ghostly apple orchards. The only person who could answer those questions was Matt. She'd find him and get the answers.

She should probably wait until Monday to confront Joe. He needed a little time and space. They both did. She needed to organize the questions and emotions tumbling through her. Heck, she had a study group to attend and a paper to write. Laundry to do. A life to squeeze in between the traumas.

Trauma. A fresh bout of grief welled up, and she ruthlessly swallowed it down. What was the reason for Joe's sudden attack? To get rid of her? No. If Joe wanted her gone, all he had to do was wait until the end of the term, shake her hand and wish her well. No need to slice her to ribbons first.

And why did he have to be so vicious? To make sure she'd leave? To get her out of harm's way? Those were more likely reasons. Good ones to focus on, too. They fueled her anger and built her resolve.

"Big, strong man, shoving the little woman behind his big, strong back so he can take all the blows himself. What a macho, thickheaded...*oooh.*" She snarled. "Slicing me up for my own good, Joe? Smooth move, you imbecile."

She guided her truck into her gravel drive, turned off the ignition and stared at the porch light. There was the bright new bulb he'd bought for her and wrapped in a silly red ribbon, the bulb he'd installed himself after another lecture.

A moth flew in tight, jagged circles around the glass, beating itself against the warmth and the light, helpless against an instinct that would kill it in the end.

Emily slumped in her seat, feeling a little mothlike herself. "Guess what, Joe? It's not going to work. You're not getting rid of me that easily."

THE SECOND HARDEST THING Emily had ever done was walking into the Caldwell High School building on Monday morning. The hardest thing was walking into Joe's classroom.

There he was, in place early for a change, hunched over his desk. He looked like hell. Good. She wanted him to suffer—a little bit, anyway. Mostly, she wanted to put her arms around him, and forgive him, and comfort him, and start working on making things right again.

The bell rang before she had a chance to say anything, so she sat down and pulled out her notebook, eager to bury her nose in her paperwork and block the stares and whispers of the students and the familiar rumble of Joe's voice. She flipped to the page where she'd outlined The Situation. There were still a lot of blanks under some of the headings, but after she talked to Matt and Joe—and her university adviser, and her parents, and Linda and Marilee, and Kyle and whomever else she needed to consult— she'd have everything figured out.

Item number one: emotional impact. She'd had twenty-four hours to boil over and simmer down, and to indulge in a couple of good crying jags. Her emotions had been examined and analyzed plenty yesterday, so she skipped recording them here. Bottom line—she loved Joe. It was his feelings—and whether he'd admit to them—that made up the biggest question mark on the outline page.

Next, she had to consider how this situation was going to affect her. Would it jeopardize her internship? Her credit at the university? Her letters of recommendation? How would her family feel if she completely botched this latest attempt at a career?

And what about Joe's job? Linda had hinted there was already some trouble with Kyle and the school board. Would this give them the ammunition they needed to get rid of him?

Then she arrived at the scariest item: the relationship. There were far too many questions and too many blanks under this topic. She took a deep breath and gave herself permission to skip to the last section.

How was she going to deal with any other problems that might surface? She wasn't going to be caught unprepared again. This time, she'd have an answer for every tough question, a plan for every contingency. From here on out, no more nasty surprises.

"Ms. Sullivan?"

Emily glanced up at the student office assistant standing at Joe's classroom door. "Mr. Walford would like to see you."

KYLE WAS WAITING for her at the reception counter. "Ms. Sullivan."

Emily winced at the sound of his voice. The first name approach was gone, along with the come-on tone. "You wanted to see me?"

"Yes." He pulled himself up and straightened his jacket. "I'm sorry to call you out of class, but this is important."

She followed him down the short hall, past Linda's basilisk stare. They entered his office, and she settled into the seat he indicated. Kyle left his door slightly ajar and took the CEO spot, behind his desk. When he clasped his hands over his leather-edged blotter and frowned, the fake mahogany closed in on her. So this was it: the first stop on the path to delinquent hell. She waited for Kyle to make the opening remarks.

"It has come to my attention that you and your master teacher have become involved on a personal basis."

She raised her chin. "Yes. That's true."

"You can imagine my surprise at this development, considering your personal policy against involvements with a coworker."

She had that coming. She took the hit, without flinching, and chose her next words with care. "I doubt I can imagine what you're feeling, Kyle."

He started to speak, but clamped his lips tightly shut and leaned back in his chair, twisting sideways to rest one elbow on his desk. After a few moments, he snatched up a pencil and began to bounce it, end over end, on the leather. "Cleverly phrased," he said at last. "But then, you're a clever woman."

It didn't sound like a compliment, so she didn't acknowledge it as such. She watched the pencil's movement, watched the tumbling yellow wand signal his shifts from anger, to confusion, to frustration and back to anger again. She waited like a game show contestant, hoping the pencil would spin back to confusion, but it stopped at anger. The tip broke off, a quiet snap in the quiet office.

"I have to wonder, Ms. Sullivan—what kind of a recommendation letter can you be expecting from me?"

Anger twisted her in one big knot, and she took a deep breath to straighten herself out again. "I would expect a letter evaluating my skills in the classroom. One that notes my cooperation with and support of the Caldwell staff. A letter noting my hard work and my many contributions to extracurricular activities."

"Yes. Your 'extracurricular activities.'" Kyle let the broken pencil drop and swiveled back to face her. "You've been quite active, haven't you? In several positions."

Kyle's office door swung open so hard it bounced off the wall and slammed shut, but not before Joe stormed through the opening. Emily and Kyle jumped out of their seats as he stalked around the big desk, scattering papers and pencils in his wake. He grabbed Kyle by his suit lapels and shoved him up against the window, crumpling the blinds.

Emily gasped. "Joe!"

His grip on Kyle's jacket tightened. "Lock the door on your way out."

"Joe, no, don't—"

"Get out. *Now.*"

"Get your hands off me," Kyle said in a strangled voice.

Joe shook him, once. "Don't you ever speak to her like that again."

"Let him go, Joe," Emily pleaded. "He's not worth it."

"No, he's not," Joe said. He lowered Kyle a bit, but kept his grip on the jacket. "But you are."

"You're finished here, Wisniewski." A fleck of foam spotted the corner of Kyle's mouth. "Both of you are. Get out of my office."

Linda opened the door behind them and leaned against the jamb. "Go ahead. Leave. I'll deal with this mess."

Joe snatched his hands away from Kyle and

stalked out of the room. Emily stood, staring at the crumpled blinds and scattered pencils.

"What are you waiting for?" Kyle shouted. "Get out. And don't come back."

CHAPTER TWENTY-TWO

HALF AN HOUR AFTER she fled Caldwell, Emily had headed for Joe's apartment. She'd pounded on his door in frustration, wanting to pound some answers out of him. He wasn't home.

But her parents were. She stood, now, at the entrance to their Seattle home, dreading what she was about to do. Twice she'd raised her hand to grasp the knocker and announce her presence, and twice she'd pulled it back. Confronting Joe about the situation seemed easier than trying to explain things to her parents.

Once again, she'd messed up. Spectacularly. Professionally, personally, publicly, privately—any way you looked at it, she'd blasted things to kingdom come. To smithereens. To—

The door opened. "I thought I saw you through the front window," said Kay. "What a surprise. I—"

Kay's greeting smile faded as she took a good look at Emily's face. Her hand fluttered up, and for a moment Emily thought she might put it against her forehead, the way she used to, as if she suspected typhoid or cholera.

She pulled Emily through the opening and shut the door. "Here, let me take your coat. Oh, I do hope you can stay a while. Dad's just getting settled in the den, watching some old war movie he's seen a dozen times, at least. I'm sure he'd much rather visit with you. I know I'd rather listen to all your news instead of guns and explosions. Can I get you something to drink? Some tea?"

"Nothing, thanks."

"It's no trouble, really. I was just going to make some for myself. It seems like the kind of day that could use a good strong cup of tea to help ease it along."

"No thanks, Mom." Emily shrugged out of her coat and took the hanger from Kay. "I can't stay long. I've got an exam to take in a few hours, and some work to do before that."

"I won't be a second, then."

Kay slipped down the hall while Emily found a spot for her coat in the closet. Lavender. Kay's closets always smelled of lavender. From around the corner, she could hear her mother's soft drawl and her father's answering grunt. Home had never felt so foreign in all its familiarity.

Everything had changed. No, not everything—just Emily, and her part in the picture. For the first time, she felt she was a separate entity, something other than an extension of Jack and Kay Sullivan. Someone who could appreciate the scent of a lavender sachet without worrying whether her own closet should smell the same. Someone whose heart tripped over the sound of a different man's grunts. Someone who could deal with anything life handed out, as long as it was her own life she was dealing with.

"Em." Dad stood in the hall, looking as sturdy as ever.

"Dad." She closed the closet door. "I can't stay long, and I—" She took a step closer. "There's something I need to tell you. To tell both of you."

Jack nodded and moved aside, letting her enter the den ahead of him. As she passed through the door, she felt him trace a finger down her spine, a featherweight brush of affection. He hadn't done that for years. She battled back the sentimental sting behind her eyes. She wanted to appear strong and in control when she told them about her weakness and ineptitude.

Kay came in with two cups steaming in their saucers and handed one to Emily. "You don't have to drink it if you don't want it."

"Thanks, Mom."

"You don't have to eat the cookies, either."

Emily had already noticed the tiny homemade macaroons wedged in beside the cup, glistening with sugar that hadn't quite dissolved into the sticky, chewy dough. Kay knew she couldn't resist those cookies. And if she ate the cookies, she'd be thirsty, so she'd end up drinking the tea.

Kay Sullivan, tea pusher, caffeine dealer. Her

yearly shipment from Fortnum & Mason must have arrived ahead of schedule. Emily took a deep breath and prepared to push Kay's world further out of whack. "I've really done it this time. I've made a mess of everything."

Kay waved her hand. "Well, if anyone can fix it, you can."

Emily stared at her mother, and then looked down at the cookies on the plate. She saw new meanings in Kay's methods today. First, something homey and comforting—tea, a cookie—to ease the situation. Then some pleasant chatter and the space to let things settle. All of it backed up by a reassuring confidence in her daughter's abilities to fend for herself. Kay wasn't a distracted or disinterested mother; she wisely chose not to be a smothering one. She stayed in the background, fussing over minor things, staying close enough to step forward and help with the major ones.

Emily looked up at her. "Thanks, Mom."

Kay met her eyes with a steady gaze. "You're welcome."

"I'm not sure I can fix it," Emily said, shifting to face her father, "any of it, or all of it, but I'm going to give it my best shot."

Jack nodded. "Sometimes, that's all you can do."

"All my life, I've wanted to please you, both of you, more than anything." She set her cup and saucer on the little pie crust end table. The rattling china sounded as fragile as she was suddenly feeling. "To make you proud of me."

"I know," said Jack. "And all your life, one of the hardest things I've had to do to was stand by and wait for you to learn to please yourself, first." He cleared his throat. "I've been proud, so proud, of everything you've done. Everything you've accomplished. We both have."

He put his big, solid hands on the chair arms and pushed himself up to stand over her, his chin in the air, every inch the commanding officer. "Are you proud of yourself, Emily Sullivan?"

She started to answer, and then stopped and looked up at him. Really looked. She saw support and unconditional love. "Yes. Yes, I am. I've worked hard, and I've learned…so much. So many things. I've made a difference in a lot of young lives, and I'm on track for perfect scores in my university coursework this term."

"You always were such a good student," said Kay. "So bright. So curious about everything. We could hardly keep up with you and all your interests."

"So," said Jack. "It would appear there are a few things you haven't messed up."

Emily's lips twitched. "How inefficient of me."

Jack grunted. He frowned and tugged at one of his ears, the way he always did when he was getting ready to say something uncomfortable. "Looks like someone else is going to have to scramble to keep up with you, now," he said. "You've earned the love of a good man."

So—they'd already figured out the hardest part of what she had to say. She should have guessed they'd be one step ahead of her. They usually were. There was no point in resenting it, and a wonderful sense of peace in accepting it.

She sat up a little straighter. "Joe's earned my love, too. I just have to make sure he understands what that means."

"God help him," Dad said.

They smiled at each other. Kay sniffled into one of the linen handkerchiefs she always had hidden somewhere in her clothes.

Jack cleared his throat. "Now then. What's this snafu you're here to tell us about?"

Emily relaxed back against the sofa cushions. Jack Sullivan didn't think his daughter's involvement with Joe Wisniewski merited official snafu status. Anything else she had to tell them would be a piece of cake. As easy as popping one of Kay's macaroons into her mouth.

She plucked one of the cookies off her saucer and prepared to take a sticky, chewy bite out of her troubles.

JOE'S FIRST IMPULSE was to get out of town. Head to San Francisco. He could make it in about twelve hours, just in time to collapse in Anna's spare bed. Time on the road to sort things out. Time to decide what to do next.

What he found on the road instead was time to worry about Emily, about what she was thinking, and feeling. Time to start missing her so goddamn much he thought he'd double over from the pain.

He only made it about a hundred miles down the highway before he pulled over and slumped in his seat, scrubbing both hands over his face. For the first time in his life, his options weren't entirely his own. Like it or not, he was tied to someone else. He was coteaching his morning classes, cocoaching a basketball team and comoderating the Garden Project. He was mentoring someone's steps toward a professional career. And the fact he just happened to be in love with that someone knotted up all the entanglements so tight he couldn't make a move without her.

So he wouldn't leave, not yet. He turned around, drove back into town and holed up in his apartment, waiting. He knew she'd come. He knew she'd give him hell. He had it coming, and he didn't expect anything less from her.

He was still in shock over the way he'd shoved Kyle against the office window. But when he'd heard the things Kyle was saying to Emily, and the way that slimy voice was oozing around those double entendres, something had shattered inside him. The ruins were still in there, rattling around like the shards of a broken wineglass. Ragged and sharp, ready to draw blood. He hoped Emily wouldn't show up until the edges had dulled.

He tossed together some salad greens and goat cheese for a late lunch, but then tossed it into the trash. He sat at the piano to improvise some jazz, and then slid into the blues. He called Anna to let her know what had happened, only to listen to her riot about what should happen next. He tried not to watch the clock, tried not to think of basketball practice, tried not to wonder where Emily might be.

Linda called with some unpleasant updates and a fresh batch of bad news: the school board had scheduled an emergency meeting, and Joe was the only item on the agenda.

"Have you heard from Emily?" he asked.

"Yes."

"Oh." He waited for more, but it wasn't coming. Linda wouldn't make this easy on him. "What did she say?"

"She wanted to be sure the team had a coach for practice this afternoon."

"Anything else?"

"What else were you wondering about, exactly?"

"Nothing. Exactly."

Linda hmphed. "What do you think's going to happen to her at the university?"

"I have no idea." The university. Finals. He'd forgotten she had exams this week.

"Joe." She paused. "About Emily…"

"Yeah?"

"Don't do anything stupid."

"Anything stupid?" He shoved a hand through his hair and choked on an ugly little chuckle. "God."

"I mean, anything more stupid than what you've already done."

"I can't imagine what that would be."

"I can. I know you. And I'm telling you… I'm warning you, Joe—"

"Thanks for the call, Linda," he said, and then he disconnected. "Thanks for the advice."

AS EMILY JOGGED into the cozy lounge near the campus information desk, Marilee looked pointedly at her watch. "Where have you been?"

Emily tossed her purse under one of the low-slung chairs and fell into the deep, foamy seat. It was late, well after nine o'clock at night, and her stomach was rumbling. She hadn't had a thing to eat since the macaroons. The cookies seemed so far away. And the scene in Kyle's office that morning felt like a lifetime ago.

It was a lifetime ago. A different lifetime, for Emily.

Marilee frowned. "You missed the exam. And the entire study group cram session for tomorrow's."

"I know." Emily sucked in a couple of deep breaths. She was still panting after her dash across campus. "Thanks for waiting."

"What's going on? Where's your briefcase?"

"I don't need it anymore."

"What do you mean, you don't need it? That thing's like a third arm. A third leg. A third—"

"I get the idea." Emily swatted the curls out of her eyes. "I'm sorry I missed the study group. I would have liked to say goodbye."

"Goodbye?" Marilee snapped to attention at the edge of her chair. "What's going on?"

"I'm out, Mare."

It hit her, suddenly, what she was giving up: the intellectual stimulation of her classes, the creative excitement of the job, the camaraderie of her fellow student teachers. Emily swallowed, hard. She hadn't cried all day, and she didn't want to start now, though the concern on Marilee's face was making her nose prickle. "I withdrew from all my classes. I quit the program."

"What are you—you can't do that. It's too late to withdraw."

"No, it's not."

"But, you—you'll fail," Marilee sputtered. "Everything."

"I know. But I need the time this week to do something more important."

"More important than everything you've worked so hard for these last few months? More important than your whole teaching career?"

"Yes."

"Oh." Marilee collapsed back against the cushions. "Who died? Someone died, right?"

"No one died. It's nothing that grim." Emily bit her lip. "Well, almost."

"What is it?"

"I was kicked out of Caldwell. This morning. And when I called the school secretary a few hours ago, she told me the school board is looking into a way to fire Joe."

"What happened?"

"We got found out. Joe and I."

"You and Joe… *Oh*." Marilee smiled a sad and knowing smile. "Oh, I see. Well. I hope it was worth it."

Emily smiled back, a wide and confident grin. "Every moment."

"So." Marilee tossed her hair back behind her shoulders. "So sue. Breach of contract or something. Get your adviser to lean on them. This is the twenty-first century. You and Joe are consenting adults. They can't do things like that."

"That's not the battle I want to fight right now." Emily leaned forward to rest her hand on her friend's knee. "There are a couple of things you could help me with. I know this is a brutal time to ask…"

"Ask. Anything."

"Thanks." Emily settled back into her chair and laced her fingers under her chin. "Actually, I think you're going to like this."

"Is it a party?"

Emily smiled. "That's one way of looking at it, I suppose."

Marilee smiled back. "What do you need?"

"An introduction to those theater arts people you know."

OUTSIDE, the early winter darkness rushed the dinner hour. Streetlights winked on near Joe's front window, casting shoppers' shadows across glistening pavement. He uncorked his last bottle of wine and made a mental note to buy a case of it in the morning.

He sat at the piano again, placed his hands on the keys and tried to concentrate on the chords and progressions of a Cole Porter ballad. The notes wouldn't come. All he heard was the ticking of his clock: Two days. Two days.

Two days, and he hadn't heard a word from Emily. He'd driven by her house, but her truck wasn't in the drive. He'd called the number on the wrinkled sheet of yellow notebook paper, but she didn't answer. He had no idea what to say to her message machine and hadn't left a recording. He'd considered contacting her parents. But if they hadn't heard from her, and he gave them a reason to think they should have, they might start having the same kinds of worries he was having.

He dropped his fingers on the keyboard and frowned at the dissonance, although it seemed as appropriate as anything else tonight. He decided on something from memory, something vaguely mournful. Debussy in the key of depression.

He played carefully, methodically, with the correct amount of expression. He played through the closing hours for the Main Street shops and the deepening darkness in his apartment. He played through the pounding footsteps on his stairs and the determined knocking at his door, through his relief that Emily had finally arrived and the regret that he was going to hurt her again.

The knocking grew louder. He heard her muffled voice. "I know you're in there."

"It's open," he called.

"Don't stop." She stepped in and closed the door behind her. "I love to listen to you play."

"No problem." He skipped to the finale. "I'd like to finish something this week."

She hesitated at the entry, and then unfastened the top snap of her jacket. "Why don't they write music like that anymore?"

"Who knows?" He shrugged and reached for his wineglass. "I'd offer you some wine, but this was the last of it."

"I didn't come here to drink with you." She walked over to the piano and ran a hand along the smooth wood. "Have they found someone to coach yet?"

"Larry Gilbert—Suze's dad is thinking about it. Dornley's helping out with the practices. They'll have someone in place by the end of the week."

"Oh. Well." Her shoulders moved up and down with a sigh. "How did you find out?"

"Linda's called. A couple of times."

"What else did she say?"

"The school board's already met. I'm suspended until further notice. They're looking into terminating my contract." He picked up his wine and gestured at the room with the glass. "Bob Dixon thinks I should look for another place to live, considering my means of paying rent is in question."

"That's not right. That's not fair." She leaned against the piano, her hands clutching the edge. "Kyle put them up to this."

"Kyle didn't have to do much talking. Walt made the motion. Bob and the others jumped on it."

"What are you going to do about it?"

"What do you want me to do about it?"

"Fight!" she said, pounding the lid with her fist.

"For what?"

She stared at him and shook her head. "What a sorry sight you are."

"If you don't want to look, you can leave."

"You'd like that, wouldn't you?" She stalked to his sofa and sat down, planting herself right in the middle, leaning back and crossing her arms. Digging in. "You're trying to push me away. Well, you know what, Joe? It isn't going to work."

"Of course not. You'd just push back." He drained the rest of his wine. "So I'm not going to push. I'm going to make it easy for you to go, instead."

"That won't work, either."

"Figured you'd say that." He stood and carried his empty glass to the kitchen counter. "You're not the first woman I've hurt."

"I'm sure there have been countless others."

"No. There was only one other. Only one other who mattered." He came back to the doorway and stopped there, between the two rooms. "And I killed her."

CHAPTER TWENTY-THREE

"No." Emily shook her head. "No, you didn't."

"Not with my hands." He looked down at them, and then slid them into his pockets. "I killed her with my carelessness. With my selfishness."

He walked to the window and stared down into the street. "Her name was Rosaria. I met her when I was in the Peace Corps. In Guatemala. I was assigned to help build a school in a small village near Flores."

It began to rain, and fat drops smeared the view. "Her father was the richest man in the district, and she was his only daughter. He forbade her to see me, but she was willful, and I was so infatuated I didn't—I couldn't turn her away."

He tried to remember that desire. He tried to bring it back, to block out the craving and the need for the woman on the sofa behind him.

"We arranged to meet, in secret. I would have taken her, made love to her that night, even though I knew the consequences for us both. But I thought I'd take her with me when I left, so I told myself it wasn't wrong."

He lifted a hand to trace the path of one of the raindrops on the glass. "I went to the meeting place, but she never showed up. On my way back, I was attacked. Clubbed in the head and tossed down a ravine. My leg was broken, and several ribs. I came to in a hospital in Guatemala City. They shipped me home. I never saw her again."

"Did you try?"

"I wrote. To her family, to a friend in the Guatemala office, to everyone I could think of. And I waited. I didn't hear anything, so I kept waiting, and took the job at Caldwell, and waited some more." Waited, for something, for his life to begin. He imagined her strolling through the school halls with his students, trailing her fingers along the edge of his scarred school desk, and he poured his heart into his lessons while he waited for the chance to promise his heart to her.

Ah, the blissful opiate of romantic idealism, of youth and innocence and dreams. Even now, it drugged and distorted the memories and visions until he wasn't sure which was which. He waited for the familiar ache to wind through his gut.

"Word came, finally. She'd entered a convent." Long black hair chopped short beneath a veil. Laughing black eyes cast down at a smothering habit. Shut away by her family, saved from temptation, saved from him. "A few months later the novitiate wing was buried in an earthquake. A landslide."

He turned to face Emily. "She wouldn't have been

there, she wouldn't have died, if I hadn't wanted her. If I hadn't ignored the risks and gone after what I wanted."

He had imagined making this confession, imagined the catharsis. Imagined what he'd see on Emily's face: shock, horror, sympathy. Grief, perhaps.

He hadn't expected anger.

It looked like his imagination was scoring about as well as all his other moves lately. He didn't feel better for having told his story. He didn't feel sordid, or wrung out. He felt…numb. And Emily wasn't scrambling for the nearest exit. She looked…

Not numb.

"So, this whole thing," she said, with frustration in her voice and fire in her eyes, "this is all about Guatemala, isn't it? About Rosaria."

"No." He shook his head. "That's too easy."

"If it were that easy, you'd have figured it out a long time ago and put it behind you. But you're stuck. Stuck punishing yourself for something you can't do anything about."

"You don't know anything about it," he said.

"That's right. That's the easy part." She stood and waved it away. "It's a whole lot easier to use your lost love as a barrier, to keep everyone from getting too close. None of us understands, so none of us gets inside. No one gets to know the real Joseph Whatever Wisniewski."

He started to turn away from her, but she stepped in close to jut her chin up at his. "You think you should drive me away before I get hurt, because you didn't do it for her. Well, you did, Joe. You did walk away from her."

"How do you figure that?"

"You told me you were hurt, you told me they sent you back home. But you didn't go after her, Joe. You didn't even try, not really. And that's the same thing."

He turned away from her then. It was completely dark now. The swish of cars passing in the street below was matched by the sweep of headlights across the ceiling. He could smell the garlic from Al's Pizzeria across the way and hear the clatter of a trash can lid in the alley. Outside his place, people were getting on with their lives, moving and talking and eating and cleaning up the messes they made.

"I'm not letting you walk away from this," she said. "I'm not letting you walk away from me. I love you, Joe. No one will ever love you more, or understand you better, than I do. I want you to fight. For your job, for us. For yourself."

Her words lanced through him on a blaze of light, fresh and pure and blinding. The weak and selfish parts of him yearned to grasp for that bright promise, to hold on with all his might, forever. But he clamped down, hard, on his desire.

"You don't always get what you want, Em. Haven't you learned that by now? It doesn't matter how hard you work, or how stubborn you are, or how wonderful your intentions may be. Sometimes life throws you a curve you can't straighten out, no matter how hard you try. No matter how hard you fight."

She reached for his arm. "You love me."

It wasn't a question. She was absolutely certain he did. He could hear it in her voice. What good would it do to contradict her now?

"Yeah. Sure." He turned his head and looked at her. A passing car illuminated her face for the space of a few seconds, lit the sapphire facets of her eyes and touched her hair with gold, and he almost lost the will to say what he had to say. Almost. "I just don't love you enough."

She shrank back, just a fraction of an inch, and he could see what it was costing her to keep her chin up. "I don't believe you," she said.

"Think about it, Em." He reached behind her and twisted the wand to close the blinds. "Think about your experiences, your values. Think about mine. Chalk it up to my childhood, to my joke of a family. To the father who died of a drug overdose in Vietnam before I was born, to the mother who dumped me on her sister's doorstep on her way to Woodstock. But why am I telling you? You already know the highlights."

She narrowed her eyes. "I don't buy that bunch of psychobabble self-pity, and neither do you. It's all just a bunch of excuses, and I know you don't work that way."

He moved away from her and flipped a light switch, and she blinked in the sudden glare from the overhead fixture. "Maybe you don't know me as well as you think you do," he said.

"I know you better than you give me credit for."

He adjusted the dimmer until the light was a subtle glow. "Leave it, Em. Give it up. I'm not an assignment you're going to fail."

He gave her a thin excuse for a smile. "Besides, the best lessons can be learned from mistakes. There," he said, tossing a vague gesture in her direction, "one last lesson from your former master teacher."

He watched her slap her hands on her hips and knew he was in for another lecture. Damn. Why had he fallen in love with the most stubborn woman in the world?

"Oh, I've learned plenty in the time I've spent with you," she said with a kick of sass that had him dousing a spark of lust. "I know I can handle anything you dish out. I'm strong enough, and we both know for sure that I'm stubborn enough."

She paced the shadowed room. "See, you really are an inspiration, Joe. You don't mean to be one, half the time, but it's the truth. You inspired me. You set me on a different path. Okay, I'm still a conservative and a Republican, but I'm different now. I am."

No, she wasn't different. She was the same Emily she'd been when she'd first come into his classroom. *Come on, Wiz. Take me on for a couple of rounds.*

He'd taken her on. And she'd probed and poked and pushed him into loving her.

"Joe." She stopped and fisted her hands beneath

her chin. "Just answer this one question. Did you ever really love her?"

No.

The answer stunned him. He'd never really loved Rosaria. Compared to what he felt for Em… *no*. No contest.

"No," he said. "I didn't love her. Not enough. Not enough to go back. Not enough to try."

He relaxed his pose, trying to look indifferent in spite of the upheaval going on inside him. Might as well take advantage of the way the conversation had spun to make one last try to make things right, to make Emily leave, to make her give up on him. "That's me, Em. That's my style. I've never really loved anyone. Not enough, anyway. I'll never give you what you need. Face it. I'm not worth the effort."

He stared through the soft light, searching for her reaction, trying to read the clues on her face. He waited for her to leave, expected her to leave, but she didn't move from her spot. Instead, she slowly unclasped her hands and undid a jacket button, and then the next. Her eyes grew cool and shuttered, and stayed level with his as her fingers slid down to undo another button.

"What are you doing?" he asked.

"Being convenient." She shrugged out of her jacket and draped it over the sofa arm. "You wanted a convenient woman, and that's me. In spite of everything you've told me, I'm still here, still ready to make love with you."

Panic welled up inside him. "You don't have to do this."

"I know." She pulled her sweater over her head, and her curls sprang around her face in disarray. "But that's the thing about us convenient women. We're simply there, no matter what. Handy to have around."

"Em, don't." He grabbed her arms as she reached behind her back to unfasten her bra. Her breath washed over him, her scent rose up from her warm flesh, and his gut twisted with desire and longing and overpowering need. When he pulled her arms forward, the sheer satin fell from her breasts. "Don't," he whispered, but then his arms were pulling her close, and his mouth was closing over hers.

One last time, he told himself, as his lips feasted on hers in a bruising frenzy. He'd let her feel the empty spaces inside him, the howling nothingness where his heart should be. He'd let himself go, let himself take, and prove to them both he had nothing to give her.

Yes, he'd let himself go—he slid one hand over the small of her back, pulling her close as he plundered her mouth. Yes, he'd take—his other hand slicked up her side to cover her breast, squeezing and molding the delicate shape of her. More, and still more he demanded of her, as he held everything back. No tenderness, no emotion. No love.

"Take me to bed," she whispered.

"I'll take you right here," he answered and dragged

her down to the floor. He clawed at her zipper and swept her jeans down her legs in one violent motion. Her long, long legs. His resolve nearly crumbled as he remembered the feel of them wrapping around him. Not this time. He wouldn't let her wrap him up. Instead, he tormented them both, licking and nipping a path from her ankles to her thighs. When she reached for him, he caught her wrists in one hand and pinned them above her head.

He was sprawled over her now, still fully clothed, pinning her to the floor. He paused, looking for her shame, waiting for her to flinch away, craving her rejection. Damn her, she wouldn't give it to him. Damn them both, he thought as he settled against her and foundered in her pliancy. And then he slipped beneath the surface of coherent thought and was lost in the ocean that was Emily.

EMILY ROLLED FROM Joe's warm bed the next morning and waited, kneeling on the floor, to make sure she hadn't disturbed him. She listened to his heavy, even breathing, and then crept to the front room and pulled on her clothes. She tiptoed out of his apartment and down to her truck to steal away while he slept.

They hadn't spoken after that first bout of passion. Joe had gathered her in his arms and carried her to his bed. His gentle care for her body, his soft caresses and sweet kisses, had nearly broken her heart. He made love to her twice more, tenderly, thoroughly, communicating without saying a word. He touched her, and loved her, with all he'd chosen to hide away inside him, all he was fighting to hide from her. His mouth could spout whatever nonsense he chose, but the rest of his body didn't lie.

Well, she had far too many things to do today to waste precious time arguing with him. Besides, he needed space and time to put Rosaria to rest, to begin rebuilding his life from the rubble of his past.

And she needed to make a phone call. There was one last bit of consulting she wanted to do before she was ready to launch her campaign. For what she had planned, she'd need the advice and assistance of an expert. She needed Joe's aunt Anna.

She pulled into her drive, jumped down from the truck and jogged into her house. Then she took a deep breath and dialed the San Francisco number she'd found on Joe's cell phone directory. Yes, she'd snooped, but it was for a good cause. The greater good—there was an idea a liberal like Joe would approve of, if not the actual deed.

"Anna Green?" she asked the woman who answered the phone.

"No. May I tell her who's calling?"

"Is this Carol?"

There was a slight pause. Then, "Is this Emily Sullivan?"

"Yes." A sweet shaft of hope arrowed through her.

Joe had cared for her enough, had let her far enough into his life to tell his family about her.

"Good. Good for you. We've been waiting for your call."

"You have?"

"Joe would never fall in love with someone who wouldn't make this call," said Carol. "Just a minute—let me go get Anna."

She smiled and flopped into her lumpy second-hand shop chair. He couldn't hide his feelings from his family any more than she could hide her feelings from her own.

"Hello, Emily," said a gravelly voice. "I'm glad to meet you, even long distance."

"Hello, Anna." She closed her eyes and sucked in a deep breath. "I'm calling to ask a favor."

"If it involves getting my nephew's head screwed back on straight, ask away."

"Actually, it involves some expert advice on a bit of political activism."

"Hmm." Anna sounded intrigued. "Activism might not be as interesting as the other project, but the chances for success are probably a whole lot better."

"What do you think about the chances of a rally to protest a certain school board's imminent decision to dismiss its best history teacher? And the chances of reversing that decision?"

"Are we talking full media coverage?" asked Anna.

"It's being discussed."

"Consider it vital. Consider the consequences, too. For yourself."

"I already have," said Emily.

Anna cleared her throat. "Joe's a lucky man."

"Yes, he is."

Anna's laugh was gravelly, too. "Make a hotel reservation for Carol and me, and arrange for transportation. We can be there tomorrow afternoon—I'll call you with our flight number so someone can meet us." She fired off a dozen questions and followed with a dozen demands, and gave Emily a laundry list of details to handle before her arrival.

"Thank you," said Emily. "For everything."

"You're welcome," said Anna. "Now, get to work, kid."

CHAPTER TWENTY-FOUR

JOE DUMPED ANOTHER armful of books into another cardboard box. He knew he'd never get all of them into his car, but he didn't want to take the time to sort through and decide which ones to give away. He just wanted to pack. Packing was exactly the sort of mind-numbing exercise he needed right now.

Seeing his possessions disappear into small boxes was cleansing, somehow. It unburdened him, set him free, gave him the chance to make a fresh start. He'd been stagnating here too long.

He only wished he could tidy up the situation with Emily. He figured arguing with someone that stubborn was pointless, but maybe he could convince her the lovemaking was his way of saying goodbye. A kinder, gentler way to dump a woman.

Who did he think he was fooling? He'd poured his heart out to her. And then he'd tried to fill it with enough of her essence to get him through a lifetime without her.

What a pathetic substitute for the real thing.

He could live a life on empty. He'd done it before. But he wanted more than that for Em. As soon as he got these boxes filled, he'd be gone. She would come looking for him, looking for one more argument, but he wouldn't be here. End of discussion.

The knock on his door surprised him. He hadn't heard her truck sputter into the alley.

It wasn't Emily standing on his tiny porch; it was the other personal problem in his life. "Hello, Matt."

"Hey, Wiz." Matt's greeting sounded a little strained. He hesitated, and then lifted the two boxes in his hands. "Pizza delivery from Ms. Sullivan. Mine's the pepperoni. She sends her regrets that she won't be able to join us for dinner tonight, and says you can shovel your load of shit in my direction instead."

"Feeling a little passive-aggressive, isn't she?" Joe stepped aside to let him in. "Why did she send pizza if she wasn't going to be here? She knows I barely tolerate the stuff."

"She warned me you'd probably say that, too." Matt frowned at the boxes and books stacked in a corner. "And she said to be sure and get enough humble pie for us both. There's plenty here. We can share."

"My lucky day."

Matt tucked the carton edges against his chest and took a deep breath. "She also said we should talk. That we need to talk."

Joe stared at the young man's face and saw the same crushing guilt he'd seen in the mirror for too many years. He rested a hand on Matt's shoulder. "It isn't your fault, Matt. None of this is."

"If I hadn't made that call—"

"If you hadn't made that call, someone else would have made a different call. Ms. Sullivan and I knew what we were doing. We knew the chances we were taking."

"Still, I'm sorry, Wiz. Even if it's not my fault, I'm sorry for what's happened. To you and to Ms. Sullivan."

"Yeah, well…okay." Joe squeezed his shoulder and pulled his hand away. "Apology accepted. Now eat that stuff before the thought of those processed pools of orange grease puts me off my dinner of…" He lifted the lid on one of the boxes. "What is this?"

"The vegan special."

"There's no cheese."

"Is there supposed to be?"

Joe took the odd-looking pizza from Matt and tossed it on the piano. "I don't think Ms. Sullivan is a good influence on young adults."

Matt stepped to the sofa, balanced the other carton on top of a pile of packing boxes and shrugged out of his jacket before taking a seat. He lifted the lid and looked at Joe expectantly. With a mild curse, Joe dragged a chair out of the kitchen and shoved it next to the makeshift table while Matt teased out the first slice. Pepperoni. Disgusting.

"So," Joe said, "why can't she come over and dish out her dirt in person?"

"She's busy," said Matt around a mouthful of sodium and cholesterol. "Very busy."

"That's right." Joe went back into the kitchen for napkins and bottled water. "Finals."

"Nope. She's all done with that."

"Done with finals?"

"Done with the whole program. She quit."

"She what?" Joe's fingers tightened around his water bottle. "She quit?"

"Yep."

"She didn't have to do that. They could have worked something out." He paced to the window and back. "No one's done more this term than Emily, or done better. She's taken on twice the responsibilities of anyone else in that program, and handled everything like a pro. They can't do that to her."

"They didn't do it to her. She did it to herself. She quit."

The loss staggered him, literally, and he sank into his chair. All that hard work, all that potential, all that energy and enthusiasm and talent, all down the drain. Joe felt like he'd taken a cross-court pass straight to the solar plexus. "When?"

"Dunno." Matt swallowed his mouthful. "Monday night, I think."

Before she'd come to him, argued with him, pleaded with him, offered herself to him. She'd already sacrificed her future before she'd come to rescue him from his past. What a pair they made. Suspended in time, no place to go.

He stared at Matt, who was helping himself to a

second slice. Matt, who was as big a fan of Emily as anyone, but who was calmly stuffing his face with molten goo. Who didn't seem all that upset by her self-destruction as he reached for another helping of pepperoni. Something fishy was going on here. "She quit?" Joe asked again.

"Yeah."

"Why?"

Matt shrugged and bit into the pizza. "She's busy."

Joe's eyes narrowed. "Doing what, exactly?"

"Stuff."

Joe shot out of his chair and grabbed Matt's jacket. "All right, bud, put this on, right now. You're coming with me."

"What?"

"You heard me. I know what's going on here. Some plot to keep me holed up while she does something she doesn't want me finding out about. Where is she? Take me to her."

"Uh-uh." Matt leaned back against the sofa cushion. "Not until I've had my dinner. I'm a growing boy. I shouldn't miss a meal."

"*Matt.*"

"Relax, Wiz." Matt laughed and held up his hands. "There's no plot. Nothing nefarious up my sleeve."

Joe felt a little foolish as he dropped Matt's jacket back over the sofa arm. He moved to the window and slouched against the cold glass.

Matt finished another slice of pizza, and then

slowly, methodically wiped his hands on a paper napkin. "Wiz?"

"Yeah?"

"That night, the night I called, I called you because I was upset. But not with you, not really. With myself."

"You were drunk."

"I was stupid." Another pause. "Stupid enough to think that getting wasted was going to make my problem go away."

Joe turned around to face him. A confession deserved the full attention of the guy on the other side of the dark box. "Didn't work, did it?"

"Nope. Just piled more problems on top."

"What happened?"

"Lindsay and I had a fight."

Joe frowned. "Lindsay Wellek?"

"My date for the winter formal." Matt wadded the napkin and tossed it in the pizza carton. "She told me she thought we were getting too serious too fast."

"Were you?"

"How should I know?" Matt shrugged. "It's not like I've had a lot of experience with females."

"Trust me, when it comes to females, experience doesn't mean shit." Joe pinched the bridge of his nose. "So, what happened next?"

"She told me she was afraid of what was happening. That I'd be leaving for college, and I'd dump her, and she'd get hurt if she fell in love with me." Matt blushed a little and reached for his soda. "So she thought we should break up before that happened."

Wiz waited, but Matt didn't say anything else. "That's it?"

"Yeah."

"And?"

"I think it's a stupid idea."

"You told her that?"

Matt looked insulted. "What do you think?"

"You're asking me about stupid ideas?" Joe raised his hand. "Don't answer that."

Matt's grin faded. "I got mad, Wiz. Really mad. I mean, why couldn't she just enjoy what was happening, instead of looking for ways to mess it up? What's the point in that?"

Joe had a sinking feeling there was a point, and that it might be aimed in his direction. "I have no idea."

"You know, we had something really special. I thought we did, anyway. I was thinking maybe I could love her, too. And then she goes and pulls a stunt like that."

"So, you broke up?"

"Yeah. That night, anyway." Matt chugged some water. "We got back together yesterday."

"How'd you pull that off?" Inquiring minds wanted to know.

"I told her it's all about taking a risk. How much do you care about another person? How much are you willing to put on the line for someone else?"

He paused and leveled a man-to-man look at his former teacher. "We agreed we care enough about each other to take the risk of getting hurt."

Matt set his water bottle on the floor and stared at the remains of his dinner. "Wiz?"

"Yeah?"

"Why'd you do it?"

"What?"

"You…and Ms. Sullivan." Matt blushed again. "You know."

"What can I say? It's that risk thing, I guess." Joe sighed. "That, and the fact that she drives me stark, raving mad."

THE ALARM.

Joe threw out his arm and knocked over an empty pizza box.

No, the phone. "Yes?" he growled into the receiver.

"Hello, Mr. Wiz."

"Mandy?" Joe rubbed a hand over his face and tried to fight his way up through the nasty haze of morning pepperoni mouth and a mild Chianti hangover. He wondered why his neighbor's little girl would be calling him at—what time was it? Ten? And what day? Friday. "What's up?"

"Mom says to turn on your TV." Joe could hear Mandy's mother yelling in the background, but he couldn't make out what she was saying. "To channel five. You're famous, Mr. Wiz."

"Mandy, what are you—"

"Gotta go." *Click.*

Joe rolled over to set the phone back in its stand, tangled his legs in the sofa throw and half fell to the floor. His head throbbed, his stomach spasmed and he couldn't find the remote.

"Damn," he muttered, and staggered across the room to push the tiny power button on his TV. He watched a sculptured blonde in a sculptured suit leaning down to shove a microphone at Mrs. Grimble's mouth. "How long have you known Joe Wisniewski?" the blonde asked through sculptured red lips.

"Oh, let me see now. It will be seven years, come next Halloween. No, no, now that I think about it, it will be eight years. I'm not sure. It was Halloween, though—I do remember that. He brought some of his young people over from the high school to clean up the mess in my yard."

What the hell was going on? Why was a reporter questioning Mrs. Grimble about him? And what were all those people doing in her yard, and spilling out into the street beyond it? He could see them on the screen, in the background, making a mess of her expansive front lawn. He hoped they'd stay out of her shrub roses, or there would be hell to pay.

"So, would you say that Mr. Wisniewski has been a good neighbor?"

"Oh, my, yes indeed. A wonderful neighbor. And a dear friend."

Joe smiled, even with the hangover. What a sweetheart.

"And now you're returning the favor?"

"Yes, I am. When that nice Miss Sullivan came to me a few days ago and asked if she could stage the rally here, I told her I was happy to help."

"I'll kill her." Joe stepped back, caught his foot on a packing box and crashed to the floor. He scrambled up and limped to the bathroom. He could hear the voices on the television—familiar voices, some of them—as he splashed water on his face, gargled with mouthwash, shrugged a jacket over his sweatshirt and grabbed his keys.

Right before he raced out his door, he heard the blonde ask Mrs. Grimble, "And how did you feel when you heard that Joe Wisniewski might lose his teaching job at Caldwell High?"

"I thought to myself, my goodness, that principal, that Mr. Walford—well! He certainly sucks eggs, big-time."

Joe made a mental note to tell the Garden Project students to stop lending Mrs. Grimble the latest teen video releases.

He clambered down the stairs and found a delivery truck's ramp blocking his car. "Damn," he muttered, stumbling in a circle and trying to figure out which store was getting the goods.

No time. He could make the few miles to Mrs. Grimble's on foot, but his queasy stomach threatened to rebel at the idea. Running was out of the question. That left just one mode of transportation: the bike. A machine he hadn't fired up since his summer camping trip. A machine he wasn't sure he could count on in an emergency. A machine that wouldn't exactly burnish his reputation if he roared into a protest rally with it between his legs.

He dashed under the stairs, yanked aside the tarp and dragged the monster into the miserly light of the raw December day. Gingerly, he stretched one leg across the bike and settled down on the seat. It felt good. It felt powerful. It felt a heck of a lot more substantial than he did at the moment. "Come on, baby," he said as he turned the key in the ignition. "You can do this."

The motorcycle hiccuped, and spat, and bucked, and then roared to life. Joe toed the kickstand out of his way and shot down the alley, spraying gravel as he took the corner into Main Street at a forty-five-degree angle.

CHAPTER TWENTY-FIVE

FIFTEEN MINUTES LATER, Joe rumbled past dozens of parked cars and television vans to bump up onto the curb beside Mrs. Grimble's driveway. As he climbed off the bike, Samuel Taggart walked over and pulled his battered whiskey flask out of his pocket to offer to Joe. It took every ounce of Joe's shaky self-control to stop himself from swiping the flask from the old man's hand and chugging the contents.

"Have you seen Emily?" Joe asked. "Emily Sullivan?"

"She the one's been passing out those posters and things?" At Joe's nod, Samuel hooked a thumb over his shoulder. "Hell of a day for a protest rally, ain't it?"

"Hell of a day," Joe agreed. He waded into the placard-waving crowd, accepting pats on the back and shaking hands. He felt like a politician—one more reason to murder Emily when he found her.

And maybe, as long as he was headed to prison, he'd take out a student or two. "Matt."

Matt spun around, a staple gun in his hand and a headset curved around the side of his face. "Hey, Wiz."

Joe narrowed his eyes. "What are you doing here?"

"Making up some more posters. They're going faster than we expected."

"I can see that." He shoved a hand through his hair. "Why aren't you in class?"

"Because I'm on strike."

"No, you're not. Get back to school before you get suspended."

"No, Wiz." Matt picked up a stake, stapled a silk-screened foam board to it and handed it to Lindsay, who added it to the stack already clutched to her chest. "This is today's lesson. Civil disobedience."

"I told you, it's not your fault," said Joe.

"I know. But it's my responsibility. You taught me the difference, and I'm grateful." Matt held out his hand. "Let me show you how much."

Wiz took his hand and shook it. "Thank you, Matt."

"Any time, Wiz." He reached up and twisted the mouthpiece closer to his lips. "Okay. I'm coming. Gotta go," he said to Joe, and jogged off into the crowd.

A young man stepped forward. "Mr. Wisniewski. Wiz. Remember me?"

"Sure, Tom." God. Tom Welton, Class of Too-Long-Ago-to-Remember. He looked…steady. Clear-eyed and successful. The last time Joe had seen him, he was lurching out of a graduation party to vomit in the bushes. "Good to see you."

"I wanted to be here today, to shake your hand.

Came all the way from San Diego. I want you to meet my wife, Denise."

Joe shook the hand of a serene brunette and listened to Tom describe how he'd changed his life. Why he, Joe Wisniewski, was partly responsible for that change.

Others crowded around him, waiting to tell their stories. People he hadn't seen in years. Parents, students, former colleagues.

A local television station's microphone angled up beneath his chin. He looked beyond it at the signs, and read the slogans. He saw Anna's hand in this, and Emily's heart.

A metallic squeak cut through the chattering of the crowd, and everyone turned to face the ribbon-and-balloon-decked stage set up beside Mrs. Grimble's garage. Emily stepped toward the microphone at its center.

"Damn," Joe said, and started shoving his way through the crush.

EMILY HADN'T BEEN in front of this many people since her junior high forensics competitions. She hoped she'd remember the techniques she'd learned. No sense in worrying about that now. Besides, she'd never made a speech outside before.

She smiled at Marilee's thumbs-up signal from the front row, and smoothed the pieces of paper on which she'd written her notes in big, bold letters. The words still didn't convey what she wanted to say, but it was the best she could do. She'd been so busy over the last few days, handling the logistics Anna outlined, contacting the media, organizing the phone calls, gathering the supplies. All she could hope for now was to put enough pressure on Kyle and the school board to give Joe his job back.

"Em."

Joe. She looked down at the faces clustered near her feet and found his. His hair was tousled, and he hadn't shaved for days. He looked edgy, and intense, and exactly like the dark and dangerous hero of all her adolescent fantasies.

He pointed at the microphone. "Turn that thing off for a minute."

She put her hand over the metal mesh and shook her head.

A little muscle ticked along his jaw. "I can't let you do this, Em."

She flinched when the sound system whined.

"I know you think you've got good reasons for doing this. Good and fine and admirable, just like you. I appreciate the gesture, Em. Really, I do. Now step down from there."

"No, Joe." She took a deep breath. "I'm going to see this through. All the way to the end."

He narrowed his eyes at her, and then his fierce look dissolved in a grin. "You know, this whole setup looks to me like the work of a bleeding-heart liberal. I should have guessed you had it in you all along."

He grasped the edge of the platform and swung

himself up, rising tall and straight to tower over her, never moving his laser beam stare from her face. "Seems to me that if you're going to see this liberal tactic all the way through, to the bitter end, it's time to start leading with your heart instead of with your head." He reached out his hand, and his fingers closed over hers, covering the mike. "I know I haven't given you too many reasons to trust me lately, but I'm asking you for a little trust right now. Trust me, from the heart, Em. And if you can't trust your own heart right now, trust mine."

She stared up at him. Everything had seemed so clouded and confused a few days ago. Terrifying. She'd taken charge, and worked through her pain, and planned every detail down to the last—well, to the last detail. Now the posters were in place and the press was in position. Only the outcome had been in doubt.

And now he stood before her, smiling down at her, and all the goals, and all the planning, and all the doubt burned away, leaving only the core, the essence of everything she had ever wanted. Everything was as clear as could be. "Okay, Joe." She stepped aside and gestured at the microphone. "Just don't turn this into a forty-five-minute lecture. We're on a tight schedule."

"Yes, Ms. Sullivan."

JOE TURNED TO FACE the crowd on a swell of applause. Cameras were settled on shoulders and microphones bristled around the base of the platform. He waited until everyone had gathered in close.

"I started teaching because I wanted to make a difference," he said into the microphone. "I thought I had a message that people needed to hear, and I shouted it out, loud and strong, every time I got the chance. Most of the time I thought no one was listening, and after a while, I got a little discouraged.

"I can see now, as I look out at all the faces gathered here today, that you were listening, all of you. Maybe you weren't listening too closely to what I was saying," he added, and got a few chuckles, "but you heard the message you needed to hear. Each and every one of you. A message that brought you here today." He swallowed, and worked his jaw, trying to get the next words out. "It humbles me."

He grabbed the microphone stand with one hand and shoved the other through his hair. He needed to take a deep breath, but his chest was plugged up so tight with emotion he wasn't sure he could. "Each and every one of you humbles me."

Some of his younger students called out, and he held up his hand for silence. "Not every teacher sees the results of his lessons. Today, I'm the luckiest teacher I know, because the fact that you're here tells me I did make a difference. And I thank you."

He waited for the applause to die down before he continued. "I'm the luckiest teacher, but I'm not the best. That person is Emily Sullivan. Because this—" he waved his hand over the crowd "—all this, is the lesson she taught me."

He reached behind him to pull Emily forward, and he hugged her close to his heart against a soundtrack of whistles and cheers. Across the street, he could see Kyle charging out of a double-parked school van, leading a contingent from the school board. From the sickly look on Kyle's face, Joe knew Emily's political maneuver had worked.

AFTER THE SPIN DOCTORS from the school board corrected the "little misunderstanding" and Kyle offered his hand in a pose for the cameras, after the journalists finished their interviews and the news crews collected their sound bites, after Joe shook hundreds of hands and the crowd began to thin, he looked for Emily.

He headed toward the rear of the speaking platform, past a scruffy group of college-aged people packing up the sound equipment, and found her chatting with the camera crew from the tiny local television station. When she bent forward to watch a portable monitor, he stopped for a moment to admire the line of her long, shapely legs and remembered the way those legs felt wrapped around him in the dark.

Samuel was enjoying the scenery, too. "Mine," Joe said.

"You can have her," Samuel answered. "Women like that are nothing but trouble."

"Sam, you have no idea."

"There's a case of the pot and the kettle," said a gravelly voice behind Joe, "if ever I heard it."

He turned to face Anna. "I knew it. I knew you were behind this."

"In a technical support capacity only." Her face split in a wide grin. "God, it's great to get back to the basics. Gets the juices flowing. Raises the consciousness to an entirely new level."

"Glad you enjoyed it."

"I did," she said with a nod. "Especially that last scene up there on the stage. You're a good-looking couple. A good match."

He scuffed the edge of his sandal against a muddy patch in Mrs. Grimble's lawn. "You think so?"

"It doesn't matter what I think." His aunt drilled a finger into his chest, just like she had when he was a boy. "It matters what you think."

He rubbed at the sore spot over his heart. "I love her, Anna."

"All right, then." She nodded, and swallowed, and nodded again. Joe was shocked to see tears filming her sharp brown eyes. "All right," she repeated softly. "So, what are you going to do about it?"

"Ask her to marry me." He took a deep breath and blew it out on a nervous sigh. "And hope to God she'll take me on."

She shook her head. "You're a lot of work, Joseph."

"I know that." One corner of his mouth twitched up in a half grin. "Good thing Emily's an overachiever."

"Like I said, a good match."

Anna spread her arms and stepped forward to wrap them around Joe's waist. "Remember this day, kid. It's not everyone who gets a sneak peek at his eulogy years before the send-off. And yours was one of the best I've ever heard."

Joe pressed his lips against the dark hair salted with gray. "I love you, you know."

"I do know. But it's nice to hear it every once in a while." She sniffed and pulled out of his embrace. "Now, go find your woman and get to work on that marriage proposal."

JOE HUNCHED DEEPER into his jacket as he waited for the television crew to climb into their van.

"See you Monday," Emily called with a wave as they pulled away from the curb. When she turned and saw him standing there, her smile sizzled right through the December chill.

"See you Monday?" he asked.

"I've got a job interview with Channel Five."

He shook his head. "I'm afraid to ask."

"It's entry level, of course, but eventually I'll put together some human interest segments, maybe do a little commentary on the local political scene." Her smile brightened. "Just think, I could be the Sean Hannity of the Seattle suburbs."

Joe groaned.

"I did major in journalism for a while before I switched to history, you know."

"You majored in every subject known to man at some point or other."

"Not quite. There were a few I skipped." She frowned. "Chemistry, for instance."

"That's okay," he said as he reached for her hand. "We'll make our own."

He led her around the corner of Mrs. Grimble's garage, tugged her against him, and lowered his mouth until it was a breath away from hers. "You know, I've been thinking about how I wanted to do this," he said.

Emily tipped her head back. "Kiss me?"

"Propose."

"Oh." She stepped back, out of his embrace, and crossed her arms.

He darted a glance around the corner of the building, checking to make sure they wouldn't be disturbed. "It wasn't supposed to be like this," he said.

"Like what?" She tilted her head to one side. "Were you planning on a more romantic setting?"

"What makes you think a protest rally doesn't have a certain romance all its own?"

"You've got a point." Then she smiled one of those big, generous smiles, the kind that made her nose scrunch, and made her eyes go wide and dark blue, and made his heart feel several sizes too big for the space behind his ribs. He stood there a moment, basking in her light, and remembered something about a dimmer switch. What a fool he'd been.

"So." Emily cleared her throat. "You mentioned a proposal."

"I did, didn't I? Guess I'm a little nervous."

"Well, you could just consider this one a practice proposal. Something to get the kinks out, so when you do it for real you'll be in better shape. Besides," she said, "it would give me a chance to practice my answer."

"You need practice saying yes?"

"What makes you so sure I'm going to say yes?"

He leaned forward to kiss her on that tender, delicious spot below her ear. She smelled of coffee, and shampoo, and essence of Em. "Aren't you?" he asked.

"Going to say yes?"

One good kiss deserved another. "Yeah."

"Is this the proposal?" she asked.

"No. The practice round. I'm going to need some time to work up to that 'till death do us part' part."

"'Till death do us part,' huh?"

"Yeah. Take it or leave it."

"That's not very romantic."

"Okay, we can leave out the 'death' part." He slipped his hands up her arms and nuzzled her neck, and listened for her soft intake of breath. "How about we go back to your place and start practicing the 'with my body, I thee worship' part?"

"Worship is good." She sighed, soft and slow, and

her arms slipped around his waist. "Worship could stand in for romance, in a pinch."

"That's one of the things I love about you," he said. "How you can toss aside your convictions when presented with a politically expedient alternative."

"Speaking of love...you haven't mentioned it yet." She raised her chin. "Not in the proper context, anyway. I think that should be part of a marriage proposal."

"Makes sense. And I think you should say it at some point, too." He took advantage of her pose to nibble his way up to her ear. "Do you love me, Em?"

She pulled away a bit and narrowed her eyes. "I asked first."

"Just once, I'd like to be the first one who asks." He sighed a put-upon sigh. "Oh, all right. Yes, I love you."

"Okay, then." She shrugged. "I guess I love you, too."

Just like that, Joe knew he'd never feel empty again. "So, does that mean you're going to say yes?"

"Not just yet." She flattened her hands against his chest and pushed him away another few inches. "I don't think I could ever agree to marry someone unless I knew his full name."

Was it any wonder he was crazy about her? "The *P*."

"Cough it up, Wisniewski."

Joe took a deep breath and tried not to squirm in embarrassment. "Pacific."

"*Pacific?*"

"Pacific. Like the ocean. Fathomless. Eternal." He

lifted a hand and wrapped his fingers around hers. "Like my love for you. There—that's romantic, isn't it?"

"Fathomless? Your love for me is incapable of being understood?"

"*Deep.* My love for you is deep. Deep and wide as an ocean." He tipped forward to nip at her earlobe, and he grew tight and hot at her tiny shiver. "Come on, Em. Say yes."

"To what question, specifically?"

"Going to make me crawl, huh?"

"If the kneepads fit…"

"You want me on my knees?" He glanced down at the slushy, crusty ground, and then bent one knee and started to drop.

"No!" She laughed, and tugged him back up.

"What do you want?"

"A proper proposal," she said. "But not on your knees."

"I thought that's how it was done."

"What are you, an expert?" Her eyes narrowed again. "Just how many times have you done this?"

He laughed and caught her in his arms and staggered in a clumsy circle. Making this proposal was a hell of a lot of fun, but there were even better ways to spend the day together, and he was suddenly in a hurry to get to those other things. To get started with the rest of his life. No—the rest of their lives. It had a nice ring to it.

The ring. "Shit."

"Excuse me?"

Joe set her down, cleared his throat, and prepared to close the deal, fast, before she could launch into some new discussion involving a ring, or his philosophical underpinnings, or God only knew what else. "Marry me, Em. Be my long-term goal. I want to argue with you forever."

"Okay."

That was too easy. There had to be a catch. "Okay, that was romantic, or okay, you'll marry me?"

She rolled her eyes. "Okay, I'll marry you."

He pulled her close to shut that sassy mouth with a kiss, but she squirmed back to get in one last shot: "Just for the sake of argument."

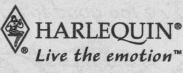

Harlequin Historicals®
Historical Romantic Adventure!

From rugged lawmen and valiant knights to defiant heiresses and spirited frontierswomen, Harlequin Historicals will capture your imagination with their dramatic scope, passion and adventure.

*Harlequin Historicals...
they're too good to miss!*

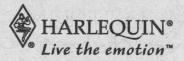

HARLEQUIN®
Presents

**The world's bestselling romance series...
The series that brings you your favorite authors,
month after month:**

Helen Bianchin...Emma Darcy
Lynne Graham...Penny Jordan
Miranda Lee...Sandra Marton
Anne Mather...Carole Mortimer
Susan Napier...Michelle Reid

and many more uniquely talented authors!

Wealthy, powerful, gorgeous men...
Women who have feelings just like your own...
The stories you love, set in exotic, glamorous locations...

HARLEQUIN®
Presents

Seduction and Passion Guaranteed!

HPDIR104

HARLEQUIN®
INTRIGUE®

WE'LL LEAVE YOU BREATHLESS!

If you've been looking for thrilling tales of contemporary passion and sensuous love stories with taut, edge-of-the-seat suspense—then you'll love Harlequin Intrigue!

Every month, you'll meet six new heroes who are guaranteed to make your spine tingle and your pulse pound. With them you'll enter into the exciting world of Harlequin Intrigue— where your life is on the line and so is your heart!

THAT'S INTRIGUE— ## ROMANTIC SUSPENSE ## AT ITS BEST!

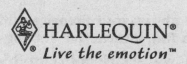

HARLEQUIN®
Live the emotion™

eHARLEQUIN.com

The Ultimate Destination for Women's Fiction

Visit eHarlequin.com's Bookstore today for today's most popular books at great prices.

- An extensive selection of romance books by top authors!

- Choose our convenient "bill me" option. No credit card required.

- New releases, Themed Collections and hard-to-find backlist.

- A sneak peek at upcoming books.

- Check out book excerpts, book summaries and Reader Recommendations from other members and post your own too.

- Find out what everybody's reading in Bestsellers.

- Save BIG with everyday discounts and exclusive online offers!

- Our Category Legend will help you select reading that's exactly right for you!

- Visit our Bargain Outlet often for huge savings and special offers!

- Sweepstakes offers. Enter for your chance to win special prizes, autographed books and more.

Your purchases are 100% guaranteed—so shop online at www.eHarlequin.com today!